T0129510

The Upside of Down

Janice Angelique

iUniverse, Inc.
Bloomington

The Upside of Down

iUniverse books may be ordered through booksellers or by contacting:

iUniverse
1663 Liberty Drive
Bloomington, IN 47403
www.iuniverse.com
1-800-Authors (1-800-288-4677)

ISBN: 978-1-4759-4098-5 (sc)
ISBN: 978-1-4759-4099-2 (e)

Printed in the United States of America

iUniverse rev. date: 7/31/2012

He grabbed her, pushed her into an open doorway and using himself as a shield, pressed his big muscular body firmly against her. "What are you doing?" Her voice sounded frantic as she stiffened against him.

"Saving your life," he responded.

His hot breath fanned her face as the sounds of breaking glass got closer. Alice's heart pounded in her chest. Was this the way she was going to die? Would she ever see her children again? Tears rolled down her cheeks as she buried her face in Andrew's broad chest and hugged him firmly.

Andrew Benton would do anything to protect the brown eyed woman he'd just met. He showed it by pressing his soft mouth gently against hers to stifle a frightened sound from her lips and give the gang of ruffians a different take on the situation as they noisily passed by.

Chapter One

Wrapped in a thick red sweater over black sweats and pink slippers, Alice Vaze stood on the balcony of her sixth floor Manhattan apartment watching the snowflakes gently flutter to the tiled floor. As the freezing wind tore through her fragile body, she hugged her chest for warmth as hot tears hesitantly crept down her frost nipped cheeks.

She was still angry, but mostly at herself; she'd turned a blind eye to everything her husband had done to undermine her character. In a fit of passion, she'd once said to him, "If it makes you feel more of a man to make me feel small, please, go right ahead and grow."

But what had put her way over the edge was seeing him in the arms of another woman.

There was no denying it. No turning a blind eye. His company was having a dinner at Tavern On The Green restaurant in Central Park and while she chatted with his colleagues, he'd stepped outside to smoke a cigarette. After half an hour, his colleague Nathan asked, "Where's Harvey?"

Alice looked around but he had not come back into the restaurant. She excused herself to join him outside.

She moved away from the lights of the restaurant, past the brightly decorated white and blue horse-drawn carriages filled with tourists wrapped in fur coats. She saw two lovers intertwined in each other's arms and dismissed them. Looking in the opposite direction, she still didn't see him. But something went off inside her brain that made her take another look at the couple. *No,* her brain said, and just out of curiosity, she walked back, slowly passing column after column of festively lit lamp-posts and trees. A few feet away, her brain still said *no,* but her eyes said, "Oh my God!"

Harvey's arms were lovingly wrapped around another woman, and his lips, the lips that had not kissed her in months, were passionately kissing the woman. So passionate was his kiss that his body pressed hard into hers making their bodies seem one. She'd seen the woman a few times with Harvey at the office and at conferences, but it never occurred to her that there was anything between them, even though at times when they spoke, the woman would be inches from his face. He always said he'd never date a white woman, and yet, now, his tongue was wrapped around hers doing the tango.

The rage radiating through Alice could have melted steel. She stood shaking, almost losing control of her bladder. Her feet felt like lead, immovable. Her jaw fell slack. Her mouth open, her brain seemed to be at the melting point. "Harvey," she whispered, still in disbelief.

Pulling his lips from the woman, he turned slowly toward her. He had not tried to shield her from the shame and embarrassment. He'd just stood there, mockingly, away from the lamp light, looking at her as if saying; *this is your life, deal with it.* The woman still clutched at his arm. In spite of the anger and embarrassment Alice felt, she turned, held her head high and without a word, walked away from them.

She dealt with it the only way she could; hailing a taxi to the train station, getting on the New Jersey Transit, and taking a taxi home to Princeton.

All lines of communication between Alice and Harvey were severed. Less than a week later, she had found herself an apartment in Manhattan.

Staring at the falling snow, she walked slowly to the railing and peered at the street below. The bed of soft white snowflakes lay undisturbed, beautiful and clean, but in the not too distant future it would become black and disgusting. To her, nothing beautiful ever lasted very long. She thought her marriage to Harvey was beautiful until it turned ugly.

Wiping the tears from her cheeks, she turned just in time to see her daughter and son standing inside the door staring at her. Phillip tugged the glass door open.

"Mommy, he said, "Are we on vacation? Is Daddy coming to see us soon?"

She shook her head as another set of tears ran down her cheek. "I'm not sure, baby." She pushed away from the rail and walked through the door. Alia caught the edge of her sweater and looked curiously at her pained face.

"Don't cry, Mommy."

Alice closed the door and bent to kiss her children. Alia wiped the tears from her cheeks with her tiny fingers, hugged her tightly, then lay her head against her mother's shoulder.

"Thank you, sweetie," Alice said smiling just for her children. "We'll be fine. Everything will be great. You'll both see your daddy," she hesitated, "soon." She lifted Alia in her arms and walked into the living room with Phillip walking by her side. She thought of watching television with the children but changed her mind. She really didn't feel like it and it was almost the children's bedtime. She walked toward their bedroom and met Delia, the children's nanny, in the hallway. "I'll put them to bed, Delia."

Delia nodded and touched her arm. "Will you be all right, Miss Alice?"

Alice stopped and turned toward her. "We'll all be fine, Delia.

Delia smiled and continued walking down the passageway.

Delia was half white with brown hair that she kept closely cropped to her small face. Her hazel eyes seemed to always smile, and her small mouth very rarely pouted. This petite woman, who never wavered in her duties, had been the children's nanny from their birth. Alice had met her while vacationing in Jamaica.

Listening to her horrific story about being raped and the death of her child resulting from the rape, Alice's heart went out to her. But as tragic as Delia's life had been, her outlook on life was still a positive one. She had inspired Alice, who promised to send for her if she could.

When she became pregnant, Alice found the need for a nanny; someone who knew her culture, not to mention one who could cook a good Jamaican meal every now and then. If she didn't go back to work within four to six months after her babies were born, she would certainly lose her job. She'd had a special connection with Delia, maybe because their backgrounds held a bit of similarity; both were part Irish, and from the same district. She trusted her. Within the year Delia was with her living in the Bronx. When they moved to Princeton, Delia didn't hesitate to move with them. That was six years ago. Delia had never gone back to Jamaica. She said she had nothing back there. Alice and her family had adopted Delia or maybe Delia had adopted Alice.

Turning into the children's room, Alice placed Alia on the bed and began taking her clothes off.

"I can do that," Alia asserted, unbuttoning her blouse and smiling at her mother. "See."

Alice smiled and nodded. "Yes, you're getting to be such a big girl."

"I can take off my own clothes too," Phillip said, hopping onto the bed and pulling his sweater over his head. Alice sat on the bed between her children and held them close to her. Valiantly, she fought the tears that threatened to weaken her courage once more.

She didn't even hear Delia come into the room. She touched her shoulder. "Why don't you let me do this? You go to your room and lie down for awhile. I'll bring in some tea for you."

Alice inhaled and nodded. She felt like a defeated woman as she hugged her children, got up and walked to her room feeling weary and strained. Sitting on her bed, she picked up the telephone receiver, dialed her best friend, Nikki, in Jamaica, but all she got was her answering machine. She left her new phone number and a short message. *I've left Harvey, call me when you get a chance.*

She realized the message was too much to the point but at the moment, that's how she felt. It had been three weeks since she'd left Harvey. She had not called Nikki sooner because she didn't want to talk about what had happened. Frankly, she didn't want to burst into tears, best friend or not. Not even her mother knew that she'd left Harvey.

Delia came in with chamomile tea and a watercress sandwich. She'd missed dinner, too upset to eat. She looked at Delia and shook her head. "Delia, how am I going to pay…"

"Hush, Miss Alice, I told you when we left the house together that I will take care of you and the children for nothing. You and those children are the only family I've got. I've been all over the world with you and…" she looked at Alice. "Sorry. Don't worry about anything. Plus, where would I go? You took me in when I had nothing and no one."

Alice smiled. "Thanks, Delia."

She nodded. "Have a good night."

"You too, Delia."

Delia closed the door behind her and Alice slipped out of her clothes and into her nightgown. She sat up, took the cup from the nightstand and sipped the warm chamomile tea. Before long, she fell into a fitful sleep.

Alice had never known what it was like to be on her own. She'd married her college sweetheart less than a year after graduation; Harvey Vaze, a very ambitious finance major from a poor background. He was determined to be rich and successful. Harvey was a very handsome man with many flaws, all of which Alice ignored, since she was blindly in love. He was vain and a horrible womanizer. Alice thought her love could have changed him, but she was wrong.

Being from an upper-middle-class Jamaican family, Alice saw firsthand what money had done to her grandmother and mother. Her grandmother was ignored by her grandfather who used his wealth to whore around. Her father did the same thing. She thought her marriage would have been different because she and Harvey were so much in love. She couldn't understand Harvey's obsession with wealth and power, but his ambition assured a nice future for her and the family they would create. Unfortunately things began going downhill as his success grew. In his quest for wealth and power, he lost his self-esteem and forgot the woman who had stood by his side for so long.

Chapter Two

At work the next day, Alice found it hard to concentrate. She kept asking herself if she could have done anything different; maybe be more spontaneous, meet Harvey naked at the door every once in a while? But she shook her head. Harvey was almost never home and when he was, he was always pre-occupied, and now she knew why.

At the end of a busy work day, she got her coat from behind the door and draped it over her shoulders. She didn't feel like taking the subway or a taxi to her apartment, she felt like walking.

She walked slowly to the bank of elevators and absentmindedly pressed the down button. She had not even heard her assistant say goodnight. She thought of her children and all the things they'd become accustomed to; having a big yard to play in and a big house to run around in. Now they were cooped up in a two-bedroom apartment sharing a room with Delia.

Getting off the elevator into the crowded lobby, she pushed through the revolving door. A gust of cold wind slapped her hard in the face. She pulled her coat tight around her and wrapped her scarf securely around her neck. She slipped on her black leather gloves and pushed her hands into her pocket. It was a horrible evening to even think of walking one block, but she was determined to walk as far as she could; she needed a lot of time to think. She needed to make definite plans for her and the children.

She couldn't really afford the apartment they were in, but she'd needed one quick.

Trying to avoid all the snow and the icy patches in her path, she walked at a slow pace. Her entire married life quickly crossed her mind in flashes as if she were about to die, and the hatred she felt for Harvey renewed in one swift blow to her heart. In a desperate attempt to save a failing marriage, she'd suggested counseling. Harvey told the marriage counselor that she was envious of his success. She'd looked at him as if he were mad. How could a wife be envious of her husband's success? What woman in her right mind wanted a husband she was ashamed of? His success was supposed to be her happiness. But in this case, his success was the downfall of their marriage. They had not gone back.

Blinded by her tears, she walked on as the cold wind whipped at her coat. It was twenty degrees, but inside she burned. The anger and disillusionment she felt drove her forward, until finally, the frigid wind got to her bones. She hailed a taxi.

When she opened the door to her apartment expecting the children to rush into her arms, the first person she saw smiling at her was Harvey. She froze and stiffened. Her lips tightened and her eyes became as cold as the outdoors when he advanced toward her with open arms.

She stood stiff and met him with accusing eyes as he attempted to hug her. "Don't you dare touch me!" she whispered defiantly. "How dare you come here thinking I would welcome you in my home after all that you've done to me and the children."

"For the children," he whispered wickedly.

"No, I will not do this to my children. I will not lie to them. We can be cordial, but don't you ever touch me."

He lowered his arms and was about to say something when Alia and Phillip ran toward their mother with open arms. "Hello, darlings." She knelt and wrapped them protectively in her arms, trying with all her might not to cry. She kissed their cheeks. "Why don't you guys wash up for dinner." She got to her feet, slipped out of her coat and gloves, then hung them in the closet.

"Is daddy staying for dinner?" Alia asked.

Not knowing how to answer, she turned to look at her daughter. "Ahhh."

"Of course, I'll stay for dinner," Harvey replied shamelessly, taking Alia's hand. "Where's your bathroom? I'll help you wash up."

Alice stood watching as Alia led her father to her bathroom. She knew exactly what he was doing. He was making her out to be the bad guy. Well, it wouldn't work. She went to her room, changed into sweats and came back to see everyone sitting at the dinner table. She sat and ate in silence praying that she could get through dinner without erupting.

On his best behavior, Harvey left right after dinner even though the children asked him to stay and read a bedtime story. "I have an important appointment tonight, but I'll come back another time," he told them and didn't notice how disappointed they were.

Harvey didn't call the next two days, but called Alice at home Friday evening to invite her out to dinner on Saturday. "We need to talk," he said.

"It would have been nice if you'd given me more time but, yes, we do," Alice agreed. "Pick me up at seven." She hung up, got out of her suit and slipped into a warm, comfortable dressing gown. There was a deep hole in her soul and she didn't know how to fix it. She no longer felt angry, just empty. The words unwillingly left her lips, *I need a divorce*. Tears rolled down her cheeks and her throat ached. *I need a divorce*, she said again covering her face with both hands. *Oh God, it's over.* She turned, climbed into bed and pulled the cover over her head.

The phone rang but she didn't feel like talking with anyone. *What's wrong with me*, she wondered. She was never an indecisive person, neither was she one to cry easily, but now she could not stop the deluge of tears. She wanted the romance. She wanted what she'd seen in Harvey's eyes when she'd caught him with the other woman. The image that she'd tried so hard to shut out, flashed before her: Harvey in the arms of another woman. *Why did I have to see them? Why did he have to stand there so uncaringly?* She placed the pillow over her head and screamed into it.

The phone rang again, and she rolled over on her side and picked up the receiver on the second ring. It was Nikki. "What's going on? Why am I calling you at this number at night? And why did you leave Harvey? What did that bastard do? It must be something real bad for you to actually walk out on him."

Alice sighed and smiled. "It's good to hear your voice. I left Harvey because I saw him in the arms of another woman."

There was a long pause before Nikki spoke. "I'm sorry, sis."

Alice wiped the tears from her eyes. "I saw him kissing another woman the night of his office function."

"Oh, sweetie," Nikki's voice caught in her throat.

"Please don't cry Nik. You'll only start me crying again. I feel as if my life is such a mess." Tears streamed down her cheeks. "I don't know what to do, Nik." She broke into sobs as Nikki silently listened.

"You will, sweetie. You will. I know you. You're strong and resourceful. I believe in you."

"I don't feel strong or resourceful right now, Nik."

"Do you want me to come up?"

Alice smiled and wiped her eyes. "Thanks, Nik, but not yet. I'm going out with him tomorrow night. I guess then we'll both say the words out loud."

Nikki didn't ask what words. "I wish I were there to comfort you. Are you sure you'll be okay?"

"Aren't you the one who just told me how strong I am?"

"I know. How are my little ones doing?"

"They think they're on vacation and given the fact that Harvey comes to visit they have no idea what's going on... I hope."

"Well, knowing you, things will be sorted out soon. Let me know if you want me to come up. I can ask another doctor to fill in for me at any time."

"Thanks Nik, I'll talk with you soon." She hung up the receiver feeling much better than before Nik had called, and just as she turned off her light, the children came into her bed and snuggled beside her.

"Goodnight, Mommy."

"Goodnight, Alia."

"Goodnight, Mommy."

"Goodnight, Phillip."

They knew their daddy would not be coming home tonight.

∞

When Alice opened the door to let Harvey into her apartment, he was holding a bouquet of white and pink roses. He kissed her cheek and handed her the roses. "I know this really nice little Indian restaurant not too far from here, you'll love it," he said, still standing in the doorway.

She looked at him and smiled. She hated Indian food.

He wore a pale blue sweater under his tan coat, and she had to admit, he looked good.

He unbuttoned his coat, took it off and slung it on the back of the off white sofa. Then he walked to the bar and poured himself a drink of cognac.

"Would you like a drink, Harvey?" she asked sarcastically, glancing at him without smiling. She looked away because after all that had happened, she felt herself still attracted to him. It was nuts and she knew it. Frankly, it wasn't just the cheating. It was all the verbal abuse that he'd heaped on her over the last ten years.

"I'm sorry. I should have asked, shouldn't I?" he said, but he didn't put the drink down. "You choose the restaurant. Where do you want to go? Anywhere."

"French," she said, sitting on the sofa and watching his expression. There was nothing there to tell her he was sorry for what she'd seen. There was no remorse.

He nodded. "Then French it is. I know a nice French restaurant on restaurant row. We don't need reservations." He swallowed the drink and picked up his coat. "Let's go." He began walking to the door.

"Aren't you going to say hello to the children?" she asked, realizing he would have walked through the door without even looking in on them.

"Of course. I just wanted to put on my coat first." He turned and walked down the hallway.

Of course you did. Alice observed him. Unfortunately, she couldn't drive away the hurt or resentment, no matter how hard she tried. She didn't know what the outcome of the dinner would be, but she knew after tonight she would go on with her life, one way or the other. *No more tears,* she promised herself.

When Harvey came back, she was standing by the window with her back to him. He came up behind her and slipped his arms around her waist. Her body stiffened as he kissed the back of her neck. "I want you," he said and she turned in his arms and looked hard into his dark eyes.

She saw the lust in his eyes and felt a little sick. "Let's go to dinner," she slipped away from him into her coat and walked to the door.

"You're a hard woman, Mrs. Vaze."

She glanced back at him. "You're a good teacher," she said clutching her coat.

He said nothing as they rode the elevator down to the first floor, through the door. Even when he hailed the taxi and they got to the restaurant, they didn't exchange a word.

Sitting across the table from Alice, Harvey reached for her hand and closed his long fingers around hers. He looked into her brown eyes and said, "We need to get a divorce."

She swallowed. *No tears, no anger.* She'd wanted to be the one to say the words. She gently pulled her hand from his and balled it into her lap as shock radiated through her. Her stomach hurt. For a moment she felt paralyzed. *I want a divorce.* She'd thought about it but had no idea he would be the one to say the words. She looked at him, heaved a sigh, smiled mechanically then nodded. "It's for the best." Actually, in her mind she had it going a different way. She had him saying, *"I'm sorry for all the hurt I've caused you and the children. I wish I could make it all go away but believe me, I love you. Please come back to me."*

"Why don't we have champagne to celebrate our amicable split."

His brows drew together. He thought she would have fought him on his decision. Cry or something to show she was still in love with him. He nodded, waved the waiter over and ordered Perrier Jouet.

"No, let's order something else. I love that champagne. We used it to celebrate good times. After all, this is the death of a marriage. Let's have something cheap."

"Cheap!" he said, his mouth set sternly.

She nodded.

"Okay." He looked at the waiter. "Not Perrier Jouet. Can you recommend something?"

"To celebrate a break-up?" The waiter asked.

"Yes," Alice said fighting back the tears. She felt her hand begin to shake as flames of anger once again licked at her. *You're doing fine. Hold it together.* She excused herself. "I need to go to the bathroom. I'll be back in a minute." She smiled politely.

The waiter pointed the way and she rushed away before anyone saw the tears. Behind closed doors, she choked on them as she let them fall. *I said, no tears. What's wrong with me? What did I expect? I'm on my own. For the first time in my life, I'm on my own.* She held onto the edge of the sink, looked at her reflection in the mirror, then breathed deeply. Again, she had this defeated feeling creep into her brain. She took another deep breath, dabbed at her cheeks and applied powder. Two glasses of champagne and she intended to make a quick getaway.

Sitting back across from Harvey, she stared at his face and knew he was angry. *Good. Why should I be the only angry one?*

He raised his glass and so did she. "We did have some good times, didn't we?" he said.

"Yes." She kept looking at him.

He swallowed a mouthful of champagne.

She gulped down a mouthful and felt the bubbles fizzing down past her throat into her belly. She needed to leave.

"What will you tell the children?" he asked.

She looked at him. "The truth."

"What is the truth, Alice?"

"I should ask you that question. Do you want to speak to them and explain this?"

For awhile, he didn't answer then he shook his head. "I wouldn't know what to say."

Alice nodded. "Then leave it to me."

"You will be kind?"

"I won't do or say anything to hurt my children or the relationship they have with you."

He nodded. "Thank you."

"I have to go," she said abruptly. I just need to go, now."

He nodded. "I did love you, you know."

She fingered the purse in her hands and looked at him with dull enthusiasm. "Once." She got to her feet and so did he.

The waiter came over with the check. Harvey looked at the numbers and pulled out a money clip. He handed the waiter a fifty and told him to keep the change. The waiter looked at him. "Thank you sir." It was a very big tip.

Alice and Harvey walked out of the restaurant and he hailed a cab for her. She got into the cab. He lit a cigarette and took a long drag, his gaze never leaving her face until the cab drove away.

Alice gave the driver the address then got on her cell phone. She dialed her attorney's number. "Gwen, I need you to start divorce proceedings."

"For whom?" she asked.

"Me."

"Huh. Are you serious?"

"Yes."

"What are we citing?"

"Irreconcilable differences."

Gwen heaved a sigh. "Okay. Do we need to talk before we do this? We've been friends for many years, Lise."

"No, no talk, just do what has to be done. I'm moving to Florida as soon as I can get a job down there."

"Wow! You're moving fast."

"I have to before I fall apart. I'll talk with you later. Call me if you need information. You still have Harvey's number?"

"Yes."

"Use it." Alice hung up the phone and looked out the window as the driver dipped in and out of traffic. *What do I say to the children? Would they blame me for the breakup? Are they even old enough to do that?* She frowned. She had to have a good explanation for the children that wouldn't diminish the roles of mother or father. She decided not to tell them just yet and realized it was a chicken shit way to go about it, but she wanted to be kind to Harvey even though he was a coward and a vermin. Right now she didn't feel very kind. She nodded. She wanted to tell them that night, but couldn't.

The next two nights the children slept in her bed. There were no more tears, just a lot of soul searching and planning. Yes, she would move to Florida to be closer to her mother and sister. Actually, she spent the rest of the weekend in bed, not because she was depressed, she told herself, but because she was tired and drained. Delia was glad she'd stopped crying and encouraged her to rest by bringing her meals to her. The children enjoyed the closeness. Watching television and playing games was their kind of weekend. They didn't even ask for their father.

Monday evening as she picked up her purse to leave the office, her phone rang. Thinking it was Harvey, she just stared at the instrument on her desk. She hesitated for a moment. However, when she picked up the receiver, she was pleasantly surprised to hear the voice on the other end.

"Hi Alice. It's Willetta."

There was no mistaking that crisp English accent. Willetta Benton had worked for her the first three years of Alice's employment with the company as personnel manager. She was born on Long Island but grew up in London. She loved to travel and for the last three months of her employment waited to hear from Lufthansa Airlines where she'd applied for a position as flight attendant. Her philosophy was, take advantage of the single life when you get the chance; to do what you like where you like, how you like and when you like. When she'd finally got the call, everyone in the department including Alice was excited for her. Willetta would have had it no other way. Getting the job was all she had talked about after her second interview. She wanted to travel the world, and this was the only way she could afford to do it.

As her friend, Alice was sad to see her go, but before Willetta left the company, they'd made plans to one day meet for dinner. Alice had never heard from her until now.

Alice leaned back in her chair, picked up a pen and tapped it noisily on the desk. "Willetta? Willetta who? I can't remember any one by that name."

"Oh come on, Allison, you remember."

Her smile broadened. Willetta was also the only person in the world who had called her Allison. She'd told her that Alice was the name given to a daffy little girl who kept running after a rabbit in a silly tale and she couldn't see her running after anything in her life except success, her children and happiness.

"Okay, so I do remember who you are, but it's been a long time. If I were waiting for you to have dinner, I would have died of starvation by now. What have you been doing with yourself?"

She detected a smile in Alice's voice. "You know, traveling, getting married," Willetta snickered.

"You got married?" Alice asked in a cynical tone. "That's wonderful. Congratulations. Who's the lucky guy?"

"I got married to a pretty wonderful man, and the name is now Zimmerman. If you laugh, I'll kill you."

"So you sold out. That's great, Zimmerman. And they said it could never happen."

"Oh come on, Vaze. You know how love is, it's color and culture blind."

"So they say." And suddenly Alice began laughing.

"Are you laughing at my name?"

"No, I'm laughing at my own memories. I can remember a friend of mine with hazel eyes and long curly hair having lunch at a sidewalk café in Manhattan and laughing or sneering at mixed couples as they walked by."

"Yeah, I thought I would have gotten married to your brother if you had one, but as I said before, love is blind and my husband is a handsome devil."

"Good for you. But it's so good to hear your voice again, finally."

"Yeah, don't rub it in, I've been thinking about you though."

"I bet you have."

"I mean it. As a matter of fact, I called to invite you to that long overdue dinner." She didn't wait for Alice to respond. "How about tomorrow? When I said we should have dinner one evening, so long ago," she laughed, "Your exact words were, *give me a few hours notice.* So this is me giving you a few hours notice. We could eat at a little restaurant in the Village, or, we can come to Jersey and eat with you guys, whatever you like."

There was a long pause before Alice answered. It would be nice to see Willetta again and meet her new husband, but she had no intentions of inviting Harvey just to keep up appearances. She didn't feel like telling Willetta her life story either. "Well, I'd love to, Willetta, but do you mind if I come by myself? Harvey's busy tomorrow night."

"Oh, then do you want to make it another night? I'll be in town for a week."

"Not at all. I'd love to come to the Village."

"Then I'll call you tomorrow morning with the name of the restaurant. I'm going to make the reservations for five-thirty. We need to chat. You know, to catch up on things. Oh! By the way, my brother will be with us."

"I'll see you tomorrow." She loved the fact that Willetta didn't probe into her business and didn't relish the idea of telling her anything. She smiled and took a cleansing breath. Going out with a good friend would be a well-deserved distraction. She needed to be around other people.

When she got home, she half expected to see Harvey there and breathed a sigh of relief that he wasn't. She hung up her coat in the closet, flicked on the fireplace, hugged her children and went to her room to change her clothes. She then had dinner with the children and Delia. She looked at the children then at Delia. They felt like a family—her family. "Do you guys mind if we move to Florida?" She knew the question would come as a shock to them but she was handling it a little at a time.

"Tomorrow?" Alia asked.

"No, maybe in a month or so."

"Will daddy come too?" Phillip asked.

"No, sweetheart. It will be just you, Alia, Delia and mommy."

He wrinkled his brow and Alice felt strong enough to answer any question they asked.

"Will we be close to grandma then?" Alia inquired.

Alice looked at her. *Why wasn't she asking about her father.* "Yes, maybe very close."

"Is it warm in Florida?" she asked again.

"Yes, very warm."

Alice looked again at Phillip. "Do you think it will be all right, Phillip?"

He nodded, but something told Alice that there would be more questions. Lots more. She looked at Delia. "What are you thinking?"

She nodded. "Yes. I will go anywhere you go."

Alice smiled. That was all she wanted to hear. "Thank you guys. I think we'll be happy in Florida."

After dinner they watched television until it was bedtime.

With the children asleep by her side, and her eyes drooping, she jumped at the sound of the ringing phone. She picked up. "Yes, hello."

"Did I wake you?" Harvey asked, his voice half slurred.

"Not entirely."

"So how was your day? Did you tell the children?"

"Not exactly." Her eyes were closing.

"What does that mean, *not exactly?*"

"Harvey, can we talk about this tomorrow when I'm wide awake?" she whispered.

"No, I want to talk about it now. I can come there right now to tell them."

"They're asleep." She yawned.

"Okay. So how was your day? Can we have dinner again tomorrow night?"

This is not good. "My day went well and no, I have a dinner date tomorrow night."

"We're not even divorced and you're dating already!"

I knew this wasn't going to go well. "I'm having dinner with Willetta and her husband tomorrow night."

"Oh, so her husband will be there but yours won't?"

"Harvey, go to sleep. Call me when you haven't been drinking. Goodnight." She hung up the receiver and looked over at the children. They were still asleep.

With Harvey's drinking problem, she wondered if this divorce would be an amicable one. She turned over, punched her pillow a couple times and settled her head in it. In spite of Harvey, she was really looking forward to dinner with Willetta and her husband.

Chapter Three

T he next day, Alice helped Delia get the children ready for school then got herself ready in a blue and white cotton-blend suit in preparation for her dinner with Willetta. Paying special attention to her long brown hair, she pulled it into a tight bun at the nape of her neck. She was never one to wear makeup except for lipstick and powder, but this morning, she dabbed just a bit of blush onto her brown cheekbones, glanced at herself in the mirror and made a face.

Running just a bit late, she helped the children on with their coats. Realizing she'd forgotten to tell Delia about her dinner engagement, she said, "Delia, I won't be home for dinner this evening. I'm having dinner with a friend of mine. I may be late in coming home."

"Okay, no problem. I'll get the children to bed at a decent hour."

"Thanks, Delia." They all went through the door together and Alice kissed her children before she dashed for the subway.

By twelve-thirty Willetta called to give her the name of the restaurant they'd be dining at that evening. "Do you know the place?" she asked.

"No, I can't say I do but as long as Manhattan has taxis, I'll find it."

"Oh, wait," Willetta said, "Did I tell you my brother was in town?"

"Yes."

"Well, at four he'll be in your area. He can pick you up at the office."

"Does he have a car?"

"No one owns a car in the Village." Willetta's laughter, again, somehow lifted Alice's spirits. "He takes the train or taxi just like all of us poor folks, but since you don't know where you're going..."

"Yes, I get the point. If he comes straight to the office and asks for me, he won't waste any time looking for me and I won't have to describe my dress to you."

"Okay, sounds good. He'll be there at four."

"Great. I'm really looking forward to seeing you."

"Me too. See you later."

In her excitement, Willetta had forgotten to tell her her brother's name. *Oh, that doesn't matter,* Alice thought. He would surely know hers. She hung up the receiver, shook her head and smiled. Willetta was one of the most punctilious women she'd ever met. If she were a few minutes late for lunch, Willetta's displeasure would almost spoil the hour. She hoped that part of her had relaxed a bit.

Leaning back in her chair, Alice wondered what Willetta's brother looked like. Willetta was a very pretty woman, maybe her brother looked a lot like her. Frowning at her own thoughts, she exhaled. *Why should I care what he looks like. I'm just having dinner with him, not marrying him for God's sake. Men are off my list for a long time. I'm going to enjoy being single.*

A few minutes later, Anna, her secretary, buzzed to say her applicant had arrived.

At four, an out of breath Anna walked into her office. She closed the door and stood against it, panting.

"What is it, Anna?" Alice asked without looking up from her work.

"There's a Greek god waiting for you in the lobby."

"A what?"

Anna fanned her face and shook her head. "You should see this guy. His name is Andrew Benton. He says he's here to pick you up."

Alice laughed. "Oh, Willetta's brother," she said unenthused. She got up, shoved Anna out of her office and made small piles of paper on her desk. She checked her lipstick in the hand mirror she carried in her purse then pulled her coat from the rack and walked out to meet Andrew Benton.

The bronze man towering over six feet to her five feet and three inches, stood as he saw her leave her office. He had thick, curly brown hair which hung somewhere past his shoulders. He wore a blue blazer over a white shirt and blue jeans. His black winter coat hung meticulously over one arm. He walked forward to meet Alice and extended his free arm.

Alice took his outstretched arm as he introduced himself. And she certainly didn't miss the deep green of his eyes and the softness of his hand that seemed to linger just a bit longer than necessary as he said "hello" and gazed deep within her very troubled, unavailable soul.

Slowly she withdrew her hand from Andrew's, dragged her gaze from his piercing green eyes, smiled at him and began walking to the elevator bank. She waved to Anna, who seemed to be dreamily frozen in time.

Getting off the elevator and reaching the huge revolving doors, Andrew stopped and handed his coat to Alice. She looked up from the coat in her hand to his extremely handsome face, but he said nothing. He took her coat from her arm, held it for her to slip into, then took back his own and slid his arms into the sleeves. Alice smiled and took a frank and admiring look at him.

"You're a man of very few words."

"Sometimes words are not necessary," he replied, and for a moment, Alice thought she saw a flicker of laughter in his eyes.

The sun's stubborn rays had pierced through dark gloomy clouds, turning the dirt-covered snow into a watery black slush which ran freely into the city's drainage system.

Andrew stood close to the curb of One Liberty Plaza and held up his hand to hail a cab.

"Are you allergic to our subway system?" Alice asked.

He looked at her and smiled the kind of smile that broke hearts and made women swoon. She was unaffected, or so she thought.

"No, but I thought we'd get there faster."

"Did you ever work in New York?" She really didn't feel like being in such an enclosed space with him, even if he looked like a Greek god.

"Yes."

"Then you've forgotten the ways of this city. No one gets to hurry at this hour."

Fortunately, it was only a short walk to the subway. And as she stepped down from the curb, they crossed the street and Andrew nonchalantly took hold of her elbow. He lightly held her hand as they descended the wet, slippery subway steps. In the overcrowded train, they stood and held onto the post. He held her casually around her waist, moving discreetly behind her just as an old perverted man with the smell of stale sweat tried to settle in behind her.

Okay, so she was wrong. They shared more of a cramped space now than they would have in a cab. What was she thinking? Embarrassed, Alice glanced up at him. "Thank you."

Holding the post with his free hand, his long powerful legs astride for balance, his strong chest touched her back.

Unable to help her emotions, for a second, she closed her eyes and exhaled. *This was her private moment.* Alice didn't mind him trying to protect her at all. In fact, with every kind thing he did for her, she became painfully aware that Harvey never did those things. He rarely held her except for during sex, which was virtually non-existent the last year of their marriage. Although he would have protected her from a pervert rubbing up against her, he would not have held her fast to him to prevent her from swaying in this crowded train. More and more she regretted suggesting the train. *He probably thinks I'm soft in the head,* she thought.

As the warmth of Andrew's soft hand seeped through her coat, she became nervously aware of the small space they shared. For the first time since they shook hands and said hello to each other, she felt compelled to speak freely. She had to, to keep from chastising herself for being so stupid. "I don't want to rush dinner. It's been a long time since I saw your sister. I'm dying to meet her husband. I thought she'd stay single longer but one never knows when they get stung by the love bug, so to speak." She was very much aware of her ramblings but talking at this very moment helped her deal with the nervousness she felt being so close to this *perfect* stranger. It was either talk or tremble. She was doing both. Fanning her face with her hand, she laughed. "Hot in here, isn't it?"

He had paid close attention to every word she uttered as his eyes took in every detail of her facial features. She had an exotic beauty and spoke with an accent, but again, both applied to his ex-wife and look how that ended. She was beautiful, conniving and selfish. Nothing he did was good enough. He glanced at Alice again, her face turned up to look into his face. Why on earth was he thinking of Darlene? He'd not thought of her in a long time. He'd tried to keep as far from her as possible. And as Alice chattered on nervously, he got the accent. She was Jamaican, but, still he wasn't quite sure because her Jamaican accent was mixed with a slight British accent.

Alice had half-twisted her body to accommodate her gazing into his eyes, but now he had her mesmerized and she was an unwilling subject. She wanted to turn away from him. She wanted to be angry with him for being a man who may have at some time cheated on his wife or girlfriend or belittled her but she couldn't, he didn't look the type. Damn him!

"It's a bit warm, and I do understand," he said, his voice deep and mellow like that of a songbird, but his eyes unsmiling.

Now, she felt so relaxed, she almost swayed in his arms. In this overcrowded train, he wouldn't have noticed, or would he? *What the hell am I thinking?* She glanced at his face one more time. *No man has the right to be this handsome. But you're a man. Eventually you show your true colors.* She tried to be angry again, and it would have worked had she not once again looked into his eyes and at the sensual curve of his magnificent mouth.

"Where do you live?" he asked.

She blinked. "Huh."

"Where do you live?" he repeated.

"Uptown, off Park Avenue."

"I'll take you home after dinner." It wasn't a question.

She gazed at his lips as he spoke then at his eyes. "If you don't mind me saying this, your eyes. I don't think I've ever seen anyone with such deep green eyes. Do you have trouble with your vision?"

His lids came down swiftly over his eyes when he laughed.

"Did I say something funny?" she asked with a shy laugh and a catch in her throat.

"No, I have perfect vision." He was peering at her now, in a lazy, sexy sort of way, and as she gazed hypnotically at his eyes, he once again averted them, shading them with thick dark lashes. *What is it about her? I just met the woman and right away she's sinking into my thoughts.* He wanted to stop thinking of her in that way and focus on the stops until they got to the village, when he could just pawn her off onto his sister then leave... No, he was also invited to dinner. Fine, he'd suffer through it.

His long, brown curls fell waywardly on his forehead and sat comfortably on his shoulder. His golden complexion looked like that of someone who spent a lot of time in the sun, which made her realize that although he had an English accent like his sister, he didn't live in England, and he certainly did not live in New York. Alice's eyes traveled cautiously to his full, perfect lips, and he smiled.

"I have my father's eyes."

She looked away from his face.

"Willetta and I grew up in London." He was breaking softly into her thoughts. She once again gazed into his dancing eyes, which now seemed to be filled with amusement. Before she looked away from his face, she caught sight of a beautiful smile, which parted his lips, showing white, even teeth, and spread across his entire face.

They both seemed to be fighting a losing battle of let's not like each other because although Alice was a tortured soul right now, Andrew had the soul of a poet and the heart of a lamb. Disappointed and angry with his ex-wife, he still didn't hate her. What made him think he could dislike this gorgeous creature beside him?

"You're laughing at me?" Alice said.

The smile faded. "Not at all."

She nodded and turned her body back into its original position determined not to be caught up in his status of a Greek god.

He lightly held her elbow as they changed trains and when they got to their destination, she sighed. In spite of herself, now she was glad they had not taken a cab because she felt very relaxed in his company. "Thank you for protecting me," she said, her voice just a bit higher than a whisper. She cleared her throat.

"You're welcome." He glanced at his watch and remembered his sister's instructions. If there was time to spare, he should take Alice to the apartment. And there was definitely time to spare. "It's still early. You don't mind if we go to Willetta's place before dinner?"

"Not at all."

"It's a bit of a walk, but the apartment is not far from the restaurant."

"All right."

Being careful not to step onto the slushy sidewalk, he guided her through different streets. She pulled her coat snugly around her as winter's harsh winds blew through barren trees on the sidewalk whistling their good nights.

"Is it always this quiet?" she asked.

"This area is, but the restaurant area is quite active. Jugglers and mimes are constantly putting on a show. I assume you've never been to the Village before?" His accent was smooth, almost with a southern drawl.

"Guilty, this is my first time. Actually, I thought they only did that in the summer."

He shook his head.

They finally got to Willetta's home and Alice wondered if Andrew had not taken the long way. After greeting Willetta warmly, Alice was introduced to her husband William, who worked as a stock broker on Wall Street.

Their cozy two-bedroom apartment had a warm, homey feeling not overly decorated, but tastefully done with what she assumed was Willetta's and William's favorite colors, blue and very light shade of green. The living room walls were filled with all kinds of paintings they'd bought together in Paris and Italy, with two Tiffany lamps on end tables framing the couch. She didn't visit the bedrooms or the kitchen for that matter. The small bar in the corner of the living room held four stools and a soft-blue tiled counter where they sat and chatted for a while. A few drinks and they were off to the restaurant.

The Italian restaurant was small and dimly lit, and the doors that would have normally been open to let the warm summer breeze in were now tightly closed against the bitter cold.

They were shown to a table for four in the middle of the room and when Andrew helped Alice off with her coat and pulled out her chair, his smooth, cool hand slightly touched her bare hand.

She breathed to distraction. "So tell me, Willetta, what's your favorite place to visit now that you're globe-trotting?" Alice asked, trying to catch her breath from the effects of the touch of Andrew's fingers. *What is wrong with me? I have never felt this way before. What way?* She asked herself. *Befuddled, stupid,* she answered.

"Greece, I love the fishing villages."

"With all the rich tycoons with their yachts and whatever they have in Greece, you love only the fishing villages? We have a few here in the States, you know. I mean places you can drive to, like Maine," she laughed.

The waiter came by, told them the specials and took their cocktail order.

"Oh, you know what I mean. The people are nice and warm, not like here."

Alice glanced at Andrew sitting across from her just as he averted his eyes. "I know what you mean but you're not thinking of one day leaving the good old USA for good, are you?" Smiling, she focused on Willetta.

"We've thought about it, but who knows?" Willetta shrugged as William caught Alice's attention and began rattling off the different dishes that he thought she'd like without even looking at the menu. It was obvious they had visited the restaurant more than once. When the waiter came back, they ordered three different appetizers: tortellini stuffed with crabmeat, turkey sausages and something green that Alice made a face at.

She sat back and listened while Willetta and William talked about the places they'd been all the while feeling Andrew's steady gaze on her face. Once again, his eyes seemed to pierce deep into her soul making her feel quite uncomfortable. If she had a million bucks to spare, she would have given it to him just to hear his thoughts.

"I often travel with Willetta whenever I get the chance, just to be near her. Willetta thinks getting away to different places at a moment's notice will keep the honeymoon going. She's right and I love her for it," William said, reaching for his wife's hand and kissing it.

"See, I told you the French would have a positive impact on our lives!" Willetta laughed.

For a moment, Alice thought of Harvey and their failed marriage and hoped Willetta and William would always feel as if they were on their honeymoon.

She listened again as Willetta told stories of her and Andrew's childhood in England. Even though Andrew's gaze was no longer on her, Alice could still feel him and her knees drummed nervously against the underside of the table. Discreetly, she removed her hands from the table and pressed her palms into her knees to suppress the shaking.

After coffee and dessert, William paid the bill and Willetta encouraged Alice to watch a bit of the sidewalk entertainment.

"I'm freezing. If I stay out here much longer without movement, my lips will turn blue," she said wrapping the scarf around her neck and folding her arms around her.

Without hesitation, Andrew put his arms around her and massaged her coat-clad arms. "We won't keep you too long," he said. Almost instantly, Alice felt warm inside. She nodded. He was true to his words. They bought roasted chestnuts and shifted their attention to the juggler and the sidewalk caricatures.

"I don't know how they stand the cold," Alice said noting how skimpily clad the performers were. She looked at her watch and realized if she stayed any longer it would be midnight before she would get home. "I'm ready to go," she said looking up at Andrew.

He nodded and she said her goodbyes to William and Willetta. "We have to do this again," Willetta said hugging Alice before William did.

Chapter Four

T urning onto Bleeker Street, Alice and Andrew had not gone four blocks when they were plunged into a frightening, unfamiliar blackness. She froze and dropped the bag of chestnuts. "Andrew! What happened? Where are you?"

He quickly held her hand and answered in an amused tone. "I'm right here. It looks like a power failure."

"No fooling, Sherlock. How am I going to get home? The trains can't run."

He read the fear and urgency in her voice. "It's all right, I have a two-bedroom apartment not too far from here. I never gave it up when I moved from New York because I'm always here."

"I think you already know that I'm not coming to your apartment. I don't go home with strange men."

"You think I'm strange?"

"No, I mean… I don't know you."

"Yes, you do. I'm your good friend, Willetta's brother."

"Oh, please, this is really not the time for levity. I'm a little scared. We haven't had a power cut in a long time, why now?"

"I know you are, and no, there hasn't been. I'm here, nothing will happen to you." He squeezed her fingers. "Let's go back to Willetta's apartment. I know she'll be worried sick."

"Okay."

When they turned to make the short trip back to Willetta's place, the entire area seemed to come alive with shouts of violence. She backed into Andrew and he held her firmly around her waist. The looting had begun. Flashes of light dominated the streets. Window and glass doors shattered as piercing alarms screamed in their ears. She heard a barrage of obscenities, but the word that stuck fast in her head was one that scared her to death and one she'd never forget.

Find the niggers.

The words reverberated in her brain and made her wince with anger and fear. Were they talking about her? Andrew and Willetta were white, and William was Jewish and pale. She struggled against Andrew and turned in his arms. He hugged her reassuringly.

The flashing lights were rapidly approaching and the words were repeated more viciously. "Why are they saying that?" she asked Andrew.

"Shhh," he said, placing a soft hand over her mouth. "It's just a word Alison."

"Have you ever faced open prejudice?" she looked into his face.

"Yes, I have." His mellow voice now held a rough edge to it as if Mississippi was burning in his head.

She was more than a little shocked. "You're white. I'm black, and there's no need for you to get angry with me. I'm the one trembling in your arms."

"I'm sorry." He breathed. "I'm not angry with you. We have to get out of here." Frankly, he had no thought to his own safety. The only thing he could think of was getting Alice to where she couldn't hear that word or feel afraid.

The lights and shouts were getting dangerously close as they hurried their pace. They didn't dare run for fear of being shot or mistaken for someone they were not, by the police. With her high heels slowing them down, the only way he could get them away fast was by grabbing her and slinging her over his shoulder. He didn't think she'd go for that. He grabbed her, pushed her into an open doorway, and, using himself as a shield, pressed his big, hard body firmly against her.

"What are you doing?" her voice sounded frantic as she stood stiff against him.

"Saving your life," he responded.

His hot breath fanned her face and as the sounds got closer, her heart pounded frantically in her chest. Was this the way she was going to die? Was she going to die tonight? Would she ever see her children again? Tears bathed her face as she buried it in Andrew's broad chest and hugged his firm, muscular waist. "I don't want to die," she whimpered.

"You won't die. We are not dying tonight. Am I hurting you?" His cheek pressed against her forehead.

She shook her head, she had to believe him. He placed a finger under her chin and raised her face to look into his eyes.

"I'm going to do something. Please don't slap my face."

"I won't."

"Do exactly as I say quickly and don't ask any questions, please. I'll protect you." The urgency now in his voice made her nod without hesitation.

"Put your arms inside my jacket."

She quickly did as she was told. "Are you going to hide my feet? I *am* wearing a skirt, in case you didn't notice."

"I noticed," he said, his voice cool and controlled.

"Sorry, I couldn't resist."

"I know. Try. I'll hide your feet." He was short and to the point.

There was no time for polite conversation; moreover, she believed he would either save their lives or get them killed. There was no doubt that the people shouting the dreaded word would have no qualm in shooting them without regret.

The voices were upon them as they stood rigid in the doorway. Alice hugged him tightly and squeezed her eyes shut. If they were going to die, she'd rather not see it coming. It wouldn't be so bad dying like this in the arms a god, but her children flashed before her eyes and she squirmed. No, she didn't want to die. There was more foul language used than Alice had ever heard in her entire sheltered life.

"Hey!" a voice called from behind them.

"Do as I say, now," Andrew whispered impatiently. Alice nodded.

"Tilt your head to the right of me."

She nervously tilted her head to the left. Her legs trembled to the point of weakness as the fear within her rose. Would she die in the arms of a stranger? She tightened her grip on his waist. If it hurt, she would never know.

Andrew impatiently moved her head to the right; his body was pressed so hard against her, breathing was optional. Before she realized what was happening, his lips pressed hard against her mouth. Her eyes flew open with questions, and her body became more rigid, if that was possible. Then she saw murky turquoise eyes gazing into hers.

"Give it to her, brother!" The hoodlums shouted. Their harsh Brooklyn accent wasn't hard to detect as their odor nauseatingly filled the air.

Alice's eyes were still open as she looked into Andrew's eyes, but he wasn't looking at her now. From the corner of his eye he stared anxiously into the streets, waiting for the opportunity to make his next move. Seeing four men in the street with a dim flashlight trained on them, he moved his body seductively against Alice.

"Take her, brother," one of the men shouted and laughed gutturally. The voices and the light slowly moved away from them, but they could still hear the laughter. Although they were now a block away, they kept the flashlight trained on them. There was more laughter, then the lights disappeared. Still, Andrew didn't move.

The voices faded, leaving just the sounds of breaking glass in the far distance. Andrew slowly relaxed his body and moved his lips from Alice's mouth. For a second, he leaned his head against her neck and breathed from exhaustion. Alice had no idea how long they stood that way. Time seemed to have stopped.

Alice's heart pounded so hard in her chest, she'd given herself a headache. Her hands dropped to her side and she felt herself sliding to the ground.

Andrew caught her as he felt her move downward against him.

"I'm sorry," he whispered, holding her close to him. "It's all right. They're gone."

"That *word* means a bit more than you're letting on, doesn't it?" she whispered, clearing her throat and standing strong on her feet. "Thank you for saving my life."

He breathed deeply. "I was called a nigger lover." He snapped the words as if they burned the inside of his mouth.

"Was your girlfriend…?"

He didn't allow her to finish before he cut her off. "No, and I don't want to talk about it now," he said with quiet emphasis.

"I'm sorry. I didn't mean to pry."

"It's all right." Still holding her to him, he flipped her around and leaned his back against the wall.

It was then that Alice realized his knees were bent in order to accommodate her height. She looked into his face. "You must have been very uncomfortable standing like that."

He gave her a little laugh and nodded. "My feet have gone to sleep." He pushed himself up while bracing the palm of his hands against the wall.

They could still hear shouting, which was now joined again either by gunfire or firecrackers. They couldn't be sure which one. However, it didn't matter; they had to get out of there and fast.

"If it weren't for you, I don't know what would have happened to me."

His voice was velvet yet edged with steel as he spoke. "You would have been home and in bed."

She began shaking and without a word of warning, he moved away from the wall and scooped her up in his arms. She buried her face in his neck, inhaled his soft cologne and held him tightly. *Aren't I supposed to dislike this guy?* "I can't go home tonight, can

I?" her voice muffled against his neck and for a brief second she felt like pulling his skin into her mouth.

"It's an extremely long walk from here. But if you want to, I'll walk with you." He laughed and continued walking through traffic where angry drivers had ditched their cars to stand on the sidewalk. What else were they going to do in this chaos?

Up and down the street taxi drivers angrily honked their horns and hung their heads out their windows cursing at the cop feebly trying to direct the traffic of cars going nowhere fast. Andrew surveyed the scene and said, "I'm taking you back to Willetta. I know she's waiting."

Alice nodded. Andrew was so focused on protecting her that he seemed to show very little concern for his own safety.

Chapter Five

P olice sirens and fire trucks dominated the dark area trying
to get to fires and looting areas. Andrew quickened his pace,
but halted for just a second as a glowing red caught his eyes. The
restaurant where they'd just had dinner was engulfed in flames.
Thick, strangling smoke rose slowly from the building. He shook
his head and continued with Alice in his arms.

"I can walk now. We're close," she said, not wanting Willetta
to see her in his arms.

He carefully deposited her on her feet, but held her hand as
they briskly walked the few yards. He knocked on Willetta's door.
It opened immediately.

"What kept you so long?" she asked. "I was sure that as soon
as the lights went out you'd come back here." She held a lit candle
in her hand and Andrew spent exactly two seconds trying to
explain why they were delayed. Willetta smiled. "Andrew, I'm
sure it wasn't a racial thing. The lights went out and there was
looting, but…"

He cut her off with an impatient wave of his arm. "I hate that
word, you know that, and you know why. I just didn't want Allison
to get hurt, that's all." His anger was very apparent as he made his
way into the living room.

Both women moved in behind him.

"No one likes that *word*. All right, all right you don't have to get upset," she said. "Alice can sleep in the guest room and you can sleep on the couch. I'm sure you'll want to protect her the rest of the night," she whispered teasingly in his ear. She said very little about the quick friendship that seemed to have formed between her brother and her friend. She turned to Alice. "I'm sorry. My big brother gets upset quite easily about that *word* we refuse to use."

Alice was now sitting on the couch watching and listening to brother and sister banter back and fourth. Candle lights flickered in the small overhead chandelier casting shadows on the wallpaper. She nodded, noticed the phone on the desk and instinctively got up and lifted the receiver. The line was dead. She reached in her purse and searched for her cell phone, but it was dead. *Figures.*

William came out to say goodnight. "I'm sorry about tonight, Alice. We all know what that *word* means. I don't blame Andrew for being angry. I would have been too." He hugged her. "Sleep well."

"I will."

William and Willetta left the room and Alice watched Andrew's back as he looked out the window at the blackness and flashes of lights. In the distance, they could still hear sounds of screaming sirens, shouts and the shattering of glass.

"Goodnight, Andrew. Thanks again."

He turned and smiled at her. "Goodnight, Alice. Sleep well."

From Allison to Alice. She smiled, nodded and walked to the bedroom carrying a lit candle. She turned and looked at him once more as he lit another candle and placed it on the window seat.

Getting out of her clothes and into the nightgown Willetta had left on the bed for her, she blew out the candle and climbed into bed. She shivered against the cold sheets and pulled the comforter up to her neck. In the dark, staring at the ceiling, she kept going over the events from four-thirty that afternoon to the present: the subway scene, dinner, the riots, her reaction to Andrew's kindness, his overall reaction toward her, his constant protection of her, even though they had just met. And what was this anger he had toward the word? *It's just a word,* he'd told her, but apparently it was more than just a word to him. She abhorred the word even if it was from one person of color to the next.

Andrew was a complex man, but she liked him. She took a deep breath, realizing she may like him too much. So the decision was made never to see him again after tonight.

Andrew's mood was as black as the darkness that had fallen all around him. He blew out the single candle and sat on the window seat looking up into the starless sky. It had been a very long time since he was in a situation to hear that word spoken so vilely. *Nigger lover! Nigger lover!* The words were fresh in his mind as if uttered just yesterday. He closed his eyes tightly as the sight of Stanley's still-bloody body swam vividly before him. He was holding his best friend in his arms, calling his name, trying to will him back to life, not feeling the knife wound in his own side until everything went black and he lost consciousness. Until this day, Stanley remained the best friend he'd ever had. *Hate is an extremely grave emotion.*

His tightly held grip on the window sill lessened as his thoughts came back to the present and Alice. Beautiful Alice. He might never see her again after tomorrow, but tonight he was glad to have protected her from the dark world of hatred and violence. When he thought of his lips pressed against her mouth, a heat radiated in his loins that he had not felt in a very long time. He shook his head; how weak the body that covers the soul.

By morning, the electricity still had not been restored. Alice threw on the blue flannel dressing gown and went into the living room to look for Andrew, but he wasn't there.

She raised the receiver and heard dial tone. Breathing a sigh of relief, she dialed her home number. To her dismay, Harvey answered.

"Where are you? Why did you leave the children alone, and why didn't you call last night?"

The harshness in his voice told her he had been waiting anxiously for her call. "I'm fine. Thanks for asking," she said sarcastically. "I'm at Willetta's home. And that's a stupid question."

"What happened to your cell phone?"

In a flat low voice, she said, "Dead battery."

"When are you coming home?" he asked again in an accusatory tone.

She took a deep breath and looked around the room to see if she was still alone. "Harvey, you are in Manhattan, not Europe. You know the situation. Please put Delia on the line."

The next voice she heard was Delia's. "Everything's fine, Miss Alice."

"I know, Delia. Sorry about last night. The children are fine?"

"Of course, Miss Alice. You don't have to ask."

"Yes or no, did Harvey stay all night or did he just get there."

"The first one. Are you all right?" she whispered.

"Yes, thanks, Delia. I'll see you soon." She hung up the receiver to see Andrew standing in the doorway with a box in his hand. She smiled hoping he had not heard her conversation. His smile told her he had not, either that or he was a very good actor.

"Well, I guess this is a forced holiday," Willetta said coming into the room.

They both caught a whiff of what Andrew held in his hands. "Fresh bagels and coffee!" Willetta exclaimed. "Wherever did you get them?"

"A well-kept secret." Turning to Alice, he smiled. "Did you sleep well?"

She smiled and noticed the tiny lines at the corner of his eyes, "Very well, thank you." Her eyes followed him into the small, clean kitchen. With his wide shoulders and tapered waistline, he was well proportioned and quite muscular. She remembered his muscles move under her hands last night.

She held her butterfly-filled stomach and took a deep breath. *Why does he have to be so damned handsome and nice?* His loose, curly hair hung freely onto his back. Their eyes met and made four; again he smiled. She bit into her lower lip and disengaged. *This is not happening. What exactly is happening? A little infatuation, that's what.* Knowing that was all it was and the fact that it would go no further, she decided that it felt good.

Willetta stood by watching the exchange then cleared her throat and moved to the kitchen to get butter out of the refrigerator. "Mmmm, coffee. Gimme, gimme," she said handing one to Alice.

She shook her head. "I'll have to pass on the coffee. I only drink tea, but the bagels look scrumptious."

"I noticed you drank only tea last night so I brought hot water for you to make tea." He reached up, opened a cupboard and took down a tea bag.

"Thank you, very much, that was very thoughtful." She stood beside Andrew, slipped the bag into the paper cup to steep and picked up a bagel. It was warm and as she slathered butter on it, she moaned a little and laughed. "I love a warm bagel."

Both Willetta and Andrew laughed. "I think he bought all this with you more in mind than us."

Andrew said nothing. He moved from the kitchen to the living room and stood looking out the window.

At eleven-thirty, after she'd had a shower and changed back into her suit, he offered to drive Alice home, then looked at his sister. She laughed, shook her head and handed him the keys to her little Volkswagen. "Good luck getting anywhere today in a car."

"Thanks for dinner and for putting me up for the night," Alice said, hugging Willetta.

Willetta smiled mischievously. "Nonsense. Why are you thanking me? We loved having you. We should do this again soon." She hugged Alice and kissed both cheeks. "Next time we'll try to keep the lights on."

Alice hugged William, who had been patiently waiting his turn. "Maybe we'll meet in Greece or France." He laughed and waved as she walked through the door with Andrew.

Willetta's car was parked in front of the building, a slushy mess running against the wheels. Andrew reached for the door, opened it and guided her into the passenger's seat.

It took them more than two hours of stop-and-go traffic to get from the Village to Alice's apartment. "Thank you so much for an interesting night and for driving me home. I would invite you up but I have no idea what my apartment looks like. Maybe another time." She knew very well there would not be another time.

"I look forward to seeing you again." He climbed out of the car and came around to open the door for her.

"Thanks again." She kissed his cheek and walked to the door of her building without looking back. If she had, she would have seen him standing there staring at her while caressing the cheek she'd kissed.

Climbing the stairs, she gave him a last thought. *He's strange in a delightful way; strong and silent.* What she loved most about him was his quick to action mentality and wondered if he was always like that. Didn't matter. She tried to push Andrew to the back of her mind as she reached her floor and pushed the key into the lock. The door jerked open. She looked into her husband's stern face and was very glad when her children came tearing toward her. She dropped to her knees and hugged them. "We were worried about you, Mama. Did you see the lights go out?" Alia said.

She laughed. "Yes, I did darling." She kissed their cheeks, got to her feet and led them inside as Harvey closed the door. She took off her coat, scarf and gloves and rubbed her hands together close to the roaring fire in the fireplace.

"Daddy stayed with us all night. He stayed in your bed," Phillip said.

Alice made a face then smiled. "Did he, now?" She turned and looked at the smirk on Harvey's face. She shook her head. "Delia, I'm home."

"Glad you're home," Delia called from the kitchen.

Alice turned to Harvey, "Are you on your way out?"

He looked at her. "I didn't know what to tell the children."

"There was nothing to tell. The lights went out and I was trapped at Willetta's place." She looked at him and shook her head. Knowing him, he was probably thinking she'd found someone and slept with him all in one night. "I'm handling it."

They kept looking at each other with the children looking up at Alice. Harvey cleared his throat. "Okay, since everything is all right here, I'll take off. I'll call you later." He pushed his hands in his pockets and tipped a little. "My cell phone is fully charged."

"And there's no power failure here." Alice smiled catching a flicker of emotion from him. "Thanks for coming over," she heard herself say knowing she really didn't mean it.

Harvey hugged the children and left.

Maybe this won't be a war after all, Alice thought turning into her room to change out of her clothes. Alia came in and began jumping on her bed. She looked at her and chuckled.

"Delia asked if you're ready for lunch."

She caught Alia in mid-air. "I could eat something." All the time she wondered if she would make it as a single mother. Tomorrow she would call the headhunter she always used and ask her to find her something in Miami or Ft.Lauderdale.

"Can we do something fun after lunch?" Alia asked.

"And what do you consider fun?"

"We could all go to the park."

She really didn't want to go back out in the cold, but the children had been cooped up in the house for too long. She didn't want them to watch too much television. "We'll see. If you still want to go after lunch, we'll go."

"I will."

"I thought you would."

They had lunch and when Alice went in to wash her hands, she came out to see them sitting with their coats and hats on. She laughed and shook her head. Delia came out of the kitchen and snickered. "Do you know anything about this, Delia?"

"A little." Delia had her coat in her hands.

"Well, I suppose I've been ganged up on, so to the park we go." She put her coat on over her sweats, and hat onto her bare head. After slipping into boots, she was once again out the door.

All the way to the park and while sitting on a bench, she wondered how she was going to pay Delia. She watched her playing with her children and guilt gnawed at her. Delia considered herself a part of the family, and rightfully so, but... *still.*

Alice didn't know how long she had sat on the bench until she felt Alia's little hand in hers. "We're ready to go back home, Mommy. I'm cold."

"Really, already?"

She nodded.

"Okay." She gave Delia a guilty look and followed behind. "Sorry, Delia, I have a lot on my mind."

"I know. Don't worry about anything. I know you'll sort everything out. I'm looking forward to moving to Florida."

With her coat open, Alice pushed her hands in her pockets, not giving much thought to the bitter cold biting through her. By the time they got home the electricity was back on. She told Delia to take the elevator with the children while she took the stairs, one step at a time. She began running and by the time she got to the eight floor, she was out of breath, but her brain was clear. She entered the open door and laughed when Alia said, "We win!"

She kissed her cheek. "Are you guys going to watch a little TV?"

She nodded.

"Okay, Mommy's going to make a few phone calls then do some reading."

"Okay."

Alice shed her coat, boots, and gloves then walked to her room and picked up the receiver. She sat with it in her hand for a few seconds then dialed her friend's number. Before it rang, she hung up. *Tomorrow at work I'll make the call. A good night's sleep—yes that's what I want.* She curled up in her bed and fell asleep, not even stirring when Delia took the children out of her bed.

At the office the next day, the first call she got was from her attorney. "Let's talk about this divorce," she said without saying good morning.

"Gwen, I don't want anything from Harvey, just a fast way out of this marriage. He can keep the house, no alimony, no nothing."

"Alice, are you sure about this?" she asked trying to persuade her otherwise. "What about child support?"

"That's up to him. I'm not putting it on the table. Just do it, Gwen. I'm giving you three months or less."

"Okay, but I may need a little more than three months."

"Listen, in less than a month, I'm moving away from New York City to as far away from Harvey as possible."

"I did not hear that."

"I'm calling my agent right after I hang up from you for her to begin looking for a position for me."

"Alice."

"Yes."

"I did not hear any of that."

"Whatever. When it's time to sign, let me know."

"I may need to talk with you before then."

"You have my cell."

"Yes dear, good luck. I mean it."

"Thanks, Gwen."

True to her word, Alice wasted no time in calling her recruiting agent to begin the search for a position in Florida, preferably in Palm Beach or Broward County. As soon as she hung up the phone, it rang. She answered to hear Willetta's cheerful voice.

"I'm not supposed to tell you this, but my brother likes you—a lot. He wants to see you again."

"Willetta, why didn't you tell him I was married?"

"I didn't get a chance. He was so busy looking at other parts of you he forgot to look at your finger."

"I wasn't wearing my wedding ring."

"Is everything all right with you guys? You never take that thing off."

"Yeah, everything's fine. I took it off to give the kids a bath and forgot to put it back on." She lied. "Your brother's a real gentleman."

"I can tell you this much about him. He's a real serious guy. If he likes you, he likes you, no matter what. He was hurt once, so he tends to be a bit cautious and withdrawn, but not with you. I was really surprised at the way he took to you. Anyway, he said to tell you good-bye and he hopes to see you again when he's back in town. So I suppose when he gets back, I'll have to repeat the evening; without the lights going out this time." She laughed.

"Willetta, I'm still married."

"I know that. What you two do as adults is none of my business. I am off to Spain tomorrow. Hey, Allison, let's keep in touch, okay. I mean it."

Alice smiled at the mispronunciation of her name. "Yeah. I'll see you soon."

By the end of the evening, she got a call from the recruiter. She had an interview set up in Ft. Lauderdale with a small investment firm.

Alice sat back in her chair and laughed. "You don't fool around, do you, Cloris?"

"Nope. When one of my best clients says find me a job, I find her a job and hope she'll remember me when she gets that job in a week."

"A week!"

"Too soon?"

"Just right. Thanks, Cloris."

A week later, a very confident, professional well-dressed woman walked into the huge, beautifully decorated office of Benjamin Frank, Chairman of Frank's Advertising, a small, ten-year old firm with all the growth potential Alice was looking for. She needed the opportunity to grow with a firm, and in the meantime get to know who she really was and her true potential. She needed the kind of job that would give her no time to think of her failed marriage.

A small, red-haired man with a pencil-thin mustache and beady blue eyes rose from behind his desk as she walked into his office. With an extended arm, and a smile, he met her halfway across the room. He led her to an uncluttered, highly polished oak desk near an open window. Offering her the chair opposite his, from which the ocean could be seen, he settled himself in a plush green cushioned oak high back chair.

The office was large and airy, with expensive paintings hanging on the wall, including a small Van Gogh original. The large oak desk in the center of the room was clean with stacks of manila folders on both sides and an expensive Parker pen set in the middle. The green, pine-scented carpet on the floor was old but obviously kept in excellent condition.

Benjamin Frank's no-nonsense attitude had kept him in business for over ten years. His company was ripe for expansion and Alice was just the person he was looking for. The company had checked her background thoroughly before the interview and after talking to her for over an hour, he'd welcomed her to the firm.

Just like that, she thought. *No, I have other people to see or I'll call you in a few days.* Seems Benjamin had made up his mind even before he'd seen her.

Ben showed her around the office, introduced her to his assistant then took her to lunch on Las Olas Boulevard. After lunch, he drove her through the wealthier parts of Ft. Lauderdale, Coral Springs and Boca Raton by way of Ocean Boulevard. He even drove her through a small part of the Intra-coastal. "You have family down here?" he asked getting onto Interstate ninety-five.

"Yes, my mother and sister live in Coral Springs."

"That's a nice place too."

He glanced at her, then back at the road. "You know, a friend of mine is going to Italy for a couple years and wants to sublet his town house. Would you be interested?"

"I would have to see it first. I really don't want my children cooped up in a place where they can't go outside and play."

"I understand. You'd prefer a house?"

"Yes." *If I can afford it.* Actually, with the salary she would be getting, she could afford to live quite well and not worry about how she was going to pay Delia.

"Okay, I'll get one of my agents to take you around tomorrow. Would that be all right?"

"Yes. I just have to get my children down here. I want to see the look on their faces when they find the house they want to live in."

He glanced at her and laughed. "You're a good mama."

"I try." *Please don't ask me about a husband. Please don't ask me about a husband.*

Purposely or not, he didn't.

"Okay, I'll drop you off at the hotel, and while you call your children I'll call my agent friend. By the way, the company will pick up the tab for all your moving expenses."

She already knew that. It was in the contract she'd signed. In two weeks she would begin her new job in Ft. Lauderdale, Florida, with Frank's Advertising Agency.

Outside the hotel, as soon as Ben's car drove off and Alice turned to go through the door, someone called her name, but it wasn't a name she'd used recently. "Alice… Alice Gregory."

She stopped and turned to see a very slim, dark man with a curly receding hair line. She didn't recognize him so she kept walking. He called her name again. She took a deep breath, stopped again and turned.

He wasn't more than about five feet eight. His clothes were loose fitting, and his pants hem puddled atop his shoes. He walked up to her, leaned back a little and smiled with his head down and cocked to one side. "You don't remember me?"

Embarrassed, she shook her head. "I'm sorry."

"It's okay. It's been over fifteen years since I saw you. But I can't forget that pretty face and the fabulous body. It's Alvin Jacob." He laughed. "We had biology together at NYU."

She nodded, still a bit fuzzy to his identity. "You look different—I think."

He nodded. "Yeah, I dropped a few pounds and dropped out of school for awhile. I tried going into business for myself." He abruptly switched the subject. "Are you staying here?"

"Yes. I was going upstairs to make a few phone calls."

"Okay, but I would very much love to see you again. We have a lot of catching up to do. Can we exchange cell digits?"

Still trying to place him, she looked into his face and slowly nodded. She listened to him rattle off his number and pretended to put it into her cell. "You'll call me, right?"

"Yes," she said nodding, waved and walked away from him. In the elevator to her room, she tried to remember who he was and if they'd ever held a conversation in college. She forgot his number and focused on calling her children. She hoped they would be as excited as she was to move from New York.

First she called the airline and made reservations for them to fly in the next morning.

The Sheraton Hotel was right across from the ocean on A1A in Ft. Lauderdale and she walked to the window and looked out at the beach. Gazing at the crashing waves, she smiled as a little tingle of excitement ran up her spine. This was her first visit to South Florida and she loved it. She'd called her mother and sister the moment she'd landed in Ft. Lauderdale and told them she'd see them for dinner. Her mother was so glad to hear that she was in Florida; she didn't even ask her if she was there for business or pleasure.

Alice glanced at her watch and realized that she had a few hours before dinner, plus, she was still full from lunch. She threw her suitcase on the bed, opened it and pulled out a long blue cotton skirt and white top. She felt like walking on the beach.

Changing her clothes, she took her wallet from her pocketbook and pulled out a few dollars just in case she felt like having tea or something cool. She pushed her pocketbook into the hotel safe and picked up the hotel key along with her cell phone, then walked out the door.

It was eighty-five degrees with low humidity and frankly, she was willing to take it over snow, ice and freezing wind. Crossing A1A at the crosswalk, she crossed the barrier and stood on the sand in flip-flops. Inside she was still smiling. The roar of the ocean, the traffic passing by and scantily clad tanned bodies made her want to do cartwheels. She took off her flip-flops and felt the cool sand under her feet. *I think I made the right move,* she thought.

She didn't walk long before Alvin joined her. She was so deep in thought, she jumped at the sound of his voice. "I don't want you to think I'm following you, but I was at the café across the street and saw you cross. You're alone so I thought I'd join you."

She looked at him, at the way he cocked his head, and his smile, and a light bulb went off. She did remember him. He was one of those guys in college who was almost never alone. There was always a girl or a few male friends with him. "What have you been doing all these years? You said you tried to go it on your own. How's that working out for you? Millionaire yet?"

He laughed. "Not quite."

She stopped and looked at him. "Wow, this is something. I never thought I'd ever see you again."

He laughed. "Did you ever think of me?"

Now it was her time to laugh. "Of course not."

"You didn't even try to boost a guy's ego."

"I thought it best not to lie."

He nodded. "Do you want to go across the street for a coffee or something?"

She remembered the bright man that walked the NYU campus as if he owned the place. Then one day he disappeared and she never saw him again. Frankly, she hadn't thought of him at all. She nodded and turned toward the café.

They sat down and ordered lemonade. Still, she kept looking at him, not sure she ever saw him before. She was certain she'd never been this close to see all the imperfections in his complexion. She tried to look into his eyes but he kept avoiding hers.

"So tell me about your," he said.

"Well, I finished college, got married, have two children and I just got a job here." *In a nut shell.*

"Wow. I heard you'd gotten married. You broke my heart, you know." He laughed, still trying to dodge her eyes.

"Excuse me?" She didn't think she'd heard him correctly.

"Yeah, you broke my heart."

"Don't you have to be in love with someone to get a broken heart?"

He nodded and looked at her for a brief moment.

She shook her head and her tone became chilly. "If I remember correctly, you had a girlfriend. And we had not even spoken two words in college. How on earth could I have broken your heart?"

"You were my girlfriend."

For a minute, he had become annoying. "How can you call me your girlfriend when we only said a passing hello— if that much?"

He nodded. "Do you know how many guys wanted to get with you in college?"

"Really?" she replied sarcastically.

"Yeah. You were kind of unapproachable because you were always around all those other girls, and always so beautiful. You had an air about you."

She was becoming more uncomfortable. "I only had two friends in college. One I'm still friends with and the other one I don't know where she is." She glanced at her watch.

"Do you have some place to go?" he asked shifting in his chair.

"Actually, I'm meeting with my mother in a little while."

"Oh, nice. They live here?"

"Yes." She took a sip of her lemonade, looked out at the crashing waves and the beautiful people walking on the beach, still smiling inside about her decision to move from New York.

"I think this is a sign that we belong together." His words seemed worn, thin, and shallow, used so often by shallow men.

"Okay, here's the thing. You need to stop saying that. It's nice that we've met again after so many years, but it's not a sign. It's just a chance meeting."

He nodded. "Okay," he said as if only to appease her.

"Do you have a car?"

"I have a rental."

He threw a few bucks on the table. She looked at it and added the tip. He laughed, but she didn't. "I don't have your phone number," he said.

"I know. I don't know it by heart, but I'll call you." She hoped he couldn't see her cell phone sticking out of her pocket. Just in case, she pushed her hand in her pocket.

"Wow," he said with a sweeping look. "You're still as pretty as ever. You know how many women would love to look like you?"

She wished he'd stop trying to flirt with her. She didn't smile. "I'll call you." She held out her hand, but was shocked when he pulled her to him, hugged her, and kissed her cheek. She smiled and wiped her cheek unceremoniously.

He pointed and nodded. "You are still as beautiful as ever."

She was getting a little tired of hearing that, but gave a little wave and walked back to her hotel.

In the room, Alice took a shower and got dressed to meet her mother and sister. She called down for the valet to bring her rental around because she didn't want to stand outside too long waiting for it just in case Alvin was hanging around. Why would he be? He must have a job. After all, it was the beginning of the week. *You broke my heart.* How can you break someone's heart without knowing them?

She waited a few minutes, made her way slowly downstairs and was glad to see the rental waiting outside. She got in quickly and drove off. Relaxing in the car and enjoying the cool tropical air, she thought again of Alvin. Maybe it won't be such a bad idea to have someone she could have an occasional dinner with or accompany to a movie. She shrugged. *We'll see.*

Following her mother's directions, it took her less than half an hour to get to her home in Coral Springs. Her sister, Gen screamed and hugged her when she opened the door and saw her standing on the step. "Oh my God, it's good to see you. Boy, you really know how to surprise your mother!"

Alice hugged back. "What do you mean, my mother? She didn't know I was coming?" she whispered. "Did you tell her anything?"

"No. I think you have to break it to her a little at a time."

"Right. If I don't, she'll start talking about dad."

Gen laughed. "On the other hand, I hear it all the time. Maybe it's time for you to get a little taste."

"No, there'll be enough time for that."

Her mother, a short, plump, almost never angry woman, was sitting in the living room. "Well," she said before standing to greet her daughter. "It's so good to see you, my dear."

Alice hugged her mother and felt like crying because she knew telling her about the end of her marriage would probably break her heart.

They sat and looked at each other. "So, where are the children and Harvey?" Merl asked.

Alice winced a little. "The children are fine. They'll be here tomorrow with Delia."

"And Harvey?" Merl asked.

Alice cleared her throat. "He won't be coming tomorrow. As a matter of fact, you'll love this. I just got a job in Ft. Lauderdale with an advertising firm."

She could tell her mother was excited by the way her eyes lit up. "Wonderful. Oh, God is good. I'll have my two girls right here with me. When do you start work? Did you find a house?"

Alice laughed, slipped off her shoes and pulled her feet onto the chair in a relaxed position. She knew how much her mother loved Harvey and was sure within the next few minutes his name would come up again. "Mom, I just got here. I'm in the process of finding a house, but I want the children to be here for that."

"And Harvey?" she smiled.

What to say, what to say? "Ahhh, Harvey will stay in New York for a while. I'm tired of the cold, Mama. And I think the kids will be better off here."

"And Harvey is okay with this? He'll visit often?"

"He's all right with it."

"Good," she nodded.

Alice looked from her mother to her sister and felt as if she'd come home from a long trip. Just looking from one to the other and glancing around the house, she smiled. *I did the right thing.* "Where do you guys want to go to dinner?"

"Oh, we get to choose?" Gen said.

"Of course. My treat."

Gen rubbed her hands together. "Okay, let's think expensive."

"You do know how to wash dishes, don't you?" Alice said.

She laughed. "I know. How about your favorite restaurant?"

"Cheesecake?" Alice asked.

"Yeah."

"Okay, let's go. Boca or Las Olas? I only know about those two."

"Ahhh, let's do Boca. I'll take you through some areas in Boca that might interest you. You know, there are some nice places in Coral Springs, too."

"Okay, I'll tell the agent tomorrow when she comes to take us around. I'm very excited. I can't wait to settle down and start working."

"Don't you want something to drink before we go?" Merl asked.

Alice shook her head. "Not really. Let's just go. I know once the children get here they'll want to visit their Grangran though."

"I'm looking forward to seeing them." Merl looked at her inquiringly, twice she'd asked about Harvey and the reply had been glossed over. She knew something was wrong but didn't want to push the subject just in case her daughter was going through a rough time and wasn't quite ready to talk about it. She got her purse and walked to Gen's waiting car. "I think your sister should drive since you don't know the areas very well," she said watching the girls go toward Alice's rental.

"Makes sense" Alice said turning around.

"What about Parkland?" Gen said.

"What's a Parkland?" Alice inquired.

"It's a very nice area west of Coral Springs. Are you renting or buying?"

"For the time being, renting until I can afford to buy. So basically it has to be something that I'll feel comfortable buying. You know, something the children love."

They got into Gen's car and rolled out of the driveway.

"You don't have to take me through neighborhoods; that's the agent's job. Let's just enjoy each other's company this evening. Why don't you guys have a pool?"

"Simple. None of us swim," Gen said.

"Fine," Gen said, getting onto the Sawgrass Expressway. "You know it's easier getting around down here than in New York."

"I'm here," Alice said. "You don't have to sell me on the place. Oh, do you remember an Alvin Jacob that attended NYU when we were there?"

Gen didn't answer right away, but had a serious look on her face. Then she said, "Short, curly hair, dark complexion?"

"Yes."

"No, I don't."

"Funny. I saw him today outside my hotel."

"Really? I thought he was in Jamaica."

"Apparently not."

"If I remember correctly, you didn't care for him," Gen said.

"Neither did you." She chuckled. "Wasn't he the one who once slapped you on your bum?" She looked at Gen. "If I remember correctly, you punched him in the face." Now that she remembered who Alvin really was, she laughed. "You're right, none of us cared for him."

"He was very fresh and obnoxious," Gen said, her tone still serious.

Merl rolled her eyes at her daughters' conversation but said nothing as they went from Sawgrass Expressway to the local ten to I-95 and got off at Glades Road to make the turn into the parking lot of the Cheesecake Factory. Luckily there was no wait.

"Let's talk some more about Alvin," Gen said.

"Now you want to talk about him?"

Gen shrugged. "You know, even if I didn't like him, I hope he turned out well." she shrugged again. "A success at his chosen profession."

Alice didn't repeat what Alvin had said about himself because she really had no interest in what he'd done or what he was now doing. "There's just something about him that sets me off. I can't really put my finger on it, but it'll come to me if I see him again. Frankly, he's not aging well." Alice picked up the menu and chose an appetizer she knew her mother would like.

"You talk as if you're an old person. You're not even thirty-five," Gen said.

Merl grunted painfully. "Can't we change the subject? It doesn't seem as if any of you like this Alvin fellow, so why talk about him?"

They both looked at her. "Mama, is something bothering you?" Alice asked.

"No." she quipped. "What should we have for dinner?"

Alice and Gen exchanged glances. "Okay, Mama, we won't talk anymore about this person. By the way, Harvey and I are separated that's why I'm here."

Merl sighed. "I thought that was it, but I didn't want to ask."

Alice echoed her sigh. "Sorry, Mom. I know how much you like Harvey, but we've gone as far as we can as a married couple. I suppose because of the children we will always be in each other's lives but one has to know when to say when, and I say when. It's for the best."

"Are you sure about this, Lise?"

Alice nodded, but as she looked at her mother, she felt as if she'd let her down. Her mother had left her father when she was twelve years old for basically the same reason. She would have given him a second chance if it weren't for the verbal abuse. Alice shook her head. Why did she feel she'd been living her mother's past life? "Mom, everything will be all right. We're better off like this. Maybe the relationship between us will be better."

"I'm sorry, dear. You guys were so much in love I never thought this would have ever happened to you and Harvey."

"As horrible as it sounds, sometimes love is not enough, Mom."

"I know. Okay, you have my permission to have a drink; wine or something. After all, you're not driving."

"No, but I have to drive back to the hotel tonight."

"You can stay with us tonight," Gen said.

"No. I'd love to be alone tonight. Plus, I have to get the children tomorrow. We have a big day ahead of us. There will be other times."

"Okay," Gen said and ordered two glasses of wine and dinner as soon as the waiter came to their table.

Alice didn't think she'd find a house the next day, not with the children anyway. Their personalities were so different that she had a feeling it would take at least a week to find a place. Her cell phone rang and although she'd made a point of not even looking at it at the dinner table, this was an exception because the children were not with her. It was a call from Benjamin Frank. "You don't mind if I take this call, do you? It's from my boss."

"Of course," Merl said.

She listened.

"Would you consider living in Parkland? It's a very nice area west of Coral Springs?"

"I suppose."

"A friend of mine has taken a jog in Nebraska for four years and doesn't want to sell his home."

"Of course, I'd love to see it, but after I pick up the children. How about noon?"

"That's fine. I'll give them a call and tell them to expect you. His wife will be there to let you in."

"Okay, I have my computer. You can email me the address. Thank you very much Mr. Frank."

"Let me know how you like the place. The rent's negotiable."

"Of course, Mr. Frank. Thank you." When she hung up, eager eyes looked at her. She laughed and told them what Ben had said.

"Wonderful," Merl said. "I hope you like it because Parkland is not too far from where we live."

"I hope so too. I really hate shopping for houses."

Gen laughed. "Now we can drive through the area," she said, as if she'd made a big breakthrough.

Dinner was served.

⁂

Driving through the city of Parkland, Alice had to admit she liked what she saw. A lot of the homes were in gated communities, which she liked and hoped the house Benjamin spoke of was in one of those areas. On her way back to the hotel she'd made up her mind that after finding a place she'd fly back to New York, resign from her present job, effective immediately, and make the move. She didn't need anything from Harvey's house. She'd left with everything she needed.

She would allow the children and Delia to help choose furnishing for their new home. As she thought about it all, she became more excited about the prospects of living as a single mother. She no longer hated Harvey, which was a very good feeling. Maybe hell would freeze over before she fell in love again. She intended to date for as long as she could. The valve to her heart was turned off. Harvey was the first man she'd ever fallen in love with, and although he was a brute, he had his good ways. In some ways, she knew she'd be comparing her dates to him, for awhile and only professionally.

Chapter Seven

After picking up the children and Delia at Ft. Lauderdale International Airport, Alice drove straight to the address Ben had given her. She was even more excited when she had to go through a manned security gate; and equally so when she got to the house. The lawn and flower garden alone sold her on the idea of living there. She held her children's hands as they walked up the driveway to the front door. It was immediately opened by the owner's wife when she rang the bell. The small woman stood aside and allowed them to enter.

Alice fell in love right away. She looked out to the pool and the lake behind the house. The high ceiling lent itself to the airiness of the house and the only thing in the house that wasn't white was the black lacquered Steinway.

Four bedrooms, split level, an open floor plan and a pool. A playground across the street, what else could she ask for? The place was perfect and the children loved it. They already picked their bedrooms. She called Ben on her way back to the hotel to tell him she'd take the house only to find out it came fully furnished. It was more than she could have hoped for. Her children weren't used to climbing on furniture and she hoped they wouldn't start now. At least she could save some money there. All they had to do now was move in with their suitcases.

Alice and the children spent the next two days getting to know Ft. Lauderdale, Coral Springs, and Parkland. Phillip asked once if his father would move down with them. Alice tried her best to explain that she and Harvey would no longer live together but it had nothing to do with the love they had for their children. "But dad will come to visit, won't he?" Alia asked.

"Of course, darling. And you and your brother can go up to spend time with him when there's no school."

"We can even go up for birthdays?" Phillip asked.

"If it's on a weekend, of course." Alice understood all the questions and hoped the children wouldn't blame either parent for the breakup.

Before she left Florida, she called Nikki and told her what she'd done. "I can come up and spend some time with you," Nikki said.

"I'd love that. Just let me go up and get things straightened out first."

"Sounds good to me. See you in a week."

They rang off.

Leaving the children and Delia with Merl and Gen, Alice went back to New York to put things in order. She resigned her job and called the movers to get her BMW, Delia's Volkswagen and paintings. She left after she saw that her things were on the truck and went back to Florida.

With a glass of iced tea in hand, she and Nikki, who had flown up from Jamaica to be with her, sat on the patio gazing out at the ducks on the lake. Nikki glanced at her friend. "Are you sure you don't want to come to Jamaica for a few days before you start your new job? We could go to the beach and eat Myrtle's fabulous fried fish and bammy." Nikki had a nostalgic look in her eyes as she exhaled.

Alice pulled her legs under her. At seventy-five degrees and almost no humidity, it was a far cry from the cold of New York City. The sound of the spa overflowing in the pool and the coconut trees swaying in the wind did give Alice a feeling for the islands, but there was still so much preparation before she started her new job. She had to get the children in school and buy new clothes for work. "Tempting, but not possible right now." She sighed. It dawned on her that she was really free to do whatever she wanted without telling or asking anyone.

Nikki noticed the faraway but still sad look in her eyes. "You're not going to sit here and blame yourself for the breakup, are you?"

Alice took a deep breath and shook her head. She was done blaming herself. She was done searching her soul for answers. "No, it's a new place, a new job. A new life, basically. There will be plenty of work to keep me occupied. Furthermore, the divorce will become final in a few months. I'm taking nothing from him and I think that will hurt him more. I have a feeling he may be looking for a fight, one that's not forthcoming." As she spoke, it was as if she were in a trance. It was a full-time job convincing herself that she wouldn't miss Harvey at all. She smiled and looked at Nikki. "Plus, I'll be with you in Jamaica in the summer or maybe end of spring. Nothing will stop me then."

"What if he suddenly decides he wants the children with him?" Nikki asked.

But Alice laughed. "Oh come on, Nik. If he didn't take them for just a weekend when they were so close to him in Manhattan, do you think he's going to want them to live with him? That would cramp his style; plus, it's too much responsibility for the poor fool. If the woman is living with him, I don't think she will be ready to become an instant mother to two children." She felt sorry for Harvey for some reason and wondered if he was still with the woman. After all, he was the one who asked for the divorce, she just sped things along. She was action, Harvey was talk.

"Why don't we go shopping?" Nikki said, breaking into her thoughts. "Because I think I'm sharing you with someone else right now."

"I'm sorry Nik. Yes, let's go shopping."

They were already comfortably dressed in shorts and cotton tops; all they had to do was slip into sandals. Alice informed Delia of their plans, then drove to the Town Center Mall in Boca Raton.

Coming out of Saks, Nikki grabbed Alice's hand. "I have an idea."

"Not again, Nik," Alice said loving having her best friend with her but not quite feeling her enthusiasm.

"No, listen. Why don't we do something we've never done before?"

Alice laughed. "What would that be, getting on a plane for the Galapagos Islands?"

"Mmmm, that's a thought, but no. Why don't we get dressed this evening and go to that gambling place in Hollywood?"

Nikki was trying to help take her mind off whatever she thought she was going through, but to tell the truth, she wasn't doing too bad or maybe the whole impact of the divorce had not really hit her yet. After all, she had not really told the children much. She nodded. "Yeah, let's go gamble. I have thirty dollars I can spare." She looked at Nikki and sighed. "Sometimes people forget what's really important in life, you know. And sometimes we're taken for granted." She started walking with Nikki by her side.

"It's sad really. Harvey and I were so in love once, then he began climbing the corporate ladder, and other things became more important. Like other people's feelings to the point where he'd embarrass me in front of them. He'd belittle me and I felt as if there was nothing I could do right." Tears stung her eyes and she gave a little laugh. It was as if all the people walking in the mall didn't exist. All the chatter around them went unheard.

Nikki held her hand, "Not now, sis. Let's go home and have a drink of wine before we go gamble. The children are always okay."

She wiped the tears from her eyes. "I know. It really won't be that easy, will it, Nik?"

"You'll be fine."

"I know."

Driving home in silence, Alice had to admit she didn't feel very lonely. Maybe it was because Nikki was with her or maybe because she had the children and a job. But one thing she knew for sure, her family would never be lost to her job.

She pulled into her driveway, got the packages out of the car and went inside with Nikki. The children were sleeping. She touched Delia's shoulder. "I bought you something."

"An old car?" Delia said laughing.

"Oh Delia, I think you've got the oldest car in the world, but it runs."

"I'm kidding Miss Alice. The car I have is fine." She laughed.

Alice chuckled and crossed her fingers that Delia's old Volkswagen would hold up until she could get her another one. Delia took the packages from her and Nikki poured her a glass of wine. They walked out to the patio and sat. It was good to talk to Nikki. "I don't know Nik," she sighed. "You know the last time I had dinner with Harvey, I thought he was going to apologize for what I'd seen. For the shame he'd put me through, but he didn't."

Nikki touched her hand across the table, her eyes sorrowful. "What would you have done if he had apologized, Lise?"

Alice shook her head. "I'm not sure."

"Would you have forgiven him and take him back?"

"I think I could have forgiven him his infidelity if I had not seen it with my own eyes, but all the years he shamed and degraded me washed over me in that one instant." She exhaled. Shaking her head she bit back the tears, then smiled. "You know, I keep telling myself that I'm handling it. I'm good, and I know with time, I will be."

"What would you do if he walked through that door right now?"

"Tell him the children are asleep." She looked at Nikki and both burst out laughing. Alice sipped her wine and for a brief moment thought of Andrew and wondered where he was, then she thought of Alvin and shook her head. She knew she never liked him in college. But one thing she remembered, she'd never thought of him once he disappeared. "Let's go spend my thirty dollars," she said to Nikki. "I'll go take a shower and change."

"Me too."

The next time Alice met Nikki, they were both dressed and ready to go out. Alice wore a smile on her face and Nikki had determination in her eyes. "I'm going to double my money tonight," Nikki said.

"And I will certainly sit and watch."

"No, even though we've never gambled before, we're going to be good at it. Delia, don't wait up."

Alice laughed. She'd never seen Nikki so fired up about anything. The very reserved doctor was about to have fun and she was about to join her. The only thing that mattered was her children's happiness and safety. Always. She had a job and a future.

She went to the kitchen where Delia was preparing supper for the children. "Things will get back to normal soon, Delia, but I won't be home for supper."

Delia laughed. "As long as you're happy, Miss Alice."

Nodding, Alice went to the children's room to kiss them good evening.

Driving on the Sawgrass Expressway heading north, Nikki leaned over and asked Alice, "Would you really have taken him back if you had not seen him kissing that woman?"

"Life would have gone on as usual because I wouldn't have known for sure that he was having an affair. It would have been pure suspicion."

"Men can be stupid." Nikki shook her head.

"Well," Alice shrugged. "Maybe he was tired of being married. Maybe he fell out of love with me and didn't know how to tell me. It's been years since we kissed." She glanced at Nikki. "I mean really kissed. Sex… maybe once a month or every other month."

"Wow! Are you sure you guys were still married? God, your kids are only six. You're in your early thirties!" Nikki refused to ask any more personal questions.

Alice nodded. "I know you're trying to help, but I'd rather not talk about it any more right now." She looked straight ahead.

Nikki nodded.

Alice got off the Sawgrass and onto the turnpike going south. "You know, there has to be a better way of getting there, but I just don't know it yet."

"That's all right, no rush. Hopefully the twenty-five cent machines won't all be filled by the time we get there."

Alice pressed down on the accelerator. "If we get a speeding ticket, you're paying the fine."

"Then go faster so that I can win some money."

Alice laughed.

In twenty minutes, they spotted the neon sign of the Hard Rock Hotel and Casino from the freeway. They got off at Sterling, got onto 441 and turned left into the parking lot. Nikki got out of her seat belt before Alice found a spot. "If you jump out of this car before I turn off the engine, I will slap you," Alice said laughing.

Nikki was quiet until Alice shut the engine off, then opened her door and waited to walk in with Alice.

Inside the casino, Nikki made a beeline for the slots dragging Alice right along with her, passing the five cent and dollar machines until she found the very stool she wanted to sit on. "Sit," she said to Alice patting the stool beside her. "Sit and feed the slot. When your thirty dollars are gone, we'll have dinner and maybe pop into one of the clubs and see if we still can shake a leg."

Alice shook her head.

Five dollars later, someone sat on the empty stool beside Alice and said, "I thought you were going to call me."

She glanced to her right to see Alvin sitting there. She chuckled, touched Nikki and said, "Nik, do you remember Alvin?"

Nikki looked at the very slim man for a while before nodding, "Vaguely." She spoke directly to him. "Didn't you drop out of school?"

Alvin laughed and pushed his hand across Alice to shake Nikki's hand. "Yes and no. I went back after a few years to finish up."

"I see, and what have you been doing for yourself?"

"A little bit of this and that."

Both women looked at him. He'd given Alice almost the same answer. "Is that all you're going to say?" Nikki said, wondering why he was being so vague about his profession.

He lowered his head and looked at her under shaded lashes. "I make a living."

"Don't we all," Alice said, not very interested in what he did anyway.

"Wouldn't you rather play the dollar machine or poker?" he said, folding his arm across his chest.

"No." Both women said in sync.

"Maybe I can get you both a drink, then?"

"Pina colada," Nikki said.

"Same for me," Alice said fishing into her purse for money to give him.

"You wound me deeply, Alice. I got this."

"Sorry," she said, noticing that Nikki was so preoccupied with the machine she didn't even hear what was going on.

When Alvin was gone Nikki took a break and turned to Alice. "He is not aging well at all. The guy can't be more than thirty-nine or forty and he's got too many lines in his face. I mean the receding hairline could be hereditary, and the salt and pepper is nice, but—wow!"

Alice chuckled. "I know."

Alvin came back with their drinks and sat down. "You're not drinking?" Alice asked.

"Not right now."

She nodded and began feeding the machine again with one hand holding her drink. She glanced at him watching her and felt a bit uncomfortable. "You don't gamble?"

"I play the horses and poker."

"Oh, well, wouldn't you like to go and play poker?"

He laughed. "It seems like you're trying to get rid of me." He got to his feet. "I can take a hint, but I'd like to see you again. Will you give me your cell number so that I can call you?"

Alice sighed and gave him her number. He walked away and she didn't look after him but wondered why she'd given into him. Would he become a pest?

"Are you sure you wanted to do that?" Nikki asked. "I know we went to the same college and all, but he's not your type, not even as a passing friend. Be careful."

"I don't always answer my phone," she replied really regretting her actions. Just then bells and whistles from Nikki's machine went off. She'd won fifteen hundred dollars.

Alvin made a beeline back to them. "Who's buying dinner tonight?" he asked, with a big grin on his face.

For the next few hours, Alvin followed them from dinner, where Nikki paid without him even offering, to the club where again he wasn't ashamed to let Nikki and Alice pay for his drinks. At the end of the evening, Alice really regretted giving him her number.

"Nice Beamer," he said when he opened the doors for the women.

He attempted to kiss Alice on her lips, but she ducked away from him. "Are you crazy!" she shouted at him.

He grinned unashamedly. "Can't blame a guy for trying."

"Try not to do that again—ever!" she said angrily and got into the car.

Driving on the freeway on their way home, Nikki said, "You either have to ignore his calls or tell him to take a hike real soon. He seems to want someone to feed off. He doesn't seem to have any ambition. He didn't even try to push his hand in his pocket to pay for drinks. Even if he were faking it, it would have looked better than standing there waiting for us to pay for him."

"Maybe he's down on his luck," Alice said. "I somehow feel sorry for him."

"Alice, really!" Nikki said, looking at her as if she'd lost her mind. "I know you're a bleeding heart, but not everyone wants to be saved. If you try to save him, he'll try to drag you down with him.

Alice shrugged. "He won't get that chance. I'm not a desperate person."

Nikki laughed. "I know you're not." She knew Alice. Love didn't come easy for her, and in her fragile state, neither did trust.

Chapter Eight

On Sunday evening, Alice saw Nikki off at Ft. Lauderdale airport and on Monday morning she was dressed in a white linen dress, her hair pulled back to the nape of her neck in a tight bun, sitting in Benjamin Frank's office.

Finishing with all the formalities of signing papers, she left his office, said hello to Lee Ann, the assistant she would be sharing with Ben, and walked into her office. She closed the door, walked to a glass desk and looked around before sitting. The brown, worn couch definitely had to go. The carpet under her feet was a rust color, that also had to go. To give the place more of a lift, she envisioned Caribbean paintings with vibrant colors brightening the office.

Alice sat down and took a breath. She'd never worked in advertising before. She'd taken a few classes in college but didn't think she'd use it. This was a small firm and each department did their own hiring; that's where she came in. She'd be doing the hiring and be involved in advertising.

She buzzed Lee Ann to come in.

With pen, pad, and a hand-full of files, Lee Ann Blake walked through the door and set the files on Alice's desk. "Sorry, I should have brought these in before."

"That's all right. Have a seat. Let's get acquainted."

Lee Ann was in her early forties, tall and slim with short blonde hair.

"How do you take your coffee in the morning?" Lee Ann asked.

"Actually, I don't drink coffee, but tea with milk is good. Black tea or green tea; doesn't matter."

"Good."

"Oh, before we go any further, I need to change some things in the office. The carpet needs to be changed to blue, and the couch needs to be changed to white. I also need some paintings on the wall, nothing expensive. I'm from the Caribbean so I'd love to have a few Jamaican country scenes."

Lee Ann wrote everything down and nodded. "I'm glad you're making all these changes. I hated the way this office looked and hoped you would too. I'll find a gallery that carries Caribbean art for you. Let me know when you want to go. In the meantime I'll take care of the rest."

"Thanks, Lee Ann." She looked down at the files on her desk.

"If you have any questions regarding that account, let me know."

"I think I'll need your help quite a lot for maybe a week or so. This is my first job as an Advertising Executive, but I'm a fast learner. Frankly, I've worked in Human Resources ever since I left college."

"That's a good background for this job. But I heard you were a fast learner," Lee Ann said with a smile.

She gave Lee Ann a quizzical look. "From whom?"

Lee Ann seemed to shuffle a little, the smile still on her lips. "That's why the boss hired you. He thinks you're a fast learner."

Alice nodded.

She worked through lunch on the files without even knowing it. She had to call legal and merchandising a few times. Lee Ann sat with her to acquaint her with the other account executive's work since one of the accounts belonged to him and he was out of town and wanted to work with her. By the end of the day, she was exhausted.

She left the office at six, went home, greeted her children and soaked in a warm bath before helping with homework and dinner.

A few days later, she opened the door to her office and found a plush royal blue carpet on the floor complimented by a small white leather couch in the corner. *All I need now is a red chair and I would be considered very patriotic.* She backed out, looked at Lee Ann and smiled. "You do work fast. This is beautiful, thank you, Lee Ann."

"You're welcome, Alice. When would you like to pick out the paintings? I found a small gallery on Las Olas Boulevard."

Alice looked at her watch. "Fantastic. Why don't we go at lunchtime?"

"Okay."

"Do you want to take the town car?"

"No, I'll drive us." She stood at Lee Ann's desk. "Unless you're afraid of my driving, then we'll take your car."

"Well, I can't say I'm afraid of your driving until I drive with you, but since I know the area better than you, I'll drive."

"Lee Ann, Las Olas is not very far away. Even I know where it is. It's all right. We can have lunch, then visit the gallery." She went into her office and began working on an acquisition file, then made a call to legal.

Andrew Benton sat comfortably on a plane bound for Ft. Lauderdale from San Francisco with the Brown file in his hands. This was a small company and although they were in big trouble, Brown himself wanted to sit still on a sinking ship. It was good that he was still open to talks; it would be a shame to wait until the place really went under from the weights of all their debts and loss of customers because of a scandal.

He closed the file and leaned his head against the headrest with his eyes closed. A vision of Alice swam before him and he smiled and wondered if he should call her. She'd given him her phone number and he had given her his, but they'd not called each other. He figured, as a lady, she was waiting for him to make the first move. But the best part would be working side by side with her. When Ben had sent him the two resumes and he saw her name on the second one, he was beyond thrilled. He'd gotten back to Ben right away and told him to hire her. "But, she has no advertising experience," Ben had said. He'd laughed and told Ben that he knew Alice and he would train her himself. "She's not a risk. Ben. She will be an asset," he'd said. Ben had agreed. He'd also told Ben not to let Alice know that he worked with the firm or had anything to do with her hiring. Lee Ann should not mention his name to her either. "Why the cloak and dagger?" Ben had asked.

"I don't think she'd appreciate my interference," he told Ben.

He was still smiling to himself about the thrill of working with the brown-eyed Jamaican woman whom he liked a lot. His sister had told him that she was married and that was fine. He still wanted to be friends with her, if nothing else. He took his wallet from his pocket to look at her phone number, then replaced it. At the request of the pilot, he buckled his seat belt and got ready for landing.

Alice had seen the painting so many times, and every time she saw it she had to laugh. It was a painting of an over crowded country bus, seemingly coming from the market and people hanging off it.

"Comical, isn't it," Lee Ann said.

"And so real," Alice replied.

They strolled over to another painting that depicted a blue and yellow country cottage with a wraparound verandah and an old

woman in a rocking chair. Another frame with a drawing of the
Rose Hall Great House caught her eyes and she nodded. She would
take all three. Lee Ann immediately made all the arrangements for
delivery, and they walked out of the gallery into Lee Ann's car and
headed back to the office. Her interviewee was waiting.

At the end of the day, Alice leaned back in her chair and a
picture of Andrew floated before her. Those eyes did something
to her that she wasn't ready for. She fished into her purse and
came up with Alvin's number. She looked at the number and
pictured the man. Did she really want to go out with him? She
shrugged and tried to convince herself that he wasn't that bad.
But as Harvey flashed through her mind, she shook her head.
Alvin was completely out of his league. Her phone rang. Lee Ann
announced a Mr. Alvin.

"Put him through," she said, picking up on the third ring.
"Hi, how are you?"

He laughed. "I couldn't wait for you to call, and I wanted to
wait until Nikki left. How are you? Am I going to see you? I want
to see you."

With the receiver away from her ear, she closed her eyes, took
a deep breath and said, "Yeah, sure. How about dinner tomorrow
evening?"

"That sounds great."

"Okay, right across from the beach and the park, there's a
restaurant with swinging booths... the Oasis, I think."

"I know the one, what time do you want to meet?" He was
still smiling.

"How about seven-thirty?"

"I will meet you there at seven-thirty. I can't wait to see you
again."

"Oh, and Alvin."

"Yeah."

"Don't call me at the office anymore. You have my cell phone.
How did you find out where I worked anyway?"

"I have my ways," he chuckled.

"Fine, but as I said, don't call me here anymore." Remembering Nikki's warning, she hung up the phone and placed her head in her hands. *What am I doing? Tomorrow evening I could be with my children or my sister and mother. What am I doing?* Would going out with this man take her mind off Andrew? She'd pushed the impending divorce to the back of her mind. She didn't want to think about it or Harvey, and she certainly didn't want to think about the word *failure*.

There was a knock on her door and she jerked back to reality. "Come in."

Ben walked into her office with his hands in his pocket. He looked around at the new sofa and the paintings on the wall and nodded. "I love what you did with the place. It looks very comfortable."

"Thanks, Ben. I'm glad you approve."

"It's not for me to approve, but for you to feel comfortable. I wanted to know how things are going. Are you settling in all right?"

"Everything's going very well. Lee Ann is helping me with things I don't know or are not sure of."

"Good, I'll be out of town for a few days next week, but if you need me, you have my cell phone and Lee Ann has the name of the hotel and everything."

She nodded. "Okay."

"The children are well?"

"They're great, Ben, and I hope your wife is fine."

"Yes, thanks for asking. Okay, well, if you need anything before I leave, my door is always open to you."

"Thanks Ben." He turned and left the office.

Alice picked up her bag and walked through her office door for home. She waved to Lee Ann and told her to go home.

She took the scenic route home, drove through the gate and saw Delia and the children playing in the park. They didn't see her car so she drove into her driveway, parked, and walked over to greet them with open arms. The park's playground had a sandy area with swings, slides, and monkey bars. She took off her heels, walked on the sand to push her son on the swing, and go down the slide with her daughter.

"Dinner's ready if you're hungry," Alia said holding her hand as they crossed the street.

"Why, are you hungry?"

"Yes, but we waited for you."

"Thank you." She held onto Phillip's hand.

They walked into the house and she walked to her room to change while Delia drove her car into the garage.

After helping the children with homework and having dinner, Alice sat on the patio with a glass of wine in her hand. She gazed at the spa flowing into the pool and the multicolored shrubbery outside the screened area. It was a bit chilly to go into the pool unless it was heated, but she didn't want go to the trouble. Maybe the cold water would shock some sense into her. What on earth possessed her to ask Alvin out to dinner? She wasn't that lonely for a man's company. Again, she thought of Andrew. *Why am I thinking of this man? He has my number and never called. He probably threw it away and has forgotten all about me.* It had taken her just a few minutes to fall in love with Harvey even before she knew the kind of person he was, and after, well—that story has been written. She hated the ending.

Chapter Nine

Alice made sure she got to the restaurant before seven-thirty. Sitting outside in one of the swinging booths, she didn't see when Alvin came up but felt his hand on her shoulder and his wet kiss on her cheek. She smiled and wiped his saliva from her cheek.

He sat beside her and put his arm around her. She stiffened and motioned to the other side of the booth. "Wouldn't it be better if you sat in front of me instead of beside me?"

He took his hand away. "You don't like me sitting beside you?"

"It's not that. But I'd rather see the face of the person I'm speaking and eating with."

He moved to the seat in front of her. His eyes met hers for just a brief moment. "You're still so pretty. You know, a lot of women let themselves go after they get married." He shook his head and smiled seductively. "Not you. You look as beautiful and young as the day I saw and fell in love with you."

She didn't know him, nor had she really spoken to him in college. "The other day you said I broke your heart. How can I break your heart when we never even held a conversation or held hands?"

"I loved you from afar."

She nodded. "I see. You loved me from afar and you imagined I broke your heart."

"No, my heart broke when you started dating that guy... I forgot his name."

"I married that guy. His name is Harvey."

He leaned back, nodded and slung one arm over the top of the seat. "That's nice. But you can't be that happy if you're here and he's somewhere else."

"Is that a question?"

He shrugged. "I suppose so. Are you happy?"

She looked at his face. It was none of his business if she was happy or not. But yet, here she was, having dinner with him. Still, she had not given him reason to get that personal. She thought of her children, her job. "Yes, I am happy." She kept looking at him but not seeing him because she really didn't want to.

"We can make love though, can't we? I've wanted to make love to you from the first time I saw you on NYU college campus."

That woke her up. "Excuse me. Are you out of your mind?"

"Oh come on, Alice. Don't you believe in fate? I mean, after all these years, we find each other again, and your husband's not around. It's God saying we should be together."

She wasn't sure what to say. Was he that simple? She knew for sure that sex wasn't all men thought about. Her husband was a workaholic who didn't think about sex very often in the last few years of their marriage; when he was with her that is. Again, she thought of Andrew. "We just met. We just began talking and the only thing you can think of is sex!"

"It's because I love you. I want to consummate our relationship."

Okay, she was pissed. "Just like that? I don't know you!" She was trying her best to keep her voice down. How on earth can someone get on another one's nerves so quickly? And why was she still sitting there? She was no longer hungry. "I'm sorry, I have a headache."

That didn't stop him from ordering and eating. "Next time come to my house. I'll cook you dinner," he said, chewing like a goat.

His voice sounded excited as if he were looking forward to doing this for her. "You can cook?" she asked, watching him crush his food. She wanted to laugh but took a deep breath and bit into her lip.

"I make the best Ackee and codfish."

She nodded slightly thinking he must be crazy if he thought she would come to his house.

"Okay then. Next time…"

She shook her head and laughed. "No. I'm not coming to your house."

"Okay, I'll wait until you're comfortable with our relationship."

She took a painful breath. "Alvin, we don't have a relationship."

"Of course we do. Okay, so you don't want us to unite physically yet, but I can wait." He kept nodding as if he had a nervous tick.

"I invited you to dinner just to talk. Along with my mother and sister I wanted to think I had another friend here in South Florida. I could be home with my children, but I wanted to be by the beach with my friend." She looked into his face and wondered again why he always hid his eyes from her.

He seemed genuinely apologetic when he said, "If I did or said anything to offend you I'm sorry. I didn't mean to. I have children of my own. I would love to meet your children."

She nodded, took a sip of wine and looked out at the ocean. "How many children do you have?"

"Five."

"Where are they?"

He chuckled. "They're all with their mothers. One is in England, one in Brazil, and three are here."

"Wow. The three that are here, are they of one mother?"

"No. Why don't we take a walk on the beach?" He smiled, revealing small smoker's teeth. He sat forward and searched his pockets. "Oh God. I don't believe this." He shuffled his feet and smiled slowly, showing very little embarrassment.

"Let me guess. You forgot your wallet."

"Sorry, I'll get the next one."

She didn't really mind paying the check. After all, she'd invited him to dinner. Unlike what he was probably thinking, she had the upper hand by paying. "No problem, but isn't it illegal to drive without your license."

"Not for me. I'll just…"

She shook her head. "Never mind, I said I'd pay the check. It's not that much." She took the money out of her purse and placed it on the table, then got up and began walking across the street.

Even though they really didn't speak to each other except for an occasional hello in college, he seemed intelligent and confident then. She still wanted to think of him that way but he wasn't making it easy.

Walking on the beach, he attempted to hold her hand but she folded them protectively around her chest.

"Where's your husband?" he asked.

She took off her sandals, held them in her hand and continued walking. "He's in New York. We're separated." She looked at the smile on his face and knew that was the answer he wanted.

"So there's a chance for me?"

"Let's just work on the friendship part, okay."

He reached for her hand again.

She moved her hand away from his reach. "I don't like holding hands. Sorry." She prayed silently for God to forgive her for the lie. She loved holding hands, kissing, and hugging. It just had to be with someone she liked. Even though she wore a sweater blouse, the chill in the air seeped through to her skin. She wrapped her hand around her chest for warmth this time.

He took off his flannel shirt and offered it to her. She shook her head. "I'm really not that cold. I have to go home now."

"My shirt is clean. It'll keep you warm," he said encouragingly and tried handing it to her again.

She saw the embarrassment on his face, but she really didn't want to take the shirt from him. "Thanks, but it's all right." She turned and walked back to her car.

He leaned against it. "I like Beamers. I can only afford a little Mazda right now until I pay off my bills."

"It's hard for a lot of people. Better will come," she offered and got into her car. She waved to him.

"I'll call you tomorrow," he said.

"I'll call you." She intended to spend the entire weekend with her children.

On her way home, she chastised herself for even agreeing to go out with him. She'd promised herself when she came to South Florida to date up a storm, not sleep around. *I'm not desperate for a man. I can do fine without a man. God!* She shook her head. She'd thought his friendship would have been a good idea even though she'd be ignoring Nikki's warning. She'd gone against the grain; her grain. This was a big mistake. She wasn't that desperate. She rolled down the window and felt the cool breeze against her face. No, she wasn't desperate at all. She could do a million times better.

When she got home, the children were still up with Delia watching television. She smiled at Delia. "Couldn't get them to go to sleep, huh?"

"They wanted to wait up for you. They have something to ask you." Delia looked at Alia. "Go ahead."

Alia gave Alice that cute little smile she used to get whatever she requested. "Can we go to Sea World tomorrow? It's in…"

Alice sat down and kicked her shoe off. "Absolutely. I think it's a very good idea."

Both children gave a cheer and asked if they could sleep in her bed. "It would be better if we all woke up together since we're going on a fun day tomorrow," Phillip said in a man-of-the-house voice.

Knowing that he was very excited but wanted to show his sister that he wasn't a baby, Alice glanced at Delia and they both stifled a laugh. She nodded. "I think that's a good idea. Should we retire now or wait until the movie ends?"

Again, Phillip had that serious look on his face. "I think we should wait until the movie finishes."

"Man a yard," Delia whispered in patois.

Alice smiled and nodded. "Yep." She then stifled a yawn and was glad when the movie ended.

The children already had their PJ's on, so they hurried to their mother's room and jumped into bed.

Alice and Delia had a good laugh before they said good night.

The cool sheets felt good against Alice's body. She took a deep breath, exhaled and cuddled her children to her. "Life will be good here, I promise," she said as she turned the lights off. She could hear the rain beat softly on the roof and hoped tomorrow the weather would hold up enough for her to take the children to Sea World. Taking a cleansing breath, she closed her eyes in peaceful slumber.

<hr />

But in the morning, as she sat with a cup of tea in her hand at the breakfast nook window seat overlooking the rose garden, the rain began again and the wind picked up. The children were still asleep and she glanced at Delia making eggs and fried plantain for breakfast.

"What was the forecast for today, Delia?"

"I didn't check. Do you want me to turn on the radio?"

"No, I'll turn on the Weather Channel." She turned, picked up the remote from the table, and switched on the small television in the kitchen. Turning to the Weather Channel, she realized that it was going to rain the entire weekend. "I suppose I'll let them decide if they want to stay home or still attempt to go to Sea World," she said to Delia.

"It won't take long for that decision to be made. Here they come."

Both children came rubbing their eyes and climbed up on the window seat. Alia sat on Alice's lap and laid her head on her breast. "Mommy, it's raining."

"I know sweetheart. What do we do about our outing today? It's going to rain all day."

Delia handed both children cups of Milo. Both women waited for their answer as the children seemed to be lost in their drink. The fruit trees swayed in the wind and the rain fell harder.

"Is it a hurricane, Mommy?" Phillip asked removing the cup from his mouth.

Alice smiled. "No, it just seems like it."

"We should stay home and watch cartoons then. We can go to Sea World tomorrow when the rain stops," Phillip said looking at his sister.

Alia nodded. "Yeah." She licked the chocolate from her lips and laid her head back on her mother's bosom. "Look, Mommy, the ducks on the lake love the rain," she said.

Alice smiled and nodded. It had rained so hard the night before that the lake had risen and now the ripples in the water looked like a river swiftly running downstream. Delia put breakfast on the table, and the children moved to their chairs.

Andrew stood at his balcony door looking out at the rain making puddles in the pool. The steam rose from his coffee mug as he stepped out onto the balcony and sat on the lounge chair. He couldn't stop thinking of Alice, no matter how hard he tried. So many times he'd attempted to call Willetta to ask if she thought it a good idea for him to call her, but stopped before dialing her entire number. What would Alice do or say if he'd called her just to say hello? He got up when the rain began blowing hard onto the balcony, but stood at the door for awhile, then walked back inside, placed the mug on the table, and picked up his cell phone to call Willetta. *I don't really want my sister to know how I feel about this woman. She'll think I'm nuts for falling for a married woman.* He replaced the cell phone on the table and walked to his office to do some work. At least work would take his mind off Alice for a little while until he saw her Monday morning. He knew he'd made the right decision by telling Ben to hire her. Maybe he was playing Russian roulette with his heart, but he kept trying to convince himself that a friendship with Alice would be better than no relationship at all.

⚬⚬⚬

Alice's cell phone rang twice and by the time she picked it up, it stopped ringing. She looked at the unfamiliar nine-five-four number and shrugged. It didn't belong to her mother or sister. "Probably someone trying to sell me something." She didn't give a second thought that it may have been Alvin.

Saturday rolled into Sunday with Alice having a good time with her children. She read to them, played games with them, and watched television with them. She loved every minute of it. And at the end of the evening while soaking in a hot tub, she thought of her own childhood in Jamaica. When it rained and the clouds refused to let the sun show its face, she would play with her sister in and out of the house. A few times per month, her mother would force them to take a teaspoon of castor oil. God, did it taste nasty, but they had very few colds.

Before bed, she spoke to her mother and sister on the phone, then Nikki. She neglected to tell Nikki about her date with Alvin because she didn't want to hear a lecture. Just like the night before, the children curled up in her bed and listened to the rain beat on the roof until they all fell asleep.

Monday morning, she helped Delia prepare the children's lunch then kissed them goodbye and hurried off to work.

She stopped by Lee Ann's desk before going into her office and the smile on Lee Ann's face told her that something was up. "What?" she asked, but Lee Ann just shook her head and smiled.

"There's someone waiting for you in your office."

She took a deep breath. "From now on, please do me a favor, whoever it is, except for Ben, have them wait out here for me."

Lee Ann nodded. "I think you'll be glad this person waited in your office."

She wrinkled her brow and kept looking at Lee Ann, hoping to God it wasn't Harvey. Her heart dropped and the color drained from her face. "Is his name Harvey Vaze?"

The smile still on Lee Ann's face, she shook her head.

For the short time she'd known Lee Ann, she'd never exhibited this kind of emotion before. She looked like she really wanted to tell her who it was but was sworn to secrecy. She knew if it was Alvin, Lee Ann would never allow him to wait in her office.

Alice held her head high, took a deep breath and pushed her office door. Looking straight to her desk, there was no one sitting on the chair reserved for clients. She walked in and immediately heard a very familiar voice, English accent and all. She turned quickly toward the sofa, and there he was, standing tall and extremely handsome with his hair pulled back in a pony tail, and a look of pure delight on his face.

Alice's breath caught in her throat. Still standing with her pocketbook slung over her shoulder, she tried to speak but nothing came out. She cleared her throat and bit into her lower lip, then finally she said, "Andrew Benton. Oh my God. What are you doing here? How did you find me?"

He didn't take his eyes from her face. "The better question would be, why didn't you call me?" He took the few steps that would close the gap between them and gathered her into his arms.

Alice stood with her hands by her side and trembled as the warmth from his body seeped into her skin. She wanted to return his hug but her hands felt heavy. She closed her eyes and smelled his soft cologne. Among the emotions she felt were joy and a little pain. Andrew held her at arms length and gazed into her beautiful face. "You have no idea how many times I've picked up the phone to call you, and now here you are."

She suddenly found her voice again. "But... how?"

"Sorry about Lee Ann. I told her not to tell you who was waiting for you."

"But…" Alice slowly placed her pocketbook on her desk and with a quizzical look on her face. "They called you Drew, and there was no name plate on your office door. I've been so busy since I got here and we didn't talk on the phone."

He hugged her again. His heart hammered so loud and hard in his chest, he hoped she wouldn't feel it. "I am so glad to have you here."

This time she slipped her arms around him. Unsteady on her feet from the shock of seeing him, she moved away and sat on the chair. "Wow! Give me a minute to process the fact that I'll be working with you." She laughed and noticed he had a file in his hand. "Is that my personal file?"

He nodded. "Yes. Why didn't you tell me you were moving to Florida when we met?"

"Because at the time I didn't know. And what are you doing with my file?"

He shrugged. "You know, we all do our own hiring." He placed the file on her desk as if dismissing it. He sat on the edge of the desk, his long legs crossed and that enchanting smile on his face. "Should I pry?"

It was obvious, he'd not really read the file. She smiled nervously noticing his attire. He wore a blue Armani jacket over white shirt and blue tie. She looked at his pants and laughed out loud, maybe to hide her nervousness. He wore a pair of blue jeans.

"Are you that happy to see me, or are you laughing at me?" he asked, his smiling eyes showing exactly how he felt. He wanted to scoop her up in his arms, dance around the room with her and tell her she was home.

"I'm sorry, I shouldn't have laughed, but what's with the jeans?"

He relaxed, reached for her hand and held it. "Oh well, you know, I'm from New York and I'm still trying to shake the Wall Street attire but it's taking longer than I anticipated. I'm relaxed and laid back, yet a little uptight." His thumb gently caressed her hand.

Feeling a bit ill at ease with his familiarity and the fact that her heart was about to betray her, she eased her hand from his. "You? Uptight? No way."

Brushing an imaginary piece of lint from his jacket, he uncrossed his legs, his green eyes still riveted to her face. "I knew I wanted to see you again, but working together is more than I could have ever hoped for. This is great... I mean." Should he tell her that he was the one who actually hired her? No, not yet. He wanted her to feel comfortable with him and the job first.

"It's okay," she said, using her thumbs to pull on each other. She glanced up at his hair. Although it was pulled back in a pony tail, there was still that unruly curl sitting on his forehead. She shook her head, got to her feet and walked around to the chair behind her desk. There were no ifs, ands or buts, her friend had come home.

"How are the children?" He moved from her desk to the empty chair across from her.

"They're wonderful. They're in school."

"So where's home now?"

She motioned to the file now lying on her desk. "Didn't you look at the address?" She shook her head. "Never mind. Parkland."

"I live in Boca, just a hop, skip, and a jump from you."

"I would say a half an hour ride, depending on what part of Boca you live in."

He wanted to ask about her husband. He wanted to know if he was also in South Florida or out of her life. "Did your husband transfer down with you?" *Good going, Benton. Real smooth. You handled that real well.* His gaze left her face for a second but noticed that she shifted slightly in her chair and her eyes fell to the desk.

"Ahhh," she inhaled, then looked at the painting behind him. Her thoughts seemed far away and arduously unpleasant. It took a few seconds for her to refocus her attention on Andrew. When she did, she bore a beautiful smile, just for him. "Harvey is still in New Jersey. That's where our home is." She had no intentions of elaborating... yet.

Now he was confused. "But you lived in New York when I met you." The look on her face told him that she felt uncomfortable. He opened her file.

"Yes, well, Harvey won't be down for a while," she said, averting her eyes from his face to look down at her clasped fingers.

He figured she wanted to keep that part of her life private and that was fine. If she felt like telling him sometime in the future, that was fine too. He is there and she is here, which spells separation. What kind of separation, he didn't know; but again, it was cool. Glancing at her open file in his hand, he nodded and smiled, then looked at her again. "Why psychology?"

She chuckled. "So you did take a peek. I'm interested in how the mind works."

He shook his head. This was going to be wonderful. But when he finished telling her what her new job entailed, it had more to do with the advertising side of the company and very little to do with interviewing prospective employees. She already knew that.

She was never one to walk away from a challenge.

Chapter Ten

At the end of the day, Andrew walked into Alice's office with his hands in his pocket and a smile on his face. He closed the door and moved to her desk. She looked up from the file she was working on and smiled. Again, she'd gone through the entire day without going out for lunch. Lee Ann had brought in a turkey sandwich on whole wheat and tea for her. Now she was hungry. One of the reasons why she'd worked through lunch was because she didn't want Andrew to invite her to lunch. Now as she looked up at him, her insides felt like jelly. She took a deep breath. "Hi," she said, and cleared her throat.

"Hi. They do work you to death around here, don't they?"

"You are my boss," she said looking up at him.

"I just got here." He seemed to search for the right words to say.

He looked at the files on her desk and shook his head then pursed his lips. "Okay, since I'm the boss, how about I take you out to dinner to compensate for working you so hard."

She broke their eye contact and rubbed her forehead. "I try to have dinner with the children as often as I can." She knew it sounded like a half-baked excuse but hoped to God he'd buy it.

He nodded. "Sorry. How could I have forgotten the children?"

His smile faded and somehow she thought she'd offended him. "How about tomorrow?"

"Tomorrow it is. Say, seven?"

She nodded. "Yes. Tomorrow at seven. It's a date. I mean..." she swallowed. "Yes."

Andrew gazed at her for a moment and saw the same nervousness he'd seen the night they'd had dinner in The Village. She'd had no idea that while she'd fidgeted, he'd not taken his eyes off her. Now his green eyes softened as he thought of his lips on hers that night, then he abruptly turned and left the office, the soft scent of his cologne lingering behind.

Alice stared after him. *Was it something I didn't say?* She gazed at the closed door, his manly strides still in the forefront of her brain. Biting into her lower lip, she reached for the phone. She picked up the receiver, held it in midair then slowly replaced it. Should she go out with Alvin? Would he be able to take her mind off Andrew? She knew in her heart Alvin could never be anything more than a friend to her. Heck, she hardly wanted his friendship. What was she afraid of? Andrew was an absolute gentleman from the first time they'd met and still was. Why was she afraid of being with him? She sighed, closed the file in front of her and moved away from her desk to look out at the ocean.

A slight knock on the door, and Andrew came in with his briefcase. "I'll walk you to your car," he said.

She turned, smiled, and all thoughts of Alvin left her. "Okay. Give me a second to collect my purse, and thanks."

"Well, I figure if I can't see you tonight, the least I can do is walk with you." His hand lightly touched her arm as she headed for the door.

Lee Ann had already left for the day and the office was almost empty except for a few people who didn't even look up as they left the building.

Outside, Andrew opened the car door for Alice and said goodbye. He walked to a blue Volvo two spots down from her BMW and she shook her head and smiled. It was a classic, almost as old as she was.

Not two minutes away from home, her cell phone rang. She didn't look at the number before answering it. "Hey girl, I missed you. When are we going to see each other again?"

She shouldn't have answered the phone. It was Alvin. "First, I'm not a girl, I'm a woman. Second, I am on my way home to be with my children."

"Sorry if I offended you, but you know, as I said before, if I meet the children we can be together more often."

"No, my children are completely off limits…"

"They can meet my children and we can have picnics and go shopping…"

She laughed. *Go shopping? You didn't even have money to pay for dinner.* "Alvin, your children don't live with you."

"That doesn't mean anything. I have visitation rights."

Why does even the sound of his voice annoy me? She answered herself. *Because you're trying to force a friendship with someone you don't really like.* "Alvin, how was your day?"

"My day was fine. Are you trying to change the subject?"

"No, but I'm pulling into my garage now, so let me call you tomorrow, okay."

"Listen, If I don't see you soon, I'll have to find someone else to hang with," he threatened.

"I strongly advise you to do so, because I have very little time for a social life."

"I'm kidding. I'll wait until you have time. Right now I'm sitting on my bed…"

"Bye, Alvin." She hung up, opened the car door and hugged her children as they ran out to greet her. Gathering them into her arms, she closed her eyes for a second. *This is my social life.* She smiled, opened her eyes to look at her pride and joy, then walked inside with each child flanking her right and left.

She called out to Delia just as she got a whiff of escoviche chicken. She threw her car keys into a small dish on the side table, while Alia took her pocketbook into her room. She walked into the kitchen, touched Delia on the shoulder and opened the saucepan. "Mmmm, I am so glad I came home for dinner this evening."

Delia smiled and began making the salad.

Alice turned and walked out of the kitchen then turned back to Delia. "Oh, before I forget, I won't be home for dinner tomorrow night. I'm having dinner with a friend from work."

Delia nodded. "Okay."

Before dinner, Alice slipped into the tub filled with warm bubbles and relaxed. For a few minutes she thought of her life and liked it. In her private life, she answered to no one. But then something entered her brain; if someone had told her that her husband was having an affair, or they'd seen him in the arms of another woman, she would have taken it with a grain of salt, believe or not believe depending on the person. But she'd seen it and he had not rushed to shield her or apologize, that was what drove her over the edge. He wasn't sorry. Did she hate Harvey? No. She was at a good place in her life. The bubbles were disappearing leaving the water flat and luke warm. She got out of the tub, dried herself off and slipped into shorts and a cotton shirt. Putting her hair in a ponytail, she rejoined her family for dinner.

The next day at work, she didn't see Andrew until it was time to leave. He pushed his head into her office and asked, "We're still on for dinner tonight, right?"

She looked up and nodded. "Absolutely."

He walked in and sat down. "I hope you like French food."

"I do."

"There's a little French restaurant in South Beach where the chef cooks anything you wish, even if it's not on the menu." He smiled and studied her thoughtfully; admiring the little twinkle in her light brown eyes and the small freckles across her nose. He wanted to reach across the desk and just caress her beautiful cheeks. Just once more… just for a little while, he'd love to press his mouth to those soft, warm, full lips. His eyes soft and exploring, he took a deep breath and got to his feet. "I have your address, so I'll be there at seven."

Alice glanced at her watch. "Then I'd better leave now. Wouldn't want to keep you waiting." She remembered what his sister had told her. He was a very prompt man.

"I don't mind waiting."

"I won't let you wait." His green eyes seemed to smile even before his lips did and her heart missed a tiny beat. *Lord, help me. My life is perfect without a man, right?* He waited while she tidied her desk and picked up her purse.

They walked together to her car and Alice almost couldn't get the key in the ignition. Good thing he'd walked away after opening the door and saying he'd see her later.

At home, she took a quick shower, no time for a bath, spent time with the children and at six-thirty she slipped into jeans and a royal blue, silk spaghetti strap blouse. She pushed her feet into blue sandals, took one last look at her reflection in the mirror; her hair was neatly pulled back from her face, her lips held a hint of mauve lip gloss and she was ready.

She glanced at her watch. It was exactly seven, the doorbell rang, and she hesitated. When Delia opened the door with the children beside her, he introduced himself to each of them. He glimpsed Alice as she walked into he living room. His eyes captured hers then approvingly ran the length of her curves. "Hello, you look wonderful," he said.

There was nothing unusual about the way he dressed. Jeans and cream silk shirt, but it was the way he wore it. "Thank you, so do you. Please come in. Would you like something to drink before we go?"

He stepped into the living room and followed her to the family room. "Just some seltzer water, if you don't mind."

"Please, sit," she said opening the refrigerator to get the water for him. "You don't drink?"

"Occasionally." He sat down and Alia promptly sat beside him. Phillip was a little more skeptical. He sat at the other end of the sofa looking at him.

"Why is your hair so long?" Alia asked, standing on the sofa and tugging at his pony tail.

He laughed. "I haven't gotten a chance to go to the barber in a long time."

"A long, long time it seems," Alia said, with her hand now on his shoulder looking into his face.

Alice laughed and shook her head. She handed him the water, "I'm sorry, Alia is only six and very inquisitive." She sat in the love seat across from him.

"I don't mind. Your children are very beautiful." He looked over at Phillip. "And this is the man of the house?"

Phillip nodded and both Andrew and Alice smiled. He didn't have any children of his own, but loved children. Unfortunately, his ex-wife didn't want to have children because she didn't want to spoil her figure. He finished his drink and held Alia's hand. "I hope to see you again."

"I can play with your hair next time?"

"Only if I can play with yours." He got to his feet.

"Yes, you can brush my hair," she said laughing.

Alice took the glass from Andrew's hand and shook her head. "You don't know what you're getting yourself into. Alia loves having her hair brushed."

He opened the door and Alice stepped through.

⁂

Under starry skies and the heavy traffic of I-95, they drove in Andrew's Volvo to South Beach. Although old, the car was clean and well cared for. The streets of South Beach were usually busy, but tonight it was fairly quiet in comparison. They parked on Lincoln Street and walked over to the strip. "I've never been to South Beach before," Alice said as they walked past Versace's mansion.

"Don't like crowds?" Andrew said.

"That would be a big part of it."

"And the other part?"

"Didn't want to come alone."

He smiled secretly. *And now I'm here to take you to all the places you want to go.*

Soft music filtered from Paolo's Ristorante. Chairs, tables and umbrellas sprawled on the sidewalk as lovers held hands to a hearty candlelight dinner.

Nestled beside a three-story historic building was Ron's Bistro, draped in white and blue pepper lights. The door opened and they were greeted by Ron himself. Ron was a middle-aged Scotsman with dull blue eyes and receding blonde hair. Both men greeted each other with a half hug and a hearty slap on the back. Andrew introduced Alice as his very dear friend. Ron took her outstretched hand and kissed it in a very French fashion for a Scotsman. They were immediately escorted to what would forever be their table. Seated, Alice was told by Ron that Andrew had made the purchase of the restaurant possible by giving him the down payment. In exchange, he'd made Andrew a silent partner. Andrew had insisted on being a very silent partner.

"Rat," Alice whispered when Andrew pulled out her chair.

He smiled. "How about a bottle of your best champagne, Ron?"

Ron bowed graciously and left, only to return within a few minutes with a bottle of Perrier Jouët. "Special night?" he inquired.

Alice glanced at the bottle of champagne and her last dinner with Harvey in New York stole a mocking kiss to her brain. Nevertheless, tonight, she would partake.

Andrew glanced at Alice. "Long story, but she's a very special lady." And with a mysterious look in his eyes, he saw her cheek warm under her brown skin.

The smile stayed on Ron's face. "I knew there was a good reason for the twinkle in your eyes, lad. Never saw it there before." He took Alice's hand again, kissed it and with another small bow, he was off.

Andrew shook his head. "Don't believe Ron. I helped out a friend in need, that's all." He toasted her beauty and she toasted his modesty.

With the menu in hand, Alice could still see the dark mysterious ocean on the other side of the street and through the hum of voices in the restaurant, she could almost hear the lapping on shore. She glanced back at him, his forehead was devoid of lines, but the corners of his very beautiful eyes held just a few. His hair had a touch of gray, beautifully displayed in curls and waves. "Should I order for you?" he asked.

She nodded. "Yes, but you don't know what I like to eat."

He glanced again at the menu. "No red meat, right?"

"Right."

"But you love seafood?"

She had no idea how he knew all that, maybe he'd been talking with his sister. She nodded slowly, watching his long, bronze fingers against the menu. Suddenly she felt fear for her heart. She didn't want to fall in love with anyone right now, but her heart wasn't listening to her head. She pressed her hands against her shaking knees and took a cleansing breath. "Fish, yes, fish. I like fish and shrimp and lobster…" she babbled.

He looked at her and nodded. "I know. All the seafood is very fresh." He didn't know anything about her personal life, but tonight she was with him, and that was all that mattered.

Alice sipped champagne and looked once again toward the shadowy ocean. Devoid of moonlight, it was still beautiful in its mysterious darkness.

When the waiter came over, Andrew ordered for them both without even asking for her approval, but then she had given him carte blanche.

Her cell phone rang once, twice. Delia wouldn't call unless it was extremely necessary. She reached into her purse and looked at the number. Given that it wasn't Delia's or her mother's, she touched the ignore button.

"Everything all right?" Andrew asked.

"Yes. So, how long have you worked at Frank's?"

"A little bit over nine years."

"And before that?"

"I worked on Wall Street until I burned out."

"Too much insider trading?" She laughed and shook her head. "Sorry. Bad joke."

"Don't be sorry. I love your sense of humor." He chuckled. "It was time to leave. What do you think about the job so far?"

She laughed. "If we continue this line of conversation, we can write this off as a business dinner. I love it."

"Okay, no more talk of work. I visited Jamaica once a long time ago. Fascinating place."

"What part?"

"Ocho Rios."

She laughed at his pronunciation. "I really love your accent. Did you go alone?" She made a face. "Sorry, I didn't mean to pry." She shook her head. "Don't answer that."

"But it's all right. I spent my honeymoon there." A darkness crossed his face and the muscles in his jaw jerked a few times. "I'm divorced."

There were no smiles on his face and his eyes visibly darkened. "I'm sorry," she said.

He shook his head and gazed at her. A smile slowly warmed his face. "No, don't be sorry."

"Why isn't your name and title on your door?"

He shrugged. "It's what's inside that matters, not a title."

"Strange."

"You think so?"

"A little. I mean when most people get to a certain position within a company they want to shout it from the roof tops, but not you. How modest."

He didn't reply, but gazed at her lips as she spoke.

When their meal was set before them, Andrew waited until Alice had taken the first bite then asked, "How is it?"

She nodded. "Excellent." She wasn't sure what kind of spice was in the sauce, but the lobster was melt-in-your- mouth sweet.

"Your shrimp?" she asked after he'd taken a bite.

He nodded. "Very good."

They ate in silence and Alice savored every morsel of the delicious meal.

For dessert, they shared a thick slice of key lime pie then each had a small snifter of liqueur. "Thank you so much for having dinner with me," Andrew said. "These days my life is nothing but work, golf, and home. You're like a breath of fresh air hopefully not passing through my life, but staying for awhile."

"I'm not going anywhere. My life is the way I want it right now. It's been a long time since I've said that."

He wanted so much to ask about her husband again, but knew that she'd eventually tell him why she was by herself. "What were you like as a little girl?" he asked, a slight huskiness in his voice. He leaned back in his chair and lightly touched the rim of his glass with one finger. He watched her keenly.

She gazed at him, leaned forward with both elbows on the table and lowered her voice mysteriously. "You don't want to know what I was like as a teenager, you want to know what I was like as a child, correct?"

"Yes."

"Okay," she leaned back in the chair. "I was shy, but a bit of a tomboy. I didn't talk a lot but I was a very determined person. My parents thought I would grow up to be a sociologist or at least something to do with children."

"Not a teacher?"

"No, I didn't have the patience, but they didn't see that."

"Your children are so well mannered."

She smiled and lowered her head. "Thank you for saying that, but I suppose it took being a mother for me to develop patience."

"Were you a good student?"

"What do you mean?"

"I mean, did you make trouble in class? Were you an A student?"

"No, I was not an A student and I was not a troublemaker. I was a shy little girl. How about you?"

"The same."

"You were a shy little girl?"

He didn't flinch. "Yeah." Then he placed a silencing finger to his lips. "Whoops! There goes my secret."

She laughed. "Don't worry, your secret is safe with me."

And just as she got comfortable being with him, she glanced at her watch. It was time to go. She didn't have to say anything. He motioned for the waiter. "I would like to see you again out of the office, so I'd better take you home."

She smiled. "This was wonderful. Thank you."

"No, thank you."

He paid the check, pulled out her chair and rested his hand slightly at the small of her back as they left the restaurant.

Chapter Eleven

It had been two weeks since Alice had dinner with Andrew, and within those days, she'd worked tirelessly on one account with him. She'd dodged Alvin's many calls by programming his number in her phone so when his calls came in she'd press ignore and delete his messages. She would have lunch at her desk or Andrew's desk. Through their close contacts and camaraderie, each day she dropped her guard a little bit more, letting him into all aspects of her life, except the married part.

She had not heard from Harvey in more than a month and was very surprised when he called her at eleven-thirty one night from California. "Sorry, I didn't call before, Alice, but I've been so busy I hardly have time to scratch my head. How are you and the children?"

"Very well, thank you. I guess the only thing in your life that changed is your marital status." Realizing that sounding a bit bitter, she said, "sorry, I shouldn't have said that. How are you?"

"I'm doing well so far. The divorce papers are ready, so I'll sign them as soon as I get back to New York. You'll still stand by what you said, right?"

"That you can see the children any time you wish except when they're in school?"

"Yes."

"Of course. It's in black and white."

"Good, because I'll be in Florida in a couple of weeks and would love to see them then."

"Sure, no problem."

"Good, do you need anything?"

She hesitated.

"I mean… money or anything?"

"That's very kind of you, but we're fine."

"Alice…" he said and she waited. She could hear him breathe, as if he had more to say, but all he said was, "Have a good night and I'll see you hopefully in a couple of weeks."

"You too." She hung up the phone but her hand rested on the receiver. Was Harvey about to apologize? She took her hand away from the phone and lay back in bed. She closed her eyes. Was he sick or dying?

The next morning at work, Andrew relaxed as he now sat before her in her office. It seemed as if he was always there, always with her.

"You seem to have had a sleepless night. May I be so bold as to ask why?" he smiled.

She looked up at him from the Garner file. This was the first client he'd brought her in on, and hopefully they'd close on the deal within the month. She and Andrew had become very close; they had an unwavering trust in each other even though she'd never talked about her marriage. But for some reason, now, she thought she should tell him that she didn't have a marriage anymore. She smiled. "How would you know whether I've had a sleepless night or not."

"Because you never had dark shadows under your eyes before today."

"You've been really paying attention to me, haven't you?"

"Yes."

She closed the file and leaned back in her chair. She knew she had to tell him. She valued his friendship too much to keep the lie

going. Now that she was faced with this dilemma, she wondered
if she had not kept it going to protect herself from him.

"Well," he pushed.

She inhaled softly, pushed her chair away from the desk, then
got up and walked toward the side table to make herself a cup of
tea. "Do you want a cup?" she asked, glancing back at him.

Gazing at her under hooded lashes, he slowly nodded, sensing
something was terribly wrong. The smile slowly faded from his
lips, leaving a furrowed brow. His eyes followed her as she made
tea for them both. She'd done it many times in the last few weeks.
No sugar, but always cream for him. She poured tea in each cup
and stirred the warm liquid, stalling. She picked up the cups
and walked back to her desk, placing one before him then sitting
heavily in her chair.

He sat quietly waiting for her to talk.

"I have to tell you something, Andrew," she said watching the
rising steam from the teacup.

"Yes," he encouraged in his casual, unhurried tone.

"We trust each other, right?"

"You're my very best friend, Allison. Everyone knows that."

She wished he hadn't said that at all. Not now. That name gave
a special closeness to their relationship, and at the moment, she
didn't think she deserved that closeness.

She looked nervously around the office from one painting to
the next, still stalling. The ivy covered English cottage standing
under misty skies with grazing horses and a barn in the far corner
of the property was one of her favorites.

Andrew lifted the cup from the saucer on the desk and sipped
the warm brew, his eyes never leaving her face.

"I haven't seen Harvey since I left New York with the children.
Before I left, I filed for divorce. He called last night. The call
disturbed me a bit because he was so nice, he almost sounded like
the Harvey I'd met so many years ago."

"He doesn't want the divorce?" Andrew asked with a scowl
on his face.

"No, yes, I mean, it's not that. He said he'd sign the papers when he got back from California, but it was just the way he spoke."

"You don't want the divorce anymore?" now he was perplexed.

She smiled. "Oh, that part of our life is over. We can never go back. I hated him at first."

"He asked for the divorce?"

"He suggested it. I executed it. He'll be here in a couple of weeks and wants to see the children."

"Are you afraid of him?" The question was very cut and dry. If she was afraid of him, he would think nothing of being with her when Harvey came to see the children.

"No, I'm not afraid of him." She sighed. "I want the divorce, but..." she looked away from him and placed a shaky hand over her lips. Now that it was all over, again, she felt as if she'd failed in some way. Unwanted tears stung her eyes. She didn't want to cry, not now, not with Andrew sitting across from her. She got up and walked to the window.

She felt his hands on her shoulders.

"I don't know what I did wrong or how I failed." Her words sounded as if she were asking herself these questions, doubting herself.

He slowly spun her around to face him but she didn't look into his face. "Don't blame yourself for this, Alice. I know how hard a divorce can be, but I've come to know you over these past weeks and even without you telling me what took place to cause this divorce I know it's not your fault."

She looked into his murky green eyes and the tears flowed. He pressed her to his chest and hushed her. "I'm here for you. Please don't ever feel that there's anything you can't confide in me."

"There was nothing I could have done to save our marriage. It was over, he wasn't in love with me anymore and I couldn't stick around just for the children. I couldn't do that to them or to me."

He held her closer and rested his cheek on hers, feeling the wetness and the warmth. "He's a fool, Alice. Whatever he did, he's a fool to let you go. He placed an index finger under her chin, tilted her face up and saw the look of pain on her face. He wanted to kiss away her pain and tell her he'd never leave her.

She smiled through her tears. "Thanks, Andrew." She accepted his handkerchief with the smell of his cologne and dabbed the tears from her face. She felt comfortable and ragged at the same time. She gently pushed away from him, but he held her hand.

"Will you be all right?" he asked looking into her face.

She nodded. "Of course, you're here." She wasn't quite sure what she wanted from him; she only knew that when he was around, she couldn't tear her eyes away from his face. He always asked about the children and made her feel very special. He opened doors for her and insisted that she eat even when she wasn't aware of her own hunger. He was very patient with her as he brought her more and more into his world.

"Yes, I am. Don't ever forget it. Anything I can do, anything you need, don't hesitate to ask." He was still holding her hand and felt her softness and warmth seep into his skin. His fingers gently touched her cheek and brushed away a stray hair from her face. Then he kissed her cheek close to her mouth and lingered.

She closed her eyes, opened her mouth and breathed, "Thank you, Andrew." It was the first time they'd ever been that close since New York, and it felt good—too good.

To Andrew, it felt like heaven. He was sorry she was hurting, but knowing that Harvey was no longer a part of her life, he felt relief.

She moved away from him and sat back behind her desk. "To answer your first question, I didn't get much sleep last night because I spent the better part thinking of my life before Florida." She smiled. "I like my life now, Andrew."

"I'm glad you do. I'd like to think that I'm in your life because I know how it feels to be alone in a new place." His voice was low, and his green eyes were soft and filled with compassion.

Alice nodded and smiled at him. "I'm not exactly alone. I have Delia, the children and my mother and sister. But I do know what you mean. Thanks." She'd found out a few things about Andrew that day. Apart from the fact that he had an understated aristocratic air about him, his eyes became a deeper green when he was disturbed.

"I bet you don't tell them half the things you tell me."

She shook her head. "I don't want my mother to worry, and my sister gets upset when men tend to take advantage. Her first advice is to dump them." She laughed.

He glanced at her under his lashes and nodded. "I'm sure I'll meet your mother and sister soon."

She wasn't sure if that was a question or a statement. Meeting her mother represented the kind of seriousness in a relationship she wasn't ready for. She wasn't very anxious for him to meet them just yet. But she nodded.

"Are you all right now?" He sat at the edge of her desk and took her small hand in his.

She looked at his face, his brow creased with concern for her, the unruly curl sitting on his forehead. *You are driving me to distraction, the kind that I cannot afford right now.* She nodded. "Yes, I'm fine, but if you don't get out of here, I won't be able to get any work done."

He mirrored her smile and took a deep breath. "Okay, but I'm just across the hall if you feel like talking."

She nodded, slipped her hand from his and opened the file on her desk once more. He began walking to the door, then turned. She shook her head. "Go, I'm fine."

He closed the door behind him and she leaned back in her chair. The lingering vision of his powerful strides caused her to shake her head again. *Just a friend, Alice, just a friend.* She was about to make a few phone calls regarding the file in front of her when her cell phone rang. She picked it up and looked at the number. It was Alvin, this time she decided to answer it. "Hello Alvin. What can I do for you?"

"Why so formal? I just wanted to know when I'm going to see you."

She took a deep breath, expelled it and smiled to herself. *I can't do this.* "Alvin, I'm sorry, but whatever we have is proving to be a little bit too much for me. So, let's just part friends."

There was a heavy silence on the other end of the phone.

"Why?" His voice sounded cross.

"You want more than I am willing to give and it's not fair for me to keep you hanging on." She purposely held an apologetic tone to her voice and hoped he would understand.

"But I said I would wait until you were ready for us to go forward."

"No, Alvin. We can never go forward." There was an unintentional edge to her voice.

"Is there someone else?"

"Alvin, I have to go. I can't see you anymore."

"But I love you."

"Nonsense, I have to go." She wanted to hang up the phone but didn't want to be rude.

"I can't accept that, Alice. You're separated from your husband, which means you don't have anyone in your life. You need a man in your life."

"No I don't." Now the edge was purposeful. How dare he try to impose himself into her life when she plainly said no. "I have to work. I'm going to hang up now." True to her word, she hung up on him and flung her phone halfway across her desk. She attacked the file as if it had done her wrong. She sighed, placed a hand to her face and closed her eyes. *I should not have called him when I did knowing there could be nothing between us. The first time he mentioned a sexual relationship I should have ended it.* Now she thought it was all her fault and blamed herself for leading him on.

Again, she tried to work through lunch, but Andrew had Lee Ann order her a shrimp salad sandwich. When Lee Ann set the plate on her desk, she smiled and said, "Compliments of Mr. Benton. He doesn't want you to starve to death."

She laughed. "Is it lunch time already?"

"No, it's past lunch time. It's two-thirty."

"Thank him for me."

"I'll make you some tea to go with your sandwich," Lee Ann insisted.

She nodded, "Thanks."

Lee Ann placed the cup of green tea before her, then left the office. It was not until four before Alice finally ate. Two hours later, Andrew came in. "Please don't tell me you're working late." He had his jacket slung over his shoulder.

She glanced at her watch. "Oops! Not intentionally." She looked at him. "Are you going to wait for me?"

"That's why I'm here."

"You know people are going to start talking about us." She got up and reached for her purse.

"There's not much they can say."

She laughed. "You're not too aware of how the human brain works, are you?"

He smiled. "I never give a second thought to what other people say or think, but if it bothers you…"

"Not at all. I'm a big girl, plus we work together. Forget that I ever said anything." She walked to the door as he held it open.

"You know, I have to pass your area to come into work, we should car pool. It makes a lot of sense." He proposed, holding the car door open for her.

He had not paid attention to one word she'd said about office gossip. She smiled. "I am west, you are east. You take I-95 and I take the Sawgrass Expressway."

"That can change."

How could she resist spending a little more time with him? "Okay, but sometimes you'll drive and sometimes I'll drive. You can park your car at my home when I drive."

He reached for her hand. "Deal."

"But not every day, because sometimes I visit my mother and sister."

"Okay."

She slipped behind the wheel of her car and he closed the door. She glanced at his Volvo beside her and jumped when he tapped on her passenger window. "In three weeks, there's a Jamaican play at the Coral Springs Center for the Performing Arts, would you like to accompany me?"

"Jamaican plays are usually mostly patois. Do you understand the language?"

"If I don't understand, you'll translate for me?"

"Yes, and yes, I would love to accompany you."

He grinned and slid into the driver's seat, then waited for her to reverse. He followed her out of the parking lot, then turned left while she turned right.

Chapter Twelve

At home with her children, Alice wondered if she should invite Andrew over for dinner the next day. She had a feeling although he may have golf buddies, he often ate alone. But again, he may be involved with someone. She sat on the patio having dinner with her family and watched the rain make disappearing puddles in her pool. She liked Andrew; she'd liked him from the first time they'd met. She thought about the subway ride with him and the way he protected her, not only then but again when the lights went out in New York City. What about that word? Should she try to broach the subject again with him? She wanted to know. There was too much of a passionate hatred there for it not to have been very personal.

As Delia cleared the table and the children went inside to watch television before bed, Alice remained outside. The bright yellow, red, and orange roses that she'd planted not too long ago seemed to be thriving, even if she'd planted the snap-dragons a little too close to them.

She got up to go inside to call Andrew and invite him for dinner on Saturday, but sat back down. *Maybe I'll wait until tomorrow. But what if he has something else to do?* She made a face. *He'll give me a rain check, that's all.* She sat enjoying the cool evening, which didn't come along very often in South Florida. Her mother and sister called and invited her to Sunday dinner. She accepted.

Through the darkness, a hazy moon cast its reflection on the ocean. Andrew sat on his balcony with his long legs propped on the railing. The breeze off the ocean tousled his long loose curls and he smiled when he thought of Alice, her sense of humor, her intelligence, and her beauty. Everything he would want in a woman. He was sorry that she'd had an unhappy marriage but glad that she was so close to him now. His sister had almost given him permission to have an affair with her. He chuckled to himself. *Willetta really likes her.*

Alice was a quick study and he had a feeling that she was getting to know him faster than he was getting to know her. He picked up his cell phone from off the table and dialed her landline.

Delia picked up. "Delia, this is Andrew Benton. How are you?"

"Very well, Mr. Benton. I'll get Miss Alice for you."

Alice was now relaxing inside with Alia asleep in her lap. She heard what Delia had said and smiled as she took the receiver. "Andrew, how are you?"

"I'm good. I just wanted to know what time you wanted me to pick you up in the morning."

"Eight would be all right."

"Good. The children are fine?"

"Yes, I'm just about to put them to bed."

"Okay, then I'll say goodnight and see you tomorrow morning."

"Good night, Andrew." Alice hung up the receiver and squinted. His soothing voice still echoed in her brain. Her eyes softened and her belly did a strange thing she had not felt in a very long time; it did a little flip. *Why didn't I invite him to dinner then?* She shrugged, tomorrow will be fine.

She got up and with Delia's help, put both children to bed.

Andrew walked into his bedroom and fell on his bed fully clothed. Why didn't he ask her out? They could have gone for a walk in Mizner Park or on the beach. *I'm not a shy man.* Something was different with him; he wanted to get to know her wonderful children, not to insinuate himself into their lives, but to be in their lives if they would have him. He closed his eyes and in his mind's eye saw Alice's face as she spoke of her marriage. She was so beautiful that it stirred something in his loins as their kiss entered his memory. It was very safe to say, he was very fond of her, maybe even more.

Alice opened the door the next morning to let Andrew in. "Would you like some coffee or tea? Delia can make you breakfast if you like."

"Breakfast," he murmured glancing at his watch. "I think we have the time."

Delia had already set another place at the table for him because Alice had told her to, just in case he agreed to have breakfast. She still didn't know if he was unattached. And as he sat, she poured him a cup of Blue Mountain coffee. He inhaled the aroma and nodded, then sipped. Scrambled eggs and toast made for a simple breakfast, but he felt as if he'd been given his favorite meal in the entire world.

Alice sat with him while Delia got the children ready for school. "You don't really have breakfast in the mornings, do you?"

"Not all the time, so this is a treat for me."

"I'm glad. Would you like to join us for dinner this evening?"

"Yes. Yes, I would," he said without thinking. After all, this was what he wanted.

Everyone left the house at the same time. Delia took the children to school in her little Volkswagen. Alice and Andrew went in the Volvo. She laughed a little, because she always had to tell the children not to spill food in her car or put their feet on the back of the seat. Would this car ever transport her children?

At the end of the work day while driving back home, Andrew asked, "What time would you like me to be there for dinner?"

"Is seven-thirty all right?"

"Absolutely."

"And you don't have to bring anything."

He glanced at her, "Not even wine?"

"No. It's fine. For a single woman, I have too much wine at home, so just come."

He laughed. "All right, I'll just come at seven-thirty with my empty hands."

But that's not exactly what happened. Alice was on the patio drinking tea and being mesmerized by the roses swaying in the light breeze when the twins came running in with a handful of fur.

"Mommy, Mommy! Look what Mr. Benton brought for us," Phillip shouted.

"Yes, look," Alia echoed.

"You said we could have a puppy. You promised!" Phillip said before she could get a word in edgewise.

And what a fool I was to say that. She looked at the ball of fur in his arms and sighed resignedly. Placing her cup back in its saucer, she looked into the droopy eyes of the puppy and smiled. She took the puppy from Phillip, smoothed its soft golden fur, blew into its face and watched as it licked at the air. She was still smiling when she looked up at her son. "And who's going to take care of this ball of fur?"

"I will, Mom."

"Me too," Alia said.

"Do you know the responsibility that comes with having a dog?" she asked both children.

"No, not really," Phillip said with sad eyes gazing at her.

"And where is Mr. Benton?"

Phillip suddenly giggled. "He's behind the door, just in case you didn't want the puppy. Oh, but can we keep him? Pleeese?"

She couldn't resist when he pleaded with her, or the charming smile that went with it.

You certainly know how to work your mother. "Yes."

Both children cheered.

Alice held up a finger. "On one condition."

"Anything," he cried, laughing.

"You have to feed him, clean up after him, and most importantly, you have to walk him. So actually, you have to clear this with Delia, because she has to go with you."

"I will, I will, I will. Delia already said she would." He kissed her cheek and hugged her tight. "Thank you, Mom."

Alice looked around for Alia, but she had disappeared from the patio. Right then Andrew appeared with her in his arms and a big grin on his face. "You only said not to bring wine; you didn't say anything about a puppy. I hope I haven't broken any rules or overstepped my boundaries."

Alice looked at his face and shook her head. She couldn't resist him either. She tried looking regal and cool, but failed. "Chicken," she said, laughing.

"Well," he shrugged and gave her puppy dog eyes.

Alia held his face and looked in his eyes, then laughed. "You're funny."

Alice was very glad she'd not begun to call him uncle Andrew; that would have been too quick for her. Caught by the turquoise green in his eyes when he looked toward her, she cast her eyes downward. "Thank you. He's very sweet."

Alia clung to Andrew's neck and pulled the band from his hair so that she could run her fingers through it. And Andrew didn't make a move to stop her, even though she was making a royal mess. He'd said she could.

"She likes you Andrew, but you should stop her from doing that." Alice said pointing to Alia.

"I like her too," he said playing with her ponytail. She giggled.

Well, if the easiest way to a woman's heart is through her children, he was doing a bang up job. Alice swallowed and held the dog in the air. "And what should we call this furry little creature?" The dog's tail went immediately between its legs.

"How about Tee Tee? It's a girl, Mommy," Phillip giggled some more.

Alice took a second look and blushed as she glanced at Andrew, who was smiling at her. "Sorry." She cleared her throat. "Wonderful," she said. "But right now we have a date at the shelter, remember?" she looked at both children. She'd taken them to the shelter a few times to help clean up or help share food to teach them values. She didn't want them to become spoiled and always wanting something, but rather to think of those who had much less than they did.

"Yes, Mommy, but can we take Tee Tee?" Phillip asked.

"No, just this once, Delia can take care of her."

Andrew bent and placed Alia on her feet. He ran his fingers through his hair and replaced the band. "I'd love to come with you. I think it's wonderful what you're trying to teach your children."

Alice didn't answer right away, then she nodded. "Sure, they can always use another pair of hands."

When they got to the shelter and Andrew realized how involved in the lives of the people Alice was, he was never more proud to be with her. She not only counseled them but did anything else that was asked of her without asking why. Some of the indigents even called her "Honey." Andrew wondered where she found the time to do all this. As his eyes drank her up, it was not without a twinkle.

When they got back home, the table was set for four. Alice wrinkled her brow, sent the children to the bathroom to get washed up and offered Andrew a drink before heading to the kitchen. She touched Delia on the arm and whispered. "I thought I told you that Andrew would join us for dinner?"

Delia had a quizzical look on her face. "Yes, I set the table for four."

"Have you eaten?"

"No."

"Then why didn't you set a place for yourself?"

Puzzled, she looked at Alice. "But, I didn't think it appropriate..."

"You are a part of this family, Delia. Whether I have company or not, your place is at the meal table." She nodded as she spoke.

"But…"

"No, Delia. No buts."

Delia nodded and watched as Alice took out another place setting and placed it on the table.

When they sat down to dinner, Andrew looked around the table and smiled. It would have been so nice for them to go for a walk after dinner, but they'd both had a long day and he didn't want to seem too anxious. So after dinner, he had tea with her and said goodnight.

———

Alice might have been finished with Alvin but he certainly wasn't finished with her because the next day at work, he called her office. Unfortunately, she picked up her phone because Lee Ann was in with Andrew.

"So," Alvin said, "when will this break of ours be over?"

"Excuse me?" A coldness slid through her veins but she kept her cool.

"You said we should cool it for a while and I miss you, so I thought I'd call and invite you to my house for dinner."

She shuddered. "I told you I didn't want to see you anymore. I won't change my mind."

"Oh. Is there someone else?"

She thought of the question and wondered if saying *yes* would do it. "Yes, there is someone else."

"That was fast, you just got to Florida. Are you back with your husband?"

She was annoyed and busy, yet worded her reply very carefully. "Alvin, I really don't have any time for this. What I do is none of your business. I have to go, and please don't call again."

Her door opened and Andrew walked in.

"You can't get rid of me that easily. I know you; you just need more time; you need a man who is patient. One who can appreciate you, and, Alice, I do appreciate you. I won't leave you. I'll pamper you and treat you like the lady you are."

What wonderful words coming from someone who cannot afford to pay a simple thirty-dollar check. The words were so kind that she was tempted to prolong their relationship, but no. She couldn't force herself to like him that way, not even to hide herself from Andrew. *Why did she still have the phone at her ear?* "Alvin, you don't know anything about me. Don't call again." The brusqueness disappeared from her voice and a tight smile appeared on her lips as she replaced the receiver in its cradle. She hoped Alvin's last statement wasn't a threat. She really didn't think she'd done anything to warrant that statement. She shook her head. She'd been very clear upfront as to their relationship.

"Trouble?" Andrew asked.

She glanced at him then at the work on her desk. "Nothing I can't handle." She smiled.

"Okay, I won't keep you, but I wanted to ask if you'd like to go for a walk with me this evening? Dinner would be my treat and the walk yours."

Trying to forget about Alvin, she leaned back in her chair and looked at his long, lean body before him. His loose-fitting, well tapered clothing couldn't hide his slim yet muscular physique. She took a breath. "You don't have to ask me out to dinner because I fed you last night, you know."

"Alice," he said with mock hurt. "I just want to see you a little bit more in a relaxed atmosphere."

Her slow laugh seeped in and tickled his very masculine bone in a way that spread throughout his body, making him chuckle to hide his need to suddenly crush her to him.

"Is that appropriate? After all, you are my boss."

He shook his head, looked into her vulnerable eyes and wondered if she knew how beautiful she was. "I am not your boss. We both report to Ben. I just love being with you."

"I know. I just love yanking your chain. But you are my teacher. How about I meet you somewhere after dinner for coffee and a walk or tea and a walk," she mused. After the disturbing conversation she'd had with Alvin, being with Andrew would more than make up for it.

"Yes, I accept. Is Mizner Park all right or would you like me to come closer to your home?"

"We could do *The Walk* on University."

"Even better, longer walk. I'll go now and see you later." He turned, looked back at her and winked, then closed the door behind him.

With her elbows on top of her desk, she rubbed her temples lightly with her fingers. She'd made a grave mistake in trying to befriend Alvin. She wasn't that lonely; she had her family. Then she remembered the fifty thousand dollars she'd taken out of her and Harvey's joint checking account. Mmmm, why had he not mentioned it in their last conversation? She had not asked for alimony although it was within her rights to do so. Maybe he thought that was her alimony and didn't want to rock the boat. She took a deep breath and called Lee Ann in to dictate a letter.

She didn't fear Alvin or his threats.

Chapter Thirteen

Sitting outside a restaurant close to the water fountain on *The Walk,* Andrew caught and held Alice's eyes. Yes, they were the compelling light brown eyes that had not left his thoughts ever since the first time they'd met. In them he could see her vulnerability and, maybe that she was even a little lost. She smiled nervously. "That phone call today at the office," he said, "Was it from Harvey, or am I being too forward in asking?"

"No," she breathed, "It wasn't from Harvey." She pulled away from his gaze and wondered if she should tell him about Alvin. There wasn't much to tell. "When I came down from New York, I met someone I went to college with and had not seen for a very long time. We went out to dinner once and although I told him there could never be anything romantic between us, he has other ideas." She shrugged and laughed.

"He wants more?" He took in the worried lines across her forehead.

"I suppose so." She shook her head. "It was a mistake to have even given him my phone number." She glanced at the fountain then back at him. "It's fine. I don't think he'll bother me again."

Andrew nodded. "He threatened you?"

"Not in so many words." She touched the saucer under the cup of tea on the table and kept the smile on her face. "Don't worry about it. Look," she said, taking a deep breath and biting her lower lip. "Maybe I shouldn't tell you this, but I will anyway." Looking at his face filled with concern, his eyes so soft and genuine, she almost cringed. "The last few years of my marriage weren't very good." She stopped talking, but didn't look at him, while she thought of all the times Harvey came home drunk and accused her of cheating when her times were spent at work and at home with the children. She looked at Andrew and smiled to mask her pain. She felt like crying, but that was not going to happen again.

He reached for her hand and held it. She tried to pull away, but he wouldn't let her. "Let's walk for awhile," he said, his voice still soft with empathy. He paid the check, moved away from the table and took hold of her hand once more as they walked.

"I never cheated on Harvey, Andrew. Not once did I ever cheat on him."

"He accused you?" His fingers swept gently across hers and he could feel her fingers gently curl around his.

She nodded. "At times, his words were very harsh and mean. He wasn't afraid to insult me in front of his colleagues and that hurt more than anything. Our marriage was over long before the day I took the children and walked away from him."

"He never hit you?" His fingers closed in a little on hers.

She shook her head. "No, never. I drank at nights to hide my pain. When the children were in bed and the house was quiet, alone in my room, I drank to put myself to sleep. When he began pushing me away, I knew that he believed his own words. I knew he was seeing other women, but I kept telling myself that what I didn't know wouldn't hurt me. But it did. His actions did."

"I'm sorry you suffered so much," he whispered above the noise of passing cars and chattering passers by.

She nodded, but said nothing more.

And he knew she had a lot more to say. She was trusting him, confiding in him, and he felt privileged. He released her fingers and slipped an arm around her shoulder. First he felt her stiffen then slowly she relaxed under his arm.

As Alice's hand touched and held Andrew's long fingers on her shoulder, her heart quickened and missed a beat as flesh to flesh their warmth mingled. She felt more relaxed than she had in a long time; more than that, she felt safe from the world that would roll over her.

It felt exhilarating to be her own person. For years, there'd been something missing in her life. Maybe it was someone like Andrew, but there were complications—always complications. They worked together in an office filled with women. They didn't socialize with them but knew tongues would be wagging. "Was your divorce an amicable one?" she asked, not wanting to talk about herself anymore.

He grimaced above her. "I packed a suitcase, picked up my briefcase and left."

She laughed. "I'm sorry, I didn't mean to laugh. It's just the way you said it."

It's all right. When I look back on that day, I laugh too, but I couldn't get away fast enough."

"You're so warm, so caring. Aren't Brits supposed to be cold? I mean—"

"I know what you mean. We have a dry sense of humor; we're not as warm as Americans, or so they say. But to tell the truth, I don't think we're any different from any other culture. Some of us are cold and some are not. It's as simple as that. Plus, I was born here. My father was British and that's why we moved to England." He smiled and brushed the hair from his face. "Not like your culture though. Jamaicans are very warm."

"See, I wouldn't go that far. There are those who are warm and those that are cold, then you have those that are hot…" she broke off and began laughing right along with him.

I would think you fall in that category. "And funny too," Andrew said. His hand dropped from her shoulder to her hands. A warm feeling shot through him and he took a deep breath and fingered her palm.

"I'm having dinner with Mom tomorrow."

"Okay, so we won't car pool?"

"Right. Delia's meeting me there with the children."

"But I'll still see you tomorrow at work." He stopped, turned her to face him and looked into her eyes. "This is one of the best times I've had in a long time, just being with you, and believe me when I say, I am extremely sorry that you were hurt so badly."

She almost closed her eyes to his breath on her face as her own breath caught in her throat. "Ahhh, no please don't apologize. Thanks for listening and not judging."

"Never. Harvey is a fool for letting you go." *But his loss is my gain.*

For a second, she stared into those clear green eyes that seemed to dance when he was happy. And just as her knees were about to go weak on her, she gently touched his cheek for a second then forced herself to shift her gaze from his face. "Thank you for saying that."

Just the touch of her hand on her face sparked a deep hunger inside him and as close as they were, he knew just a small taste of her lips wouldn't be enough; but still, he hugged her and felt her heartbeat in sync with his. *One kiss*, he told himself under a tree where the birds chirped.

But he was slow and she was fast in disentangling herself from him.

"We'd better go," she said, her voice a little bit above a whisper.

He nodded and steeled his body. "On Sunday, why don't I make lunch for you and the children at my home? Do they love the beach?"

"Yes."

"My condo is right across from the ocean. We can even picnic on the beach." *Good recovery.*

She nodded. "Yes, I think they'd love that. Alia seems to be quite taken with you already."

"And what about Alia's mother, does she like me even a little?" He held her hand.

There was a sudden swoosh in her stomach as butterflies seem to flutter their wings, but she kept calm. She released her sweaty palm from his hand and gave a nervous laugh. "I think Alia's mother likes you—a little."

He smiled and squeezed her hand. "Would you like to walk on the beach with me?"

How romantic. "I would love to, but can I take a rain check? I'm a little tired."

"Of course." They kept walking to his car. He opened the door for her, walked around and slid into the driver's seat. The woman who felt like crying not too long ago felt comfortably wrapped in the aroma of this man sitting beside her.

⁕

Alvin pulled up into his apartment complex, got out of his car and looked around to see the squalor he lived in. Funny, he'd never even thought of it before Alice. He leaned against his car, lit a cigarette, took a deep drag and crossed one leg over the other. How could he be so stupid as to invite her into the ghetto. She was out of his league. He shook his head and looked up at his fourth-floor apartment window. Beside his apartment, several shirts and trousers hung on the railing. A few windows over, the glass was broken and replaced with cardboard. He filled his lungs again and exhaled a fog of smoke. She wouldn't judge him. He knew she was down to earth; they'd just gotten off on the wrong foot. He could make it right. He threw the cigarette butt on the ground and crushed it out with the heel of his shoe. A woman sauntered up to him with a wide grin on her face. Her skin a deep cocoa brown, her plumpness made him remember last night when she lay beneath him writhing with legs spread to his liking. He'd had an itch that she could scratch, that's all. She stood before him with hands akimbo. "What's up?" he said.

"Last night was good, wasn't it?"

"Yeah."

"Can I come up later?"

He laughed. "Sure, but I have something to do first." He walked away from her without a backward glance and took the stairs to his apartment two steps at a time.

He knew where Alice worked; he'd asked for the address of the building before he'd asked her secretary for her. That was a smart move. He had to see her again. He pushed through his door, straight to the bathroom. He picked up the damp towel he'd left on the floor this morning and threw it on a peg behind the door, then walked to his bedroom and sat on the bed. What a mess he'd made of his life. He watched a roach climb the wall and didn't even make a move to squash it. He just kept watching the wretched, nasty thing until he began thinking of prison. He didn't want to go back there. He cringed as he thought of the beatings, the threats. He blinked. He'd made bad investments, one after the other, and the last one landed him in jail for real estate fraud. Little old ladies had more money than they knew what to do with. What was the harm in borrowing a few thousand? But it was much more than a few thousand. He would have paid it back eventually.

He groaned, got up from his bed and walked to the tiny bathroom to take a shower. Alice was his ticket out of this hell hole. *I can be charming. I can make her love me.* He didn't really believe she had a man in her life.

Alice turned against the cool sheets in her bed and stared in the darkness at the ceiling. She could hear Tee Tee fussing in the children's room. She got out of bed and pushed the door to their room. Tee Tee was marking time and she knew that was a sign that she wanted to go out. She picked her up and opened the back door allowing her to run to the grassy area close to the pool. She stood waiting until she came back, sat down and stared up at her. Alice smiled. *I knew they'd slip up. Someone gave you water, didn't they?* She picked up the dog, closed the door and placed her back on her dog bed in the room, then returned to her bed.

She didn't fall asleep until three in the morning. She couldn't get Andrew off her mind. The feelings he stirred in her made her wonder if it was too soon to have romantic feelings for another man. *You can only control those feelings if you're cold*, she told herself, and she was far from it. But didn't she promise herself that she wouldn't fall in love again? She smiled, hugged her pillow and took a cleansing breath. Her eyelids fluttered then flew open. What would her mother say about Andrew being white? *Oh, don't be silly. Your mother is not a bigot. Actually, she's a romantic just like you.* Her eyes fluttered close.

During the next day at work, Andrew made several trips to her office for little things that could have been handled over the phone. "I can't get enough of seeing you," he said.

She never tired of his accent or the warmth in his beautiful eyes. "I keep telling you, if you're not careful people will begin to talk about us."

"Then let them." He pressed his hands on her desk and leaned over. "Oh, sorry. Do you mind?"

She shook her head. "Andrew... No." She blinked and palmed her face. "Did I just say no?"

He nodded, and smiled as if he'd just won the lottery and strolled out of her office.

At the end of the day, she picked up her purse and headed out of the building before Andrew. She felt as if she were running away, but he would probably find that funny too when he called her later on.

Backing out of her parking space, she was blocked by a blue Nissan, so she sat and waited for it to pass, but it didn't. She jumped at the tapping on her window and turned to see Alvin standing beside her car. He made a turning motion with his hand.

Her hands shook as she half rolled her window down. "Alvin! What are you doing here?"

"You wouldn't return my calls. You wouldn't call me, so I decided to visit."

"This is where I work for God's sake. I have nothing to say to you, Alvin. Now if you don't mind, please remove your car," she said, not knowing what he would do.

"Not until you agree to have dinner with me one night. We need to talk." He bent and placed an arm on her car. "Listen, I know what you're going through left with two children and no man in your life. But I want to be that man for you. You're a beautiful, intelligent woman," he shook his head. "To tell you the truth, I don't want to see you unhappy."

Eyes like ice drilled into him, wondering what his angle was. "Okay, you've said your piece. I keep telling you, you don't know anything about me."

"I know that you have class, more than anyone I've ever known. I want to be with you."

She was repulsed at the thought of his skin even touching hers. She shook her head. "I should have kept on walking the first day I saw you outside that hotel. I am not lonely and you really should go before security realizes that your car does not belong here. This is a closed parking lot. Now, please go away. I don't ever want to see you again." She was angry yet a little afraid of him. She'd never been in a situation like this before.

"Not before you agree to have dinner…"

"I believe the lady asked you politely to leave." Andrew's voice had a dangerous edge that Alice had never heard before, which startled her more.

She froze with fear. She didn't know what either man was capable of.

He stood imposingly at least five inches above Alvin's small, round-shouldered stature. "Who are you? I'm having a conversation with my girl."

To this, Andrew clenched his fist as he ground his teeth. He knew this was the man Alice spoke of so unfavorably, and wanted to grab him by the scruff of his neck and throw him against his dirty looking car. He could see Alice's provoked face in the mirror and wanted to touch her and tell her that she had nothing to fear. She shook her head and spoke up, her voice deceptively calm. "I'm all right, Andrew. Alvin was just leaving." She looked up at Alvin's blazing red eyes. "Weren't *you*, Alvin?"

He nodded. "But…" He looked from Andrew to Alice, smirked and again nodded calculatingly.

"Weren't you, Alvin?" Andrew said menacingly.

Alvin looked to his right to see a man in uniform coming towards them. He nodded, hurried to his car and sped off.

Alice gave a big sigh of relief as Andrew waved to security who made a U-turn back into the building. It was then he noticed that Alice was shaking. He opened her door and crouched beside her. "I thought you were being car jacked. I'm sorry, I didn't see you leave. I was in a meeting. Was that the guy you spoke of?"

"Yes, that's Alvin Jacob, but he's harmless, really."

"No, he's not, because you're shaking. Did he threaten you?"

She took another deep breath and leaned her head against the headrest. "Oh Andrew. I think I was just surprised to see him here, and when you came up, I didn't know if he had a weapon." She shook her head as she tried to calm herself.

He took her moist hand in his and caressed it. "Are you all right?" he didn't wait for her to answer. "You don't have to deal with people like him on your own. I am here," he reassured her.

She nodded. "I don't know what I did or said for him to think…"

"You didn't do anything." He kissed her hand. "You didn't say anything." He could feel the blood pumping in his temple.

Again, she looked and saw turquoise eyes staring back at her. "I'm sorry, Andrew," she whispered watching his temple pulse.

"Why do you say that? I'm the one who should apologize. I should be protecting you."

She smiled as his reassurance calmed her. "I'm not your project, Andrew. I can take care of myself."

"I know you can, but I'm bigger and stronger than you are." He smiled.

She laughed shakily. "Yes, you are. Now I have to be on my way." She kissed his forehead and almost lingered as the musky scent from his hair caught her nostrils.

"Alice," he whispered. "You're still shaking. I can't let you drive like this. Let me take you to your mother."

"Really, that's not necessary."

"Alice, please. I can drop you at your mother's and you can drive home with Delia. I'll pick you up tomorrow morning."

"Andrew, please." She took another calming breath. I'll be fine. I don't think he's waiting for me around the corner."

"I don't want to take that chance. Please let me do this for you." His eyes were beseeching and troubled.

"Okay." She got out of the car, followed him to his, and directed him to her mother's home. Delia and the children were already there.

She hoped she'd never see Alvin again, because somewhere in his delusional brain he'd think that Andrew was her man.

"Are you all right?" Andrew asked again when he parked outside her mother's home.

Her mother had done a very good job of taking care of her garden and planting as many fruit trees as the property would allow, including mango and Ackee. She remembered her mother once saying, "No Jamaican home is complete without at least one mango tree." The red brick walkway leading to the white front door held on either side a colorful variety of flowers, for half of which, Alice didn't know the proper name. She knew the crotons because she had some in her own walkway.

"Yes, I'm better." She turned to look into his eyes. "Thanks. I'll call you when I get home."

He leaned over and kissed her cheek. "I'll be waiting for your call."

"I would invite you in, but I'd have to…"

"I know. Another time." He slipped from behind the steering wheel and opened her door for her.

Even though the sun was still high in the sky, he waited until she was inside. She turned and waved as his Volvo slowly moved away from the gate.

She took a deep breath and smiled as her children rushed out to greet her. "Where's your car, Mama?" Alia asked.

"Something was wrong with it so Andrew gave me a lift." She walked in with both children by her side to the back patio where her mother and sister sat waiting for her. She saw Delia in the kitchen and laughed. "Delia, we were invited to dinner, why are you in the kitchen?"

Delia smiled. "I'm just making tea."

Alice kissed her mother and sister and sat.

"I heard Alia ask about your car," Merl said.

"Yes, Mr. Benton gave me a lift. My car wouldn't start." She looked up and asked God to forgive the lie, but if she'd told the truth, her mother would have gone to pieces.

Gen looked at her and winked. "Got an admirer already? What does he look like?"

"Funny. He's just a friend. He's Willetta's brother. We actually met in New York before I had even thought of coming down."

"And now you work together?" Merl asked.

"Yes."

"It's good to have a friend," Merl said. "So how is Harvey doing?" She looked at her daughter with more than inquiring eyes.

"Mom, I told you that we're not together anymore."

"What does that mean? Are you guys getting a divorce?"

She was thankful when Delia brought the tea and set it on the table.

Gen looked at Alice and shook her head. "You woke the sleeping giant again."

They both laughed.

"Well you know, I wish I had a friend when your father and I broke up," Merl began.

"And we're off," Gen said, laughing.

That didn't stop Merl at all as she went into the familiar story that the girls had heard a million times. "There were so many women in your father's life, and he was such a rough man, I was afraid of him."

"We know, Mom. He was seventeen years your senior. You ran away from him," Alice said sipping the warm brew and focusing on her mother.

"You girls never heard us, but we quarreled a lot."

"Thank you for doing that, but maybe you should have warned us a little."

She shook her head. "You've got brothers and sisters in Jamaica."

"We only know of one, Mom," Alice said.

"Yes, the one he had with the maid."

"You're still angry with him, Mama. I've told you so many times to write your thoughts down as if you were talking with Daddy. Tell him on paper how you feel since you can't say it to his face. Dead man tell no tale and answer to no one," Gen said.

Merl took a deep breath and exhaled. Both her girls knew for some reason she was back there with her dead husband. Then she said something that no one expected. "He was a real stud. He had a..."

"Mom!" they both shouted, putting their hands to their ears.

"I really don't want to have nightmares tonight. Please do not paint a picture for us," Alice said.

Her mother burst out laughing. "He knew how to use it too."

"Mother!" Gen said joining in the laughter that erupted from both Merl and Alice. "I speak for Alice when I say, it's really a good thing that you kept all this from us. No child wants to know that her father was a stud inside and outside the home."

Merl became serious and turned to Alice. "So, it's really over between you and Harvey?"

Alice nodded. "But, you don't have to dislike him. He's not divorcing you, he's divorcing me."

"Who asked for the divorce?" Merl touched her daughter's hand.

Alice looked into her mother's kind eyes. For her sixty eight years she should have had at least a few lines in her forehead, but she didn't. Her mother's complexion was a shade lighter than hers, and her plump figure didn't stop her from eating what she wanted even though she had hypertension and was borderline diabetic. "I wanted it, he asked for it, but I won't tell you what he did, not yet. Can we please change the subject? He will take care of the children. He may be a lot of things but he still loves his kids."

She looked from Merl to Gen, and they both nodded.

Delia came out with the children who were quietly watching television. "I've set dinner on the table."

Chapter Fourteen

On her way home, she called Andrew. "I was waiting for your call," he said. "Did you have a good time with your mother?"

"Yes, I did, and now we're on our way home. Actually, we're a few minutes from the gate. I'll see you tomorrow?"

"Bright and early."

"Come for breakfast."

"Thank you, I will."

"Good night," she said, disconnecting the call.

At home, she helped Delia put the sleeping children to bed, read from their favorite story book then took a shower and slid between the cool sheets. She fell asleep thinking of Andrew.

Alice had an established time for everyone to have breakfast so that she could leave for work before eight-thirty. That was the time Andrew stuck with every morning when they carpooled.

Two days later when Andrew dropped her home, Alice noticed a brown registered envelope on the table. She looked at the postmark and knew exactly what it was. She didn't want to open it just yet. "Delia, when did this get here?"

"This morning." Delia touched her hand. "Is it…?"

"Yes." She didn't open the envelope but kissed her children and went in to take a bath. She lay in the warm water and shook her head. There were no tears this time. She'd shed them all, or so she thought. But in the tiniest space in her brain, again, she wondered if anything that caused the demise of the marriage was her fault. Was it her fault why he never stopped running around? She had always shown him how much she loved him except when she was angry with him. After all, she was by no means a saint and she wasn't very good at hiding her feelings. *There was no recourse. We went as far as we could and a few days after I left there was another woman in my space for all the world to see.* She took a deep breath and sat up in the tub.

Suddenly, she didn't want to be alone. She needed Andrew. She got out of the tub, dried off and hurriedly slipped into jeans and a T-shirt. She stopped herself from dialing his number when she picked up her cell phone. *What if I'm disturbing him?* She looked at the phone in her hand then automatically dialed his number.

He answered on the first ring. "I was just going to call you…"

"May I come over? I don't want to be alone right now. I need to be with you."

"Of course. I'll pick you up. Is everything all right?"

"Yes and no. You don't have to pick me up, just give me directions."

He rattled off his address and directions of how to get to his house. "I'll call the gate for you. Are you coming now?"

"Yes."

"Have you had dinner?"

"No."

"Okay. I'll wait for you."

Alice hung up and sat heavily on her bed. *This is what I wanted. I wanted to divorce Harvey, so why do I feel this way?* Her hands shook as she slipped the phone in her purse and walked into the living room. "I'm going to have dinner with Andrew, tonight, but you guys be good for Delia, okay," she said to the children and kissed each one. They could never know she was extremely close to tears. She wanted her children to be happy, not see their mother fall to pieces once again. She waved to Delia and walked through the door.

It took her less than half an hour to get to Andrew's home. He was standing at the door waiting for her. She fell into his arms, and he kicked the door closed and held her. He didn't ask what was wrong, he just held her and felt her body shake against his.

She released her hold and smiled, then wiped the tears from her eyes. He slid an index finger under her chin and tilted her face up to his. Still he said nothing.

"My divorce papers came today."

His forehead creased with concern and confusion. "This is not what you wanted?"

"Yes, but... you know... it's like a death in the family, only no one dies."

He understood. "I know. I know." He held her as she placed her head back on his chest.

The warmth of his embrace soothed her and fired up emotions that she was more than ready for. She lifted her face to his.

His eyes drifted to her mouth and he felt an ache in his groin. This was not the time, he told himself, but when he looked into her eyes, what he saw changed his mind.

Slowly, his lips brushed hers, and her insides went soft as a surge of lustful longing went through her body. She wanted to stop, but she couldn't. She closed her eyes and waited for his soft mouth to drive her to distraction. His warm mouth gently closed around her lips, sucking softly, driving a rush of desire to the pit of her stomach. She grabbed his face with both hands, pulled him closer into her and let herself go, to swim in the sea of this amorous feeling that she'd not felt in such a very long time. She clung to him. He backed her against the wall and pressed his hard body against her, holding back with all his might the urge to grind his body into hers. He broke away and cupped her small face in his hands. "It's all right?"

"Yes," she whispered with urgency and a little out of breath. "It's all right. And she reached up and slipped her arms around his neck, pulling his lips to her waiting mouth and kissed him so deep she felt giddy. Yes, she was free and ready. She needed the warmth she knew he was capable of giving. This time she broke away before it became necessary to pull him into his own bedroom and beg for him to make love to her.

He gazed dreamily into her face, the primitive sexuality glowing so bright, it was like a beacon of light to follow. But as a man of calm and patience, he took a deep breath and slowly exhaled. "It was good for you to come. I wanted to kiss you from the first day I entered your office and saw you," he said, smiling at her. "You're okay?"

She nodded. "Better than okay."

He slid his arm around her waist and moved away from the door to the brightly lit living room. He sat beside her on the couch and she leaned her head against his chest while his fingers twisted the curls in her hair. "I'm sorry you hurt."

She looked up at him. "No, don't be sorry. You're here."

"Yes," he whispered. "I'm here always for you. Are you hungry? I can fix us something to eat."

"No, not right now." She got up and walked to the balcony which overlooked million-dollar homes and scanned the ocean and the Intracoastal which ran along the side of the building. "This is such a breathtaking view. No wonder you love to come home." She turned and smiled at him. "I'd love to walk on the beach. It's not too late, is it?"

"No, it's not too late, and this view is so much more beautiful with you in it." He looked down at her shoes.

She looked down at her shoes then back at him. "I will take them off." She smiled sheepishly.

After crossing the street to the beach, he took her shoes and they began walking on the cool, beige sand. He asked the question she didn't want him to ask but knew he eventually would. "What happened to the marriage, Lise?"

She shrugged. The cold water lapped at her feet causing her to gasp. He lifted her as if she were a feather and placed her on dry sand. They began walking again.

"He stopped loving me, I guess."

"He cheated?" Andrew asked.

She nodded. "And other things. I think in the end he didn't care." She just wanted to walk and he respected her privacy and didn't ask any more questions.

Andrew was just glad that she'd chosen to come to him at this particular time in her life—to trust him with her vulnerability, her hurt. Not forgetting the incident with Alvin, he slipped a comforting arm across her shoulder.

He walked with her until they came to a boulder. She sat and he sat beside her, both looking at the ocean foaming and thrashing against the rock both with their own thoughts.

He remembered when his wife had cut his hair off and left him bald then laughed in his face. He wasn't a heavy drinker but she'd invited a few of her friends over for drinks. She'd asked him so many times to cut his hair but that was the only one thing that he refused to do for her. That night, she slipped something in his drink and while he was out, she and her friends had a wonderful time shaving his head. He wore a hat for months after that until it grew back to a desired length. The day he had had enough, she'd told him that he should leave because he bored her and she no longer had feelings for him. He threw a few pieces of clothes in a bag, got his briefcase and took a taxi to his sister's house. Good thing Willetta was away for the week. He didn't feel like talking to anyone about the death of his marriage.

Alice took a deep breath, got off the rock and walked in the soft sand. For a moment she just stood in the surf and watched her feet sink as the tide came and went. She smiled bitterly and thought, *If I had not left, this is exactly what would have happened to me, a little bit at a time.* The smile stayed on her lips as she saw

Harvey's face smiling back at her. She looked at Andrew looking at her. Her feet buried deep in the sand past her ankles.

"Would you like to be rescued?" he asked.

"Is that your favorite thing to do?"

"For you." He nodded, "Yes. I know you're a very strong woman, but I like your vulnerable side, when you let me in; today, all the way." He got up and stood beside her, his feet sinking in the wet sand. "I like the way you take charge at the office, when you stand up for yourself. You're so eloquent, so intelligent."

She laughed and held his hand as she wavered by the pulling sand. "Good thing this isn't quicksand. We would both be in trouble. But you do know that all I know about the business is what you've taught me."

"You learn fast."

Holding his hand tightly, suddenly, she opened her mouth and expelled a piercing scream. He gasped and before she could say anything, he grabbed her, lifted her out of the sand and carried her to dry sand. She laughed, glanced at his alarmed face and laughed some more. "I'm sorry, I just wanted to release all that pent up anxiety. I didn't mean to scare you," she said almost out of breath from laughing.

A smile formed on his lips. He'd thought she was bitten by a sand flea, a jellyfish or something because where she'd stood there was quite a lot of water. He was prepared to suck a poison out of her foot; instead here she was, laughing lightheartedly. He began laughing, and suddenly, they both couldn't stop laughing. She let go of his hand and slid to the sand, him beside her. Eventually, their laughter subsided and she leaned against him. It was okay. Everything was all right. She wasn't going insane, she was right where she should be and so was he.

"It wasn't a very easy decision, you know," she said.

"It never is," he shrugged. "At least for those few people who married for love."

"I turned my head the other way so often I forgot to look at what was right in front of me."

He didn't say anything.

"My grandmother did it. My mother did it and it seems, I fell right into step."

"Did your grandmother and mother get divorced?"

She shook her head. "No, they didn't. Grandmother stayed. Mother ran away to this country. Grandmother never stopped loving her husband." She shook her head. She didn't want to think of her grandmother anymore.

"What are your feelings for Harvey now?" he had to know.

She exhaled as if she'd been holding her breath. "I don't know." She laughed bitterly as memories flooded back of how she'd longed for Harvey's love. "When we were married and I didn't see him for awhile, I used to watch romantic movies, get in the mood for some affection and couldn't wait for him to come walking through the door." She stopped talking.

"Then what?" he encouraged.

"He came home." She shrugged. "He'd inevitably say something or be so cold that the feeling got lost in the dust."

"I'm sorry."

She nodded.

He felt he had to do something to cheer her up, but frankly, she didn't seem that sad, just a little angry. He knew what that felt like. But he needed to change the mood. "You haven't given up on marriage, have you?"

"Ask me again in a few months." She looked into his eyes. "Have you?"

"No. There are still some wonderful people in this world. I'm sitting with one of the most wonderful women I've ever met in my life."

She dragged her eyes from his face and looked out at the endless ocean, her fingers digging into the sand. "I can be moody."

"Me too. Where would you like to have dinner?" he asked, pulling her fingers from the sand.

"I don't care. But, although I love whatever Ron prepares, I don't want to go to South Beach tonight." She looked into his face, his very handsome face. There was a part of her that wanted to be happy that she was with Andrew, but another part of her that was unhappy about the divorce. As the image of kissing him focused in memory, she felt torn. *Was it fair to have done that?* She felt conflicted and wanted to stop thinking of her failed marriage. It was done.

"Then we can go to Mizner Park. Are you familiar with it?"

She nodded. "I love the seafood restaurant there."

"Then that's where we'll eat." He hugged her warmly and breathed in all the hopes he had for them. "And so, we write our own book."

She nodded. "Handprints in the sand." She pushed her hands in the sand and he pushed his between and to the left of hers. They got up, brushed the sand from their behinds and walked back to his condo to freshen up for dinner.

Sitting across from her on the patio at dinner, he reminded her of their upcoming date at the Coral Springs Theater.

"I remember."

At that time of night, the restaurant wasn't very crowded and they waited for their meal to be brought to their table. Andrew looked at Alice. Her jubilant behavior on the beach had not taken away from the tears she'd shed before, and he still felt that she had not truly forgotten why she'd come to him. He touched her hand. "Are you all right, I mean…"

"I know what you mean," she smiled. "Don't worry," she took a breath. "I'm fine." *Or I will be.*

"You can stay with me tonight."

Her gaze stayed on his face, the concern he felt plainly displayed there. She would have loved to stay with him, making the last thing she felt before she closed her eyes in sleep his warm protective embrace, but shook her head and looked away from his engaging eyes. "I can't stay with you, Andrew. The children will wake up tomorrow morning and wonder where I am. Plus the implications…" she didn't know how to finish that sentence.

"Then I'll come home with you and stay until you fall asleep."

She shook her head. "I'll be all right and I promise I won't cry again."

"Promise?"

She nodded.

When their dinner was put before them, they ate in silence except for a few glances and smiles. Through those smiles, he saw her shyness and again her vulnerability. She was wise to say no to his request. He wasn't sure he could be that close to her and not want to ravish her warm body. He looked at the rise and fall of her bosom and called upon his own strength. She was no longer married and his thoughts and feelings were now unbridled.

After dinner, they walked over to Starbucks and ordered two green tea lattès, then walked to a wrouth iron bench in the park, sat and listened to the jazz band.

They'd driven separate cars and when she said she had to go, he walked her to her car, pressed her against the closed door and kissed her longingly, again, calling upon his waning strength as his body became hard against her. He pulled his body away from hers, kissed her hand and opened the door. Before her car rolled down the incline, she looked at him mischievously. Why wouldn't she feel his longing?

He mouthed *I love you, Alice.* She didn't see.

On Saturday, the children were delighted with their picnic on the beach. Alice lay under a thatched umbrella on a lounge chair reading and periodically glancing at the children. But mostly, she couldn't take her eyes from the tall, bronzed, handsome figure in the baggy trunks. His chest chiseled to perfection, his arms solid and his thighs... she bit into her lower lip. Even if he wore a wet suit, he would still drive her crazy; actually, no, a wet suit would just get her imagination going. *Can this really work? Will he someday walk away from me the way Harvey did?* She shook her head. She was in the fast lane when she should be cruising in the slow lane. She tore her eyes away from him and looked at the book in her lap, but she kept reading the same line over and over. She laid her head against the chair and tried to relax, then looked out at the ocean undulating onto shore. Rising waves crashed against

the shore line again and again. She shook her head again. *Damn!*
It's been a long time.

Andrew and Delia were busy playing with the children until
Andrew decided to wade into the cold water with them. Delia
looked on from shore. No one could get her in that cold water.
Alice laughed and waved her over.

"The children are very taken with Mr. Andrew," Delia said,
sitting on the sand under the thatched umbrella.

Alice nodded. She knew that even if they loved Andrew,
Harvey would always be number one with them. She had to see
to that.

"Harvey will be visiting in the week," she said, glancing at
Delia's face just in time to see her grimace. She laughed. "He's not
that bad."

Delia shook her head. "I guess not."

Andrew and the children came running, their lips blue. The
children trembled with goose bumps all over their little bodies.
Delia and Alice were fast in drying them off and wrapping the
towels around them while Andrew stood in the sun trying to
dry his thick long hair. Alice glanced at her daughter watching
Andrew and knew she would just love to make a mess of his hair,
but right now, she was too cold and shivering to move. It was time
to eat the delicious meal that Andrew so painstakingly prepared
from the nearby bakery.

Sunday evening, Andrew picked up Alice and they headed
for the Coral Springs Theater. And as the performance unfolded,
Alice found that she didn't have to translate much to him. The
players spoke patois but most times they spoke English. At
intermission, instead of going for a drink, they sat in their seats.
"I can't remember when I've laughed so much," he said. "I have
never been to a Jamaican play, but now I know what I've been
missing. Are you enjoying it?"

"If my laughter tells you anything, it's that this is hilarious. I
love these things. There's a comedian by the name of Oliver, now
that's a funny guy. Of course, I'm sure I'll be translating a lot for
you because his skits are ninety percent patois," Alice replied.

"I'll look out for him. I'm glad I came."

"Me too. Thank you." She looked at him questioningly. "Did you do this for me?"

"Yes." He looped his fingers through hers and didn't miss the look he got from the plus-size woman who sat beside them. "She's my wife," he said to her.

The woman didn't smile but said, "Uh, huh," rolled her eyes and turned front.

Alice bit into her lips to smother her laughter as Andrew squeezed her hand. "I could do this all night," he said to her. "I can deal with this."

"I know you can," she said, straightening her shoulders and looking back at the actors as they once again took their places on stage.

She was glad they'd chosen seats in the middle of the theater because the people who sat at the front were picked on by the actors and she knew Andrew's green eyes would have sparked a rich conversation. With his hair hanging loose on his shoulder and the first two buttons of his shirt undone, he was stunning. When the performance was over, the young woman to her right made sure when she passed Alice, to linger beside Andrew touching his shoulder with her breasts and trying to catch his eyes. It didn't work. *Good boy, Andrew. It would have worked on Harvey. Now why did I think of him?*

On Tuesday, Harvey called her office. "I'm here," he said. "Can we have lunch?"

She was silent for a few seconds then she said, "Yes, of course."

"I know where your office is, I'll pick you up at one. Is that all right?"

She was about to say she'd meet him at the restaurant but knew he'd ask why he couldn't pick her up at her office. "Yes." She hung up, but with her hand still on the receiver, she wondered if he'd changed just a little or if he was still the same old combative person she left months ago.

Lee Ann came into her office with tea and a steno pad. Alice had been looking at a small cosmetic firm ever since she began working with Franks. The owner did most of her public relations but her business wasn't growing as fast as she'd like. This one was all Alice's and she was going after it with gusto. The Deveraux account was proving to be a challenge. It was a family owned company. Maloney Deveraux, her two sisters and her daughter ran the company. Maloney, the CEO was an African American woman who was always so busy, it was hard to pin her down on a time to meet even though they'd spoken on the phone a few times. But Alice had no intentions of giving this up. She knew Mrs. Deveraux was doing a full check of the company and their competitors. That was all right, Alice had been doing her homework too. The company did a lot of business with beauty supply stores and beauty salons across the country, and although she reached a lot of African American women with her products, she wasn't making the money she'd hoped. Alice had bought and used the product and actually liked it. She knew she could turn this company into a money-making machine.

In the middle of going over the company's background, Lee Ann buzzed and told her Mr. Vaze was in the waiting area.

Alice took a deep breath. "Send him in, Lee Ann." She didn't get up to greet him when he came through the door, but she did close the file. Looking at him framed in the doorway, she had to admit, he was still handsome. His dark smooth skin looked radiant with the budding salt and pepper hair. His wide smile showed white teeth.

He came over and stood across from her. "So this is where you work?" he said nodding and walking toward the window.

"And you've finally decided to let your hair go natural. I suppose you broke up with Miss Clairol."

He turned and laughed. "I deserved that. You'd been trying for years to get me to stop dying my hair. I woke up one morning and just decided not to do it anymore." He shrugged. "So, here I am."

"Or was it the other woman who…" *Bad Alice.* "Never mind. Let's go to lunch." She picked up her purse to go.

Harvey noticed that she had the children's photo on her desk. "So I'm completely out of the picture for you?"

"Oh come on, Harvey. Do you really expect me to have a photograph of my ex-husband on my desk?"

"I still have yours in my office."

"Get rid of it. Let's go." Expecting him to open the door for her, she stood for a second; when he didn't, she opened it and walked through with a smirk.

Andrew was standing at Lee Ann's desk. She'd told him that she'd be going out to lunch with Harvey, but didn't say what time. This was not awkward at all. His back was to them and he turned when she came out of her office. He smiled and so did she. "Andrew, this is Harvey, my ex-husband."

Andrew extended his hand and firmly shook Harvey's hand. "It's very good to meet you."

"Likewise," Harvey said, giving the man a quick sweep.

"Not to prolong anything," Alice said, "I'll see you later, Andrew."

"Yes," he said in a very professional manner.

Halfway down the hall, Harvey asked. "Who was that guy?"

"My boss," she replied.

He nodded, and lightly touched her elbow as they exited the building. "Do you want me to drive?" she asked.

"No, I've got a rental." He pointed, "Right over there. He pointed to the BMW in the parking lot. "I can't wait to see the children. I really miss them." He opened the door for her then, went around and slid into the drivers seat.

This was not Harvey's first visit to Florida so she wasn't surprised that he knew his way around. He drove onto Las Olas and parked close to H20. He'd made a reservation and the restaurant wasn't very full so they were taken immediately to their table. He touched her hand as they sat down. "I'm selling the house. It's too big for just me."

She nodded and ordered bottled water.

"I want to set up a college fund for the children."

"That's very admirable of you, Harvey," Alice said. She didn't want to be suspicious of him but she couldn't help herself. What was his angle? When would the shoe drop? She kept looking at him for a sign of nervousness, but he seemed quite relaxed.

"If I did anything to hurt you I'm sorry." He held her hand. "Alice, I was a damn fool to let you go."

"No argument there." She figured that was all the apology she'd get. Why hadn't he said that to her when they were in New York? She didn't know what good it would have done, but it would have appeased her a little. Right now, she was just a tiny bit angry with him. She sighed and wondered if she would really have gone back to him if he had; maybe not.

He laughed. She slowly withdrew her hand from his. She felt a pleasant vibe coming from him now, but she was not about to drop her guard.

"Are you getting married?" she teased.

He laughed. "I just poured out my heart to you and that's all you can say?"

"And I appreciate that, but are you?"

"No, but I got engaged."

She almost choked on the water going down her throat. They were no longer married, so what he did was his business. She laughed but this time it was not of sarcasm. It had only been months since the divorce. Finding someone else, yes. She expected that, but getting engaged, that was different.

"Are you engaged to the same woman?"

He studied her thoughtfully for a moment, his look challenging as if to say, it's none of your business. "No."

"Wow, you work fast."

"It's not like that. It's someone I knew a long time ago in Jamaica. We met right out of high school, but before the relationship had a chance to grow, I came here. Actually, she looked me up on Face book and we began corresponding. She's a teacher."

"So this is a long distance relationship?"

She took a sip of her water.

He nodded.

"How did you get engaged?" her brow wrinkled inquiringly wanting to know if he'd become engaged before they'd divorced.

"We've both been going back and forth from New York to Jamaica and last week, she popped the question and I gave her a ring."

Alice bit into both lips to keep from laughing. "She what?"

"I know, seems she made up my mind for me." He moved back in his seat. "I mean, I don't want you to keep the children from me because there is someone else."

She shook her head. "Harvey, I wouldn't deprive you of seeing your children at all. They love you and you love them. I'm glad for you."

"Thank you. When you walked out, I wanted you back but didn't know how to ask. I made a mess of things at the restaurant and drove you further away. It was then that I realized that it was really over, Alice."

"Harvey, you asked for a divorce!"

"I know."

"I must add that you were a pompous ass back there at the restaurant." She couldn't believe what she was hearing from him. "I'm glad you didn't get engaged while we were still married." She looked searchingly into his eyes and knew he wouldn't have admitted it even if he did. But it didn't matter.

He chuckled. "I wouldn't have done that."

It was her time to chuckle. She mimicked his chuckle as she shook her head without looking at him. "Of course you would have." Then something made her really laugh. "Wait, did you cheat on the woman who actually broke us up, or did you dump her before your fiancée sought you out?"

He grinned, but admitted nothing. "I still love you, Alice."

His lips hardened and she knew that he was still resentful of her no matter what he was willing to admit or not. She didn't return the sentiments. "One more question. Did you get engaged to be married or just to hold onto the woman for awhile?" She didn't know why she asked the question because she knew he wouldn't respond truthfully, but of course, time would tell. He'd changed all right. But he still didn't know when he was hurting her. Either he thought she was made of stone or still didn't know what real love was. He was still selfish and self absorbed.

"So, have you found anyone?" he asked.

"I'm not looking." She kept gazing at him. She knew he would have asked.

"Andrew is a handsome fellow."

"Do men really say things like that?"

"Of course, when their wife is involved with someone else."

She nodded and was glad when the server came to take their lunch order.

"The children are very excited at the prospects of seeing you. I told them this morning that you were coming, but I didn't exactly say when."

"You're not going to talk about Andrew?"

"No."

He nodded. "I can't wait to see them. I'm staying at a hotel in South Beach. I'll be here through the weekend. You don't mind if they spend the weekend with me, do you?"

"No, not at all. I think they'll love that. So you're here on business?"

"Uh huh." He looked at her and smiled. "Pamela is here now, but she won't be here for the weekend. I want the weekend to be just for the children and me."

She nodded. Although she was glad that he was moving on with his life, she wasn't sure she wanted him to introduce the children to his fiancée just yet.

"You don't mind if I tell them about her, though?" he said.

"No."

Their meal was served and while they ate, Alice decided that this was the most civilized time she'd had with Harvey in years. She was in no way a purist, but for his sake and the sake of the new woman, she hoped he'd really changed.

After lunch, they talked some more about the children and he took her back to the office promising to see the children in the evening. She gave him directions to her home. Pamela would not be with him.

As soon as she got to her office, Andrew entered. She was standing by the window and turned. "Are you all right?" he asked, capturing her eyes and taking her in his arms.

She smiled against his shoulder. "I am great. I had a nice lunch."

His brow knitted into a frown as he gazed down at her questioningly. He had an unfamiliar feeling, a pang of jealousy. *This is the man whom she'd once been in love with; the man who broke her heart. Why was she so happy to have had lunch with him?*

"He was nice." She pushed away from Andrew and he followed her. She turned. "I don't think I ever met this Harvey."

"You're not…" He tilted his brow looking at her uncertainly, hoping to God she wasn't falling back in love with Harvey.

"No, Andrew, that ship has sailed, but he seemed to have changed into a human being. He still doesn't quite know what love is, and he's still selfish, but I suppose he's making strides." She smiled, held his hand and kissed it.

"Up here," he said with relief, pointing to his lips. He drew her to him, cupping her face in his hands to tilt it towards his waiting mouth.

She went on tip toes to kiss his lips. He caught her waist, lifted her off the floor and as his lips lingered on her mouth, his tongue slowly, gently pierced through her mouth to drive all thoughts of Harvey from her brain. She responded as a kick of lust ran to her most private part. Only he could do that to her now; only Andrew could awaken in her this undeniable passion that had lain dormant for so long. But this was the office and they had to cut before they got to a point of no return. Her couch was not for making love. His lips slid to the hollow in her throat, which made her want to giggle and swoon at the same time. She closed her eyes, opened her mouth and breathed. "He's engaged," she whispered

"Who?" he asked, lost in his desire for her as his lips moved to her earlobe.

Now that tickled and she laughed. "Harvey, he's engaged."

"That's wonderful for him." His words sounded dreamy as if he wasn't really listening.

She gently broke away from him. "I know you're very strong, but I'm not as strong as you are. This, that we're doing, will get us in trouble. At least it will get me in trouble."

"I'm sorry," he said, "I should curb my appetite for you at the office."

She smiled. "Sometimes." She slipped away from him and sat behind her desk. "Were you a little jealous?"

"A little."

"There's never any need for you to be jealous."

"I know, but I'm human and I'm glad that Harvey's moved on. And I'm glad that the relationship between you two is better."

"Thank you. I suppose now I'll stop having nightmares about him choking me." She laughed and shook her head. "I'm joking."

He left her office a little lighter than he'd come. When he'd seen Harvey place his arm on Alice's hand, he feared that he could have eventually won her back even though they were now divorced. But there was still a little voice in the back of his mind saying, *she would not have kissed you the way she did if she didn't have strong feelings for you.* He was a man, and very human. She was a very beautiful and intelligent woman. He sat in his office with his eyes closed, feeling her breath on his face and her lips on his. He took a deep breath, leaned over his desk and picked up the ringing phone. Time to get back to work.

Who said men don't daydream about their woman?

Chapter Fifteen

While Harvey visited his children, Andrew kept a respectful distance, but that didn't stop the children from talking about him. As soon as Harvey came through the door and the children saw him, they ran to his open arms calling, "Daddy, Daddy! We missed you."

Alice stood aside while they climbed all over him, and was pleasantly surprised to see that he wasn't impatient with them at all. After a while he said, "I would like to speak with your mother in private, but, we'll play again before I leave."

They nodded, yet still didn't move away from him until they got him on the carpet. "Oh, you guys got a puppy," he said when Tee Tee joined in the game.

Before the children could say where they got the puppy, Delia rushed in and picked up the dog. "I'm sorry, Mr. Harvey. I'll hold her so that you can play with the children undisturbed." Alice would have been very proud of her.

He nodded and she walked away with the puppy in her arms. The children forgot about the question and began laughing and playing with their father once again.

Alice sat outside waiting for him, watching the ducks in the lake dip in and out every now and again sitting on the irrigation ducks in the water.

"So there is something between you and Andrew," Harvey said to Alice when he joined her.

"Where's that little dog?" she said looking all around. "I haven't seen him all evening."

"You're trying to evade the question," he persisted. He was wearing the same outfit he'd worn at lunch.

She assumed he'd gone to a business meeting after he'd left her. She didn't ask. "I never denied it. I just didn't say anything."

"You weren't trying to hide it, were you?"

"He's been to my house. We carpool to work. We have an occasional dinner..."

"The children don't call him daddy, right?"

"Harvey, you're reverting to the old you," she said calmly lifting the cup of tea to her lips.

"I'm sorry. I'm being selfish. I just don't want them to be closer to him than me."

"They won't if you treat them with respect and don't stay away too long."

He cast a hand across the chair and looked back into the house. "This is nice. You're making a nice life for yourself. Good job, new boyfriend. But how can I spend time with my children when I live in New Jersey and you have them here?"

She responded to his last statement. "I'm here because of what you did to me and them." Her voice dulled. "I know this might sting a little, but you weren't much of a father to them when we lived together."

There was no rebuttal. He knew she spoke the truth.

She wished it were the weekend, because she knew from past experience that they couldn't share the same space for too long before he began to find something to quarrel about or to criticize. Like now. He didn't say much more.

After he'd had a cup of tea and a sandwich, he went back inside and spent more time with the children. To be fair, Alice hung back so that he would have their undivided attention. Before he left, he promised to come back for them on the weekend. He had to meet Pamela for dinner, but he didn't tell them that. He told Alice and asked that she didn't tell them. "I want to be the one to tell them," he said.

"Of course," she replied, walking with him to the black BMW he'd rented. "I wouldn't dream of telling them about your fiancée."

"Are you going to run and call Andrew as soon as I leave?" he asked, standing with one foot poised to enter the car.

"Are we back in high school again? When do we start college?" she passed her hand over her face and laughed. He got into the car and pushed the key into the ignition, then proceeded to look her up and down. "You still look great. Florida agrees with you."

"Thanks."

The children came out, stood by Alice and said goodnight to their father.

He waved. "I'll see you guys real soon. We're going to have a lot of fun this weekend." He drove away.

—————

After work the next day, Alice decided to go to the shelter. She didn't tell Andrew she was going because he had a late meeting with Benjamin.

When they got to the shelter, Delia went to the back with the children to sweep and help tidy up while Alice helped serve food. She barely looked up at the faces as she placed chicken on their plates, but this voice made her almost drop her spoon.

"Hello, beautiful."

She looked at the man with the plate in his hand and was mortified. "What are you doing here?" she shook her head. "I mean, really, why are you here?"

He laughed and shrugged. "Sometimes I like to eat out. I hear the food here is very good."

For the first time she could see his eyes and they were as red as if he had just finished smoking ganja. "But you can afford to feed yourself. You have a job, but these people aren't that lucky."

"As I said, sometimes I don't feel like cooking for myself and I don't feel like going to a restaurant either." He smiled wickedly. "You know, I could give you more than a lot of guys can."

She decided to humor him. After all, what could he do to her here, talk her to death? He didn't look any better than the homeless she was serving food to. "Alvin, what can you give me that I can't give myself? You're here stealing from the homeless."

"If you give me a chance to make love to you, you won't ever want anyone else and I'm not a thief."

She felt nauseated. "Okay, you've said enough. I don't know how many ways to say I'm not interested in you." At the moment, giving him food that was meant for the homeless, she pitied him, but still felt uneasy that he felt she would want to be with him.

"I will rock your world, girl."

She sighed and shook her head. "Go away, Alvin, or I'll call the police."

Hoping she wasn't serious, he laughed. "And tell them what? That I tried to talk to you?"

"No, that you're stalking me." For the sake of where she was, she kept her voice low, a wary smile on her face. "You know what? If you don't leave me alone, I'm going to shoot you myself."

He chuckled. "You don't have a gun."

"Do you really want to find out? I don't want to have anything to do with you. I don't like you."

At her strong declaration, his face fell. He really thought he could have worn her down enough for her to start liking him. "Is that really how you feel?"

"Yes, it is, Alvin. As I said before, If you come within thirty feet of me, I'll call the police."

He nodded. "Okay. I won't bother you again." He was angry that she'd rebuffed him, but he was on probation; one mistake and he'd be back in jail. He shuffled and glanced behind him at the other three people in line. He had waited until the line had thinned, but now a few stragglers had wandered in. They were getting impatient and because Alice had kept her voice low, she knew they were all wondering why she was having such a long conversation with this one man. As a matter of fact so was the woman who shared the vegetables and rice. She glanced at her. "Sorry."

"Some are still in denial, honey." She looked Alvin up and down then shook her head. "Don't hold a conversation with him. He thinks he's your equal."

She nodded, looked back at Alvin and wondered if he was really down on his luck and in denial.

He smiled benignly as if she were a petulant child, looked down at his plate, then back at her.

She rolled her eyes and took a deep breath. "Right," Alice said, placing the chicken on his plate. She didn't know if he'd followed her or he was really down on his luck but it was none of her business. She was here to do a job. She watched him walk away and sit at a table by himself. She numbly served each plate one by one. Every time she caught his eyes, they looked menacingly at her. She sized up his small frame and wondered if she had to, could she fight him off?

Even after he'd finished eating, he didn't leave. He walked over to another table and sat down with a few of the regulars and entered their conversation. Through the corner of her eye, Alice still watched him. When she thought he wasn't looking, she hurried to the back and told Delia to take the children to the car through the back door. "Is everything all right?" Delia asked, a bit scared by the look in Alice's eyes.

She nodded. "I just have to help clear the tables, then I'll be with you guys. But go now." She tried to keep the fear she felt for her children out of her voice and didn't move until Delia and the children were out the door.

She turned, looked through the peephole in time to see Alvin coming toward the door. She pushed the door hard and he jumped back. "You can't go back there," she said, standing guard.

One of the male volunteers came over—a big white man with beefy hands and a protruding stomach stood by Alice. "Everything all right here?" he said.

They both looked at Alvin.

He laughed, avoided the man's eyes, gestured with his hands and backed away. "I was just looking for the men's room." He looked at Alice. "You need to lighten up. We used to be friends before you became afraid of me."

"You don't get it do you? I'm very serious about what I said. And for your information, we were never friends, and I'm certainly not afraid of you." Now standing among five volunteers, two of whom were men, she wasn't lying at all.

Alvin nodded. "Sorry. It won't happen again." He moved away.

Roger walked beside Alice as they both cleared and cleaned the tables. "Is that guy bothering you?" he asked her.

"Not really. It's okay. Thanks, Roger."

"Anytime. If you need me to walk with you to your car, just say the word."

She glanced at him and was about to refuse when she thought better. "Thanks Roger, that's a good idea." She knew they could have thrown Alvin out of the place and called the police, but that was not what she wanted. She only wanted him to leave her alone.

They piled the dishes in a plastic container and carried them to the back to be washed. She looked over at Roger. "It's beginning to get dark outside. Will you walk with me? The children and Delia are waiting for me in the car."

Roger knew that she and her children usually walked out together after they were finished helping and wondered why she'd sent them away, but didn't ask any questions.

When she got to her car, she turned and saw Alvin standing at the door. He waved to her but she didn't reciprocate. "Thanks, Roger," she said and got behind the wheel.

He nodded. "Don't allow that thug to stop you from doing the Lord's work."

She smiled. "I won't."

Delia shot her a glance, looked at the man standing at the door and realized she'd never seen him there before. They had no set time to really volunteer at the shelter, but she would have remembered the small, bearded face with the ill-fitting clothes. She turned and buckled the children in their booster seats.

Alice wanted to tell Delia what was going on but decided it was not a very good idea. No use having her look over her shoulder every time she left the house with the children.

As soon as she walked through her door, her cell phone rang. Thinking it was Alvin, she took a deep breath. It was time to put a stop to this idiocy. But when she got the phone out of her pocket and looked at the number, it was Andrew. "Hi."

"Hi, am I interrupting anything?"

She laughed. "No. We just got home from the shelter."

"Why didn't you call me? I would have come along with you."

She shook her head. "You were in a meeting with Ben, and I didn't know how long it would take. I didn't want you to hurry because of me." If Andrew was with her, she would bet any money that Alvin would have thought twice before even coming into the place. "Sorry."

"No, it's all right. Just wait for me next time. The shelter is not in the safest neighborhood. Have you guys eaten?"

"Not yet, but I think Delia is about to prepare something. Do you want to come over?"

"Yes, but why don't I take you all out to dinner in Ft. Lauderdale by the beach."

Envisioning his smiling face, she wanted to be with him. "Thank you. I think Delia will be glad for the reprieve."

"I'll be there in half an hour. We'll go to the Oasis. The children will love it."

She was about to dismiss the Oasis, but decided not to. Alvin didn't own the place. He probably forgot they'd ever gone there. And she was sure he wouldn't be there. "Yes, they will."

"You know the place?"

"Yes."

"Okay, I'll see you in a few." He hung up.

"Delia," Alice said going toward the kitchen.

"Yes." She had a bag of frozen shrimp in her hand.

"Put that away, Andrew's taking us out to dinner..." Before she could finish what she was saying, Delia laughed and happily threw the shrimp back into the freezer.

"I'll just get the children ready." She was about to walk away then stopped next to Alice. "Who was that guy at the shelter? Is he a threat to us? I mean, I know most of your friends and you don't have any enemies, so..." she tilted her head to one side with concern in her eyes. "Is everything all right with you?"

"Yes, Delia, everything is fine. He's just someone I met briefly in college. He won't be bothering us anymore. Don't give it a second thought."

"Okay." Again she was about to walk away, then turned with a frown. "He went to college with you?"

Alice laughed at the look on Delia's face. "Not everyone who attends college becomes successful. Some fall on hard times, I suppose."

She shook her head, touched Alice's shoulder and walked past her to get the children ready.

By the time the children were freshened up, Andrew rang the door bell. Alia saw him through the glass door, shouted his name and flung the door open. He scooped her up in his arms and Alice made a mental note to add an extra lock higher than her daughter could reach. She had no idea Alia could open the door by herself.

Alice took a deep breath and adjusted her smile when she noticed that Andrew had two booster seats in his Volvo. "Andrew! Did you do this for the children?"

His face brightened as he looked at her enigmatically. "Of course. I wouldn't want anything to happen to our precious cargo."

She felt her flesh color and wondered if he realized that he said *our precious cargo*. She watched as he belted Alia in while Delia did the same for Phillip. She didn't miss the smile on Delia's face and had a feeling that before the evening was over she would comment on Andrew's kindness and concern for the children's safety. She liked him.

Andrew didn't get on the expressway but took the scenic route to the beach, which didn't make any difference to Alice or her family as the children kept asking, "Are we there yet?"

At the restaurant while the swinging lounge chairs moved, powered by the excited children, Alice ordered their meal then talked about the Deveraux account with Andrew.

"This is supposed to be a relaxing evening for you, Alice. You don't have to talk about business."

Sitting across from him, she played with the gold ring on her middle finger and grinned. "Sorry. This is my first solo account and I'm a little nervous." She glanced at him, then at her daughter sitting beside him. For the last year and a half before she left Harvey, he'd stopped taking the children out to lunches or even to the park. Now looking at Alia, she found that her daughter was getting closer to Andrew than she was comfortable with, at the moment.

And as Alia climbed into his lap, Andrew knew for sure that he was falling in love with this family. "If you hit a rut, I'm always here as your sounding board."

She nodded. "I know, but I want to do this on my own."

When hamburgers, hot dogs, salads, French fries and crab cakes were set on the table, Andrew laughed. "I promise I won't do this too often."

"It's all right. They love this kind of food... once in a while," Alice said, watching her children eat something that they rarely got at home. For the time being, she pushed Alvin to the back of her mind.

After dinner, Andrew suggested a walk on the beach, but it was getting late and close to the children's bedtime. "Can we take a rain check? I know the kids would love to, but they have school tomorrow."

He nodded. "Okay." He paid the check and they piled into his car and drove home.

Andrew helped to put the children to bed and stayed for a night cap. "I'll pick you up tomorrow?" he said before leaving for home.

"Of course."

He kissed her lightly on the lips. And after he left, Alice walked out onto the patio and looked up at the star- filled skies. She thought of Alvin and almost scared herself by wondering if he was dangerous. After all, she didn't really know much about him apart from the fact that many years ago they'd attended the same university. She had no idea that just a friendly drink would turn into him stalking her. She turned, went inside and made sure she locked the door and turned on the alarm.

Chapter Sixteen

Thursday morning, Alice received the call that made her nervous and excited at the same time. Mrs. Deveraux wanted to meet with her. "She wants to know if you can meet her in New York," said Lee Ann, sitting across from Alice in her office.

Alice took a deep breath and a soft smile ruffled her mouth. She didn't want Lee Ann to know how excited she was and how much getting this account meant to her. "I'll meet with her Monday morning in New York. I think her office at ten-thirty will be a good place to start."

"I'll call her office right now," Lee Ann said while leaving the office.

When Lee Ann walked out, Alice wanted to call Andrew and update him but decided to tell him in person. She got up from her desk and sauntered into his office. This would be the second time since she began working with the firm that she would enter his office. She knocked lightly on his door.

"Come in," Andrew said, relaxing in his chair as she entered. "Welcome. I wondered how long it would take for you to visit me again."

"Why? You always visit me, so I didn't think it was necessary." She glanced at the huge mahogany desk with the glass inlaid top; files neatly piled on each side in the in and out trays; the paintings on the wall, one of a man and a woman on horse back; and the huge, double-glass window that let in lots of sun light. She walked to the painting and looked closer. "Your parents?"

He rose from his seat and stood beside her. "Yes, they both liked to ride."

"Are they still alive?"

"Dad passed away a few years ago." He slid his hand around her waist. "No one comes in without first being announced," he said, turning her to face him.

His smile had a spark of eroticism. She averted her eyes from his and laid her head on his chest for a moment. Hearing the beat of his heart and feeling the warmth of his body on hers, she closed her eyes and willed her body not to move against his as her heart hammered in her chest. She took a deep breath and looked into his soft, green eyes. A smile found its way through her mask of uncertainty. "I go to New York this weekend to meet with Mrs. Deveraux on Monday. I thought a morning meeting at her office best."

He knew how very important this was for her and hugged her to him, inhaling a trace of baby powder. "We can fly up on Sunday and come back on Tuesday."

The enthusiasm in his voice was infectious and the uncertainty she felt about going by herself to this very important meeting melted away. "You'll come with me?"

"Of course. I know you don't want me at the meeting, but I would be a fool to give up this chance to have you all to myself. Plus, I want to be there to share your joy when you get the account."

"You're very confident."

"Yes, I am." His mouth curved with tenderness as he brushed her lips.

She flashed him a smile of thanks, then welcomed his mouth on hers and felt a depth of satisfaction.

He wrapped his arms around her midriff and pulled her closer into him.

Her skin tingled as his tongue penetrated her mouth and she groaned at the strong hardness of his lips and the sweetness of his kiss knowing that if she didn't pull away, she would swoon in his arms. "Andrew," she whispered against his mouth.

"Mmmm," he responded, hardly able to tear his lips from hers.

"We have to stop," she said, her mouth still warm from his kiss, her face still upturned to his.

"Yes," he whispered while brushing a soft, gentle kiss across her forehead.

She took a step back from him and looked into his eyes, her heart still pounding in her chest. He held her still. "I like the way you make me feel, but I'm also afraid of the way you make me feel," she confessed, her eyes gentle and contemplative. Was she ready for him? Her entire being said yes, but her brain was still sending cautious waves. He was a gentle, beautiful, wonderful man who obviously cared a lot for her and her children, but she just came out of a marriage to a man who she thought would love her forever.

"You have doubts about us?"

His gentle voice penetrated her brain, bringing her back from the land of doubt. "I don't know Andrew. I just got out of a marriage that…"

"I am not Harvey. I can't predict the future but I know that I would never hurt you in any way possible."

"You don't know that."

"Yes, I do. I've been married before. I know what it's like to hurt so badly you don't think you'll recover, but you do." His big, soft hands held her face and his green eyes met her liquid browns. "I would never hurt you."

And in that moment, that very moment, she believed him.

"I know how vulnerable you are, but I'll protect your heart." He pressed his lips against hers. "Trust me."

Feeling his warm hands on her, and his lips on her mouth, turned her brain to mush and made her legs weak. "Yes," she whispered, lifting her face for him to kiss her again.

He did, long and wanting. They broke apart and breathed together. Her hand went to cover her mouth and she smiled. "I have to go. I have to make arrangements to go to New York."

"You have a lot to do before you go. Allow me to make the hotel arrangements, or would you like us to stay at my apartment?"

"Hotel is good." She smiled knowing very well what would happen if they stayed at his place. But again, they'll be alone in a hotel room, in New York City. Again her body tingled and she turned and left the office.

In her office, sitting behind her desk, her mind replayed his lips on hers, his hard body pressed against her weak body and she shivered with desire. She shook her head, picked up the Deveraux file and went over it page by page. Her eyes left the file and bore into the painting of daffodils on her wall. The children would be with their father on Friday night, back on Sunday. She would make sure they were back home before she left. She was still so excited, she trembled. She got up, rolled her neck from side to side, then flashed her hands to release the tension. She wanted to hold on to this day for a long time for more reasons than one.

~~~

On Friday, Alice took the day off to work on her presentation to acquire the Deveraux account. She helped Delia with the children by making their breakfast and packing their backpacks for them to take to their father's when he picked them up after school.

When Andrew came over, she made him breakfast of oatmeal and coffee. "I won't bother you today although I will be tempted to call and ask how you're doing," he said before leaving.

"Don't call, but I promise if I need you I'll call. Delia will be spending the weekend with a friend she has not seen in years, so I'll be all by myself."

"You promise you'll call?" he said before walking to the door.

"Yes, now go." She laughed and pushed him through the door, then went to take her shower. Ever since she'd thought of getting the Deveraux account, she'd been playing around with different ideas from a woman's point of view. But the company also made products for men so she had to rethink her strategy.

After she'd showered and dressed, she walked into her office and got to work.

The day went by so fast, the sandwich Delia had made for her lunch went uneaten, but the gallon of water on her desk was almost gone. At three, Harvey called to say he'd picked up the children. "Will you please bring them back before four on Sunday?"

"Why?"

"I have to fly up to New York on business on Sunday and I want them back home before I leave."

"Oh, I wish I was going up on Sunday. We could travel together."

She smiled. *No we wouldn't.* "Mmmm, don't change your travel plans."

"You sound a bit distanced. Am I disturbing you?"

"Yes. I stayed home to work on a project for my trip." She rolled her head from side to side. She was tired but the job still wasn't finished.

"Oh, okay, I'll see you on Sunday then. I'll take good care of the children."

"I know you will. Take care... oh, wait. May I speak to them real quick?"

He passed the phone to Alia first. "Mama, I'm going to miss you, but I love Daddy."

"I know you do sweetheart. I know you'll have fun with your Dad. So be a good girl and I'll see you on Sunday, okay."

"Okay, Mommy. Here's Phillip." She passed the phone to her brother.

Alice said the same thing to Phillip and hung up the phone. She knew she'd miss her children but she still wouldn't spend time with them until she got back from New York.

―――

Pouring over all the hard work she'd put into the presentation, she was finally done. Without looking at the clock, she got up from her desk, stretched and took a deep, satisfying breath then exhaled slowly. She looked at the presentation again and decided that she'd done a very good job in the short amount of time she'd allotted to herself. She smiled as she envisioned Andrew waiting for her call, then picked up her cell phone and dialed his number.

He picked up on the first ring. She could hear shuffling as if he was in bed and his voice had a sleepy sexiness that she'd never heard before. "Did I wake you?"

"Mmmm. No, not at all."

"Andrew, I'm sorry, I did wake you." she glanced at her watch and gasped. "Oh, my God! It's 1 a.m. I am so sorry."

"No think nothing of it. Is everything all right? Do you want me to come over?" He was now sitting up in bed.

"Oh Andrew," she said, regretful that she'd called so late. "I had no idea it was that late."

"Okay, now I'm wide awake. How is the presentation going?"

"I'm finished, I think. I wanted you to come over and take a look at it, but go back to sleep, you can look at it tomorrow. We have all day."

"No. I can't go back to sleep now knowing that you want me to come over. I'll be there in half an hour."

"Andrew, it's…" but he'd already hung up. She wrung off and placed her hand to her forehead. She should have looked at her watch before calling him, but even looking out at the starlit skies, she didn't realize that it was after midnight.

She unlocked the front door so that he wouldn't have to ring the bell and wake up the dog, then brewed a cup of chamomile tea, turned on the patio light and walked outside. There was a chill in the air and the leaves rustled on the trees as the wind blew.

With her hands wrapped around the warm cup, she wondered if she'd done all that she could have done with the presentation. This was one thing she didn't want to fail at. She wasn't the only one who had expressed interest in procuring the account but Ben had given her the go ahead. She was doing it all by herself and that was very important. On the other hand, the other woman who wanted to go after the account was Mary Jones, a woman who'd made no bones about not liking her. That didn't matter to her either.

She didn't jump when she felt Andrew's arms circle her waist. After all, he was the only one on her list at the guard gate who could come in at any time of the day or night. She rested her head on his chest and he nuzzled her neck. "Mmmm, that feels very nice," she said, staring out into the dark night lit by lamp posts in the empty lot across the lake. The smell of her freshly planted gardenias permeated the space and she smiled. "I love gardenias," she said. Her fingers touched Andrew's hand still around her waist. And the warmth of his body against hers gave her a warm, erotic feeling inside. She moved away from him and turned to look into his face. His hair was tousled and a slight stubble covered his cheeks and chin, but God, did he look sexy. "Is this really how you look in the mornings?" she asked, lightly touching his cheek.

"Sorry, I should have shaved, but I wanted to get to you as quickly as possible." He rubbed his chin.

She laughed. "I'm not complaining. I think you look very sexy."

A pleasant pink rose to his cheeks and he ran his fingers through his curly hair pushing it from his face. She reached up and pulled it back the way it was and he laughed.

"I can't believe you've finished the presentation already. Did you take a break? Did you eat anything all day?"

"A little break, but I didn't eat anything. I was too pumped to stop once I got going."

"I like that word, *pumped*," he said laughing. "Okay, first I'll make you something to eat then we'll look at the presentation." Even though she looked a bit tired, to him, her brown eyes had that sexy sparkle that he loved so much. He couldn't help himself. He bent and kissed her lips but moved away before he started something they couldn't finish. He was at her home. They were alone, but he didn't think she was ready for a sexual relationship with him quite yet.

He took the unfinished cup of tea from her and guided her to the kitchen. "Okay, you sit on the stool and I'll make you the best omelet you've ever had."

He placed the cup in the sink, opened the well-stocked refrigerator and took out red peppers, cheese, broccoli and eggs. He placed them on the counter, and as if he'd been in her kitchen before, opened drawers and pulled out a knife and cutting board.

"Wow, you seem to know your way around my kitchen better than I do!" She raised an eyebrow. "I had no idea you could cook."

"Then prepare to be wowed, my dear, because I am a whiz in the kitchen." He winked at her, spinning the very sharp knife in his hand.

She almost jumped off the stool. "Andrew! Please, you're scaring me."

He laughed. "If I cut myself, I know where the nearest hospital is. I have them on speed dial." He blew her a kiss and proceeded to chop the vegetables.

"So, you've visited the emergency room before?"

"No, I just think it's safe to have them on speed dial." He chuckled.

She sat quietly watching him. When the very pink tip of his tongue shot out and wet his lips, she bit into her lips and felt her nipples tingle. She closed her eyes and took a few cleansing breaths, then opened them and saw him looking at her in a most curious tone. "What!" she said laughing. "I was just resting my eyes."

"That's what I thought. Am I keeping you up? I know you've worked all day, but…"

"No, I love that you're here." *Even if my body is doing things that it's not supposed to do right now.*

When he began sautéing the vegetables, now that woke her up even if she felt tired. Her stomach growled and she hoped he had not heard it. She couldn't wait to sink her teeth into whatever the outcome was.

He beat the egg mixture, poured it into the pan and covered it. "Do you want more tea or wine?" he asked, washing his hands.

"Tea, please."

He placed the kettle with water on the stove and came to sit beside her. Before he could hold her hands, she jumped down from the stool and said. "While we have this lull, why don't I get the paperwork for you to start looking at."

His smile was boyishly affectionate as he touched her bare arm and nodded. "Good idea." He watched her walk to the office and wondered if she was really afraid of their developing relationship. Her kisses told him that she liked him a lot, but she was still holding back. Frankly, he couldn't blame her, but little by little he felt her layers of fear peeling back one layer at a time.

She came back with the paperwork just when he got up to take the skillet off the stove. "It's done," he said. When the kettle whistled, he made two cups of chamomile tea and plated the omelets.

He sat beside her and ate while reviewing her presentation. She ate and surveyed his face for any scowls or frowns. So far she didn't see any.

Now, she felt the weight of the long day behind her as she stifled a yawn. Andrew looked at her. "You can go to sleep, you know. I'll clean up and continue going over the presentation."

"Are you sure?" she asked, her face almost brightening at the suggestion, but felt guilty about leaving him by himself.

"Absolutely, I'm wide awake. If I get tired I'll take a nap on the couch, if you don't mind."

"Oh, Andrew. The couch is not the most comfortable place to sleep." She searched his face to find a hint of tiredness, but all she saw was eagerness for her work and tenderness toward her. "Okay, but you can sleep in the guest room down the hall on the right. There are fresh towels in the closet on the right." She still felt guilty when she pressed her lips to his, hugged him and said goodnight. "Don't run away in the morning. I'll make you coffee. Thanks again for the delicious meal," she whispered in his ear and walked to her bedroom.

"I'll be right here." His fingers lingered on hers until the tips were a distance away.

Alice fell asleep as soon as her head hit the pillow.

Andrew cleaned up the kitchen, washed and stacked the dishes in the dishwasher, then relaxed in the guest-room bed with only the hanging lamp turned on. The smile on his lips was truly from his heart as he kept reading and looking at the drawings. Feeling so proud of her, he beamed with pride. This was not from his teaching. This was from her heart. He could tell, even from the male point of view, she'd put a lot of heart in it.

She'd left him a message. *I would like to make a lot of noise with this. Do you think we could get Mr. Frank's daughter to be a part of the campaign?*

She left a little smiley face with a pucker at the bottom. Andrew had no idea she knew that Ben had a daughter. He was up to the challenge of getting her to the States from Paris, but wondered how hard he had to work. No one knew that Danielle had not spoken to her father in years. Ben referred to her leaving as the day she ran away.

Andrew had worked with the company long enough to have met her before she'd left. He had gotten to know Danielle well enough to know even though she was young, she could be a tough lady.

He placed the papers on the nightstand, and folded his hands across his chest. He wished he could tiptoe into Alice's bedroom and just watch her sleep for a few minutes. He didn't know if she was a light sleeper and didn't want to betray her trust in him. His eyes slowly closed as he drifted off to sleep at four-thirty in the morning.

Chapter Seventeen

Alice was awakened by the smell of coffee brewing. She turned over on her back and remembered that Andrew was still there. She hid her head in the pillow. She'd told him that she would make coffee for him. She stretched, got out of bed, slipped her arms into a flowing robe, and pushed her feet into slippers. She ran to the bathroom, brushed her teeth, splashed water on her face and went to the kitchen.

He was standing on the patio with a cup in his hand. She walked out and pushed her hand around his waist along with an apologetic head on his arm. He smelled of soap and water and the nightly stubble was gone. She smiled, realizing he'd planned to stay over. "I'm sorry. I should have made you coffee."

He hugged her and kissed the top of her head. "No, I wanted you to sleep in today." He pulled her closer. "I loved your work. The woman would be foolish not to give you the account. But…"

"What!" she stiffened. "Something's wrong?" she released her hand from him and stood a foot away from him. "I should have spent more time on it? You don't think it's well stated?" She felt deflated.

"Stop, stop," he laughed. "There's nothing wrong with it." He set the cup on the wrought iron table and placed his hands on both shoulders. "You need just a little shot of confidence, darling. Your work is magnificent…"

"But, you said…"

"You didn't allow me to finish." His eyes grabbed hers and wouldn't let her look away. "What I was going to say is that, I'm not sure about Danielle. She and her father have not spoken in a very long time." He felt her relax and pulled her into his arms.

She giggled. "Sorry, I kinda jumped the gun there."

"Good thing I'm coming to New York with you. Once you've gotten the account I will be waiting to celebrate with you."

"Thank you for the shot of confidence. You're good for me."

"I've been telling you that for a while now." He wondered if she got the full implication of his words. Whether she did or not, she didn't show it. Until Monday, she had blinders on.

"I know you can get Danielle back here," she said, cinching his waist.

His laughter filled the air as he looked down into her upturned face.

His lips pressed against hers then gently covered her mouth. She could taste the freshness of toothpaste as she gave herself freely to the passion of his kiss. But when his lips became hard and searching, she released her mouth from his. Her stomach flip-flopped as she felt that old familiar weakness creep in every time she was this close to him. "Andrew," she whispered.

"I know," he said, fighting his own need for her. "Maybe we can take a side trip to Paris after the meeting." He tried to get his mind and body off the softness of her gentle curves that fit so perfectly into him. *Oh God, help me.*

Inside at the kitchen table, she took his hand. Her eyes scanned the face she thought was perfect. She smiled. "In fairness of full disclosure in our relationship, will you tell me what happened to your friend? And why do you hate that word so much? You're white; it has nothing to do with you." She wasn't going to let it go until he explained it to her. She knew there was a dark secret somewhere; a secret so forbidden that it caused his green eyes to turn a deep shade of turquoise. Like now.

A regretful sadness crossed his face. "Do you like that word?" His mouth pulled into a sour grin as his eyes pierced into her.

Crestfallen, her smile quickly faded and she moved her hands away from his. "No." She backed into her seat, avoided his eyes and looked down at the table.

"It doesn't stand for anything good, Alison."

The mispronunciation of her name made her cringe because she knew this time it wasn't meant to bring them closer.

"It was created by the white man to demoralize people of color. It doesn't matter if people of color use it in friendship, a white person shouldn't use it against a black person."

She glanced at him, then back at the empty table in front of her. Even though she knew it would be painful for him to divulge this secret, she wanted him to talk about it. She managed a tremulous smile and avoided the strained look on his face. "I thought maybe there was some kind of bond between us and…"

"There's always been a bond between us, love. Didn't you feel it the first time I held your hand?" The corner of his mouth twisted upward.

She said nothing.

The pain was clear and the fact was, he'd never really spoken to anyone about the way he felt toward the death of his friend. He'd been carrying around the burden of guilt for too many years. The memories he'd locked away for so long came flooding back. His jaw tightened, his body tensed with anger, and without looking at her, he spoke. "When I was in my teens, my best friend was a black fellow. We did almost everything together." A melancholy frown flitted across his features as he remembered the good times he had with Stanley Falloway. "There were certain unsavory characters that didn't like the fact that I was so close to him, but I didn't care, and neither did Stanley. I loved him as I would my own brother if I had one. You could say he was the brother I never had. He was the kind of fellow that could charm the pants off you. He was the most genuine person I ever met in my life."

He turned dark, sorrowful eyes towards her and it tore at her heart. "You don't have to…"

It was as if he hadn't heard a word she'd said. He couldn't stop. "Not like you, darling. You know that."

She nodded.

"My parents always invited him to family outings, dinners and to the theater along with his parents. His mother and Dria, my mother, became the best of friends over the years. His sister was quite sweet on me, I was told." He smiled a little. "But I was ten years her senior. For a teenage boy, that was a lifetime."

"Lucky for me," Alice said, trying to lighten his mood.

He laughed bitterly. His eyes became darker than Alice had ever seen.

"We went to London one weekend. Mother had told us we could go to the theater and use the apartment we had there. I remembered feeling so proud, because I was finally a man. My mother had trusted me enough to be on my own. When we came out of the theater, there was a crowd of white boys waiting for us. They were from our school in Halifax. Seems someone had told them we were going to London alone that weekend."

Andrew broke off, got up, and looked around for a small bag he'd brought over with him. He began searching in the bag for something. He pulled out everything he had in there—shaving cream, toothbrush, toothpaste, then pulled out a box of cigarettes that must have been years old. Alice said nothing, but watched him as he rolled it around with his fingers as if contemplating lighting it.

She said nothing.

He was fighting the tears as the anger he had felt inside threatened to erupt and cloud his vision and voice. He got up and walked to the glass patio door, looked out at the lake and the birds across the open field. "We didn't have a chance. There were six of them. We fought like hell. It was my first fight and I wasn't very good at it. Stanley wasn't a fighter either. We were only seventeen." He opened the door, lit the cigarette and took a drag. It crackled its age. His voice dropped to a whisper and Alice joined him on the patio. She stood watching his face, but made no attempt to touch him.

"Two pinned me against the wall while four had Stanley on the ground. I couldn't move; there was a knife pressed to my side."

The tears rolled down his cheeks and he exhaled as if he had the burden of the entire world on his shoulders. He made an attempt to wipe the tears away as his face distorted in anger. He took another drag of the cigarette and blew the smoke into the air. The wind rustled the dried leaves on the ground and whistled through the trees as rain clouds threatened above.

Even though the chill had disappeared, Alice wrapped her arms around herself.

Andrew stood ram straight, looking out as if consumed by hell's fire. "I could hear Stanley screaming my name; calling for me to help him, but there was nothing I could do. They were too strong for me. They pinned me there to watch as if they were murdering Stanley because of his sins. The sin he committed in being my friend. I shouted his name over and over. I tried to pull away from them, but I couldn't help him… God! I couldn't help him."

Andrew raised his clenched fist to his temples, almost crushing the lit cigarette in his hand as his breath came in short gasps. The overwhelming, gut-wrenching feeling was tearing at his insides.

Alice reached for and held his face in her hands. He turned wretched eyes toward her. She had asked too much of him. "You don't have to go on. You don't have to say any more, Andrew. I'm sorry, I didn't know." Tears fell to her cheeks. She couldn't bear seeing him this way. She watched his expression grow hard and his face set in a vicious expression. She wanted him to stop.

Reluctantly, he pulled away from her, but still looked into her beautiful face; the face that was giving him the courage to speak. She wanted to know and he needed to bare all. He shook his head, he had to go on. He kept talking as if she wasn't there, as if he were back in that time in London. He was reliving his nightmare. He turned away from her and took a last drag of the bad tasting cigarette before throwing it to the concrete and crushing it out with the tip of his shoe. "I must have fainted, because when I opened my eyes, I was lying on the ground. The boys who had held me before were nowhere to be found. There seemed to be at least fifty policemen standing over Stanley's still body. He had been stabbed five times in the upper chest. I felt numb, paralyzed at the amount of blood that seemed to be everywhere. I screamed his name not knowing he was dead. I fought my way to his side." He paused, took a deep breath as a dull ache developed in his head. He continued. "He was so still, I saw the blood but nothing registered. I didn't want to believe he was gone."

His voice trailed off again to a whisper. "His body was covered with blood. He was dead." He stood silent for a moment his heart wrenching with pain and feeling as numb as he'd felt on that faithful night.

"I picked up his lifeless body and cradled him in my arms for—I don't know how long, Alice. I wanted to will him back to life—I must have fainted again because when I regained consciousness, I was in a hospital bed. That's when I realized that I'd been stabbed once in the side. I'll never forget the look on my parents' faces or the look on Stanley's parents' faces."

The entire tragedy had made Andrew weak, but what he had not told Alice was that after graduating from college, he took his first trip to the Far East to study martial arts. He had refused to talk to anyone about the murder. He had locked it away in the furthest regions of his brain. "Stanley's father died recently. His mother still lives in London."

Alice looked at him through her own tears, regretful that she had ever asked him to explain that stupid word. "I'm sorry, Andrew. I didn't know there was such pain in your past."

He nodded. "Of course not. How could you know?" He took a deep, cleansing breath and exhaled. "Before I became unconscious, one of the boys called me a *nigger lover*, just before he stabbed Stanley twice. He wanted me to feel the guilt. He wanted me to know that it was because of me why Stanley had to die. He wanted me to feel the pain." His voice trailed off again to a whisper as he felt the pain of losing Stanley.

"No," Alice shook her head, wrapped her arms around him and laid her head on his massive chest. "No, it was because of their ignorance and black hearts. It wasn't your fault."

"I know that now," he whispered. Wrapping his arms around her, he leaned his head against hers.

"Were they ever caught?" she asked in a shaky voice.

"Yes, they were. I knew them all, and I didn't care what they did to me—and believe me, they threatened, but I gave the police every last name. They were caught, tried and found guilty. The two that stabbed Stanley were convicted of murder in the first degree. They were tried as adults because they were over eighteen. One swore that if he ever got out of prison he would hunt me down and kill me. Mother sent Willetta and me to France until things calmed down."

She held his hand and pulled him back inside as the rain began to fall, but he didn't want to sit. He needed to walk in the rain. He needed to run. "I have to go for a while. I have to walk," he said, pulling away from her and toward the front door.

"But it's raining," she complained. "You'll be drenched."

"But I won't die," he said. "I need this Alice."

She nodded and watched him disappear through the open door. She flopped down on the sofa, held her head in her hands and cried. "What have I done? Why couldn't I just leave well enough alone? I had to force him into talking about the worst thing that ever happened to him in his life." And as guilt ate at her, she pulled herself into a tight ball and cried herself to sleep.

———

Andrew sat silently beside Alice and she opened her eyes to see him smiling down at her. He had changed his clothes.

"You went home?" she said.

He nodded.

"I'm so sorry," she said, her voice a whisper.

"No, thank you. I have never really talked to anyone about it. I kept all those dark feelings bottled up inside me all these years, and now I feel as if I'd just laid Stanley to rest." He bent his head toward her face and his damp hair tumbled to the sides of her face as he kissed her lips tenderly, took her into his arms and carried her to her bedroom. He laid her on the bed, took off his shoes and crawled in beside her. And while the rain fell softly on the roof, they rested silently in each others arms.

In spite of the tumultuous emotions he'd just gone through, Andrew laid watching Alice sleep. This is what he'd wanted to do since the night before. She looked so peaceful, so beautiful, and he was so deeply in love with her it hurt. His body was on fire and he knew she trusted him with her body and soul. She had to make the first move. She had to give him the sign that she was fully ready, for them. He lightly touched her smooth brown face and her eyes fluttered open.

It took several seconds for her eyes to adjust and now she stared at him with rounded eyes. "Did you rest at all?" she asked holding the soft fingers that had caressed her cheek.

"Yes. Thank you so much for not freaking out. I was pretty graphic." His gaze rested on her questioning eyes and he smiled with an air of pleasure. "Do you know how wonderful it is just to lie here with you? Watch you sleep? I don't want this day to end." His fingers moved lightly over her cheek and he kissed her mouth hard and searching.

She felt the heady sensation of his lips and her calm was shattered with the hunger of his kiss as she responded in a way that frightened even her. "Tea," she said against his lips. "I'll make us tea." She moved away from him, her small hand on his cheek as he lay looking at her with a demure smile on his face.

"Don't be afraid of me, please. I love you. I will never hurt or disappoint you in any way. Nor will I take you for granted."

She stared at him as the words played over and over in her brain. *I love you, I love you.* She smiled nervously. She wanted to move, but didn't want to. She wanted him to repeat the words she wasn't ready to say to him. His face was so damn beautiful and he was such a good man, she didn't know what to say. She felt she had to say something, anything. "I'm a little hungry." She heard herself say the words and covered her face with embarrassment. *I'm hungry? The man just poured out his heart to you and you say, I'm hungry!*

He laughed and pulled her back to him. "You don't have to say the words until you're ready." But he knew she felt something real for him. "What would you like to eat?" he turned and looked out at the rain, still falling pretty hard.

"We can send out for pizza or Chinese. I have old movies we can watch." Her voice squeaked.

He laughed at her. "Relax, please. Pizza."

She nodded and picked up her cell. "What do you want on your pizza?"

"Pepperoni and pineapple." He rolled onto his back and looked at the forty-two inch flat screen on the wall.

She dialed and ordered pizza then got off the bed and opened a white oriental cabinet. She took out a few movies and rattled off the names. "*Sabrina* with Harrison Ford, An *Affair to Remember...*"

"Okay," he said. "Let's watch that one." He looked around the room with white oriental headboard, vanity and nightstands. Even the lamps were oriental with flowers and birds painted in blue and green. To the side, close to the glass doors, was a white lounge chair with a single blue pillow on it. "This is beautiful. I love this room."

She smiled. "The house came completely furnished but I had to have this for myself, so I placed the owners' furniture in storage and bought this," she said proudly.

He nodded then remembered he had not seen the dog since he got there. "Where is Tee Tee?"

"You think the children would have left her behind?" she slipped the DVD in the player and turned it on, then sat on the bed beside him.

He pulled her up against the headboard and hugged her. She laid her head on his chest and wondered if he was really all right. Maybe he was a little like her. He spilled his guts, got everything out and now he felt lighter. Nothing else to say regarding the matter. She figured she'd tormented him enough.

Sitting there with his arms around her, she couldn't help thinking of her work for just a few seconds. All she had to do was get on a plane tomorrow and make the presentation to the woman on Monday. Lee Ann had arranged the flight; Andrew had made the hotel reservation himself at the Waldorf. Lunch was set for eleven-thirty.

The movie began and the rain pounded harder on the roof. "Wine," she said, not feeling the most comfortable lying beside him. It wasn't that she didn't love curling up in his arms, she just didn't trust herself. This was the perfect time and setting for love making, but in her head, she was still saying no. He was very different from Harvey, and she knew he wouldn't say those faithful words just to get her to make love to him. If he did, he would be all over her the way Harvey was when he wanted sex. *Shut up with the Harvey business*, she told herself. Although not wanting to, she noticed she was comparing Andrew to her ex-husband.

"Love to," he replied. "But let me get it. I know where it is." He got out of bed and was back within a few minutes with a bottle of red and two glasses.

"When did you become so aware of where things are in my house?"

"This is not my first time here and I'm very observant."

She laughed. "I know that you're very observant." She kept looking at him. He'd taken off his shirt before lying with her and now all he had on was a close fitting T-shirt which showed his well-defined muscles. *Why on earth would I compare you to Harvey? Oh God, show me a sign that this is the man for me.* She closed her eyes and opened them, resisting the urge to touch his powerful thighs that ever so slightly touched hers.

He knew her because he listened to her and watched everything she did when they were together. He knew her frailty and her strengths. He would like to think that he also had her heart.

Forty minutes later, they were eating pizza in bed, sipping wine and hardly watching the movie, but watching the rain fall steadily, making puddles in the pool. *This is perfect*, Alice thought. She remembered only a few times when she and Harvey had spent the entire day in bed watching old movies and eating pizza, but it didn't feel like this at all. Now, she felt light and safe as if nothing could touch her.

Andrew left Alice's home at midnight after he'd gone over the presentation once more at Alice's insistence. "I want everything to be perfect," she'd said.

He agreed.

— ⊶∞⊷ —

Sunday morning, Alice carefully packed for her trip. Delia got home at midday, and at three in the afternoon, Harvey brought the children back home.

Alice hoped he would have just dropped them off and left. Instead, he asked her to take a walk with him onto the patio, then closed the sliding glass door behind him. She checked her watch. "Harvey, I have a plane to catch in a few hours."

"I know," he said, folding his arms across his chest. He frowned, his eyes level under drawn brows.

"Now what?" she said taking a deep breath and adjusting a vanishing smile.

"You still deny that you're having an affair with Andrew?"

His face was marked with that familiar loathing that she used to see whenever he came home from one of his late nights with *friends.*

"How can you stand there and ask me that question? If I have a relationship with Andrew, it really is none of your business."

"I sat down and told you my situation, yet you won't come clean with me regarding your life. I've never been able to trust you, that's why we broke up." His voice rose an octave as the familiar mask descended once again.

"Aren't we being a bit hypocritical, Harvey?" she said trying to keep calm, but feeling demeaned.

"No. The children told me that Andrew has breakfast with you every morning before you two go off to work."

"Yes, he does. We carpool in the mornings. I think I told you that—"

"But not of the affair." His lips tightened with disgust.

"You're engaged, Harvey. Before the ink on our divorce paper dried, you got engaged. I have a life to live and yes, Andrew will be a part of my life whether you like it or not." Her words stunned even her, because she'd just told her ex-husband that she was in love with the man she was so afraid to admit her feelings to.

"Now, was that so hard? You're not as pure as you'd have me think. Did he sleep with you last night?"

"You're disgusting." She kept looking in his face, challenging him. She visibly saw his mask drop.

His voice softened. "So I've lost you for good then?" He dropped his hands from his chest.

"Harvey, you have another woman who you intend to marry," she said, befuddled by his words and action. "Did you want me to be your fallback person? Did you not want me to move on with my life? What is this constant need you have to butt into my private life?"

He nodded then shrugged. "Habit," he said then did something quite out of character. He hugged her then let go and walked inside. "I'll call you in a few days." He turned and looked at her with an unnatural smile on his face. "I'm just trying to protect you."

She'd been so surprised and angered by his hug, her hands stayed pinned by her side. She watched him go through the door and wondered why he wanted to protect her, and from whom, himself? She didn't feel love for him, she felt guilt. Why did she feel guilty? Their marriage had been on the rocks for years; she catching him in the act was the one thing that opened her eyes to her stupidity. She knew he'd said those words on purpose. He was good at making up things and believing them. She took a deep breath and tried to wash the guilt feeling away, but it stayed through his goodbye and her ride to the airport with Andrew.

But, she'd be damned if she would allow Harvey to interfere with this very important step in her life. What on earth did she have to feel guilty for?

Andrew held her hand as they walked to the plane and her fingers automatically curled around his soft, warm hand. She smiled up at him, but still she couldn't get Harvey's face and words out of her mind. *Damn him!*

Chapter Eighteen

The entire plane ride, all Andrew said to her was, "Are you comfortable?"

She'd nodded, but didn't speak.

He kept glancing at her face and the faraway look in her eyes, and the constant furrowing of her brow, but said nothing, hoping that eventually she would open up to him.

Landing at JFK, they took a taxi to the Waldorf Astoria hotel. Gazing out at the snow-covered landscape, the fast-moving traffic mixed well with the dominating yellow of New York taxis, and her mood changed somewhat. She had to admit, she never grew tired of New York City. With Andrew constantly holding her hand, she was finally aware that he had been caressing her fingertips the entire time. She looked at his inquiring face and smiled. "I'm sorry."

He nodded. "You've been distant ever since I picked you up from home. Is everything all right?"

"Yes. No—" She shook her head, smiled, and kept looking at his soft lips, his serenely, compelling eyes, and said, "Will you kiss me, please?"

Not a man to deny her anything, he moved closer, closing the gap between them, lifted her waiting face and softly kissed her lips. His kiss was surprisingly gentle but she didn't want gentleness right now; she wanted a wake-up call that would leave her wanting only him. Her mouth hungrily claimed his and he responded to her as his lips matched her demand. She slipped her hand around his neck and pulled him closer to her, feeling the intimate ecstasy that reminded her of her deep feelings for him.

The taxi hit a bump and they abruptly parted. She placed a shaky hand to her mouth and laughed. "I'm sorry, but I needed to do that."

"Please don't apologize. I was beginning to wonder if I'd done something wrong."

She could see the concern on his furrowed brow and in his green eyes. She shook her head. "No, I had a little argument with Harvey that kind a left a pellet in my gut. My mood had nothing to do with you."

His mouth swooped down to capture hers quickly then parted. "Thanks for telling me."

They arrived at their destination. He paid the taxi driver and gathered their things, as she pressed her coat closer around her to keep out the frigid cold.

He checked them into the hotel. He'd reserved only one room with two double beds, but when they went up to the room there was one king-size bed. She looked at him, then the bed.

He shook his head apologetically. "I'm so sorry. This wasn't what I'd requested. I'll call down and have this rectified." He dropped the bags on the floor, and reached for the phone.

She stopped him with a gentle hand, and smiled. "It's fine. Maybe the universe is trying to tell us something. It's a big bed." *Plus we already slept together and nothing happened.*

"Are you sure?" he asked, "Because I can have them change us to…"

"No, this is very cozy. We shared a bed at my home, this is no different." But she knew it was, this time they'd sleep together for an entire night, touching and…

Clearing the lump from her throat, she looked around the room; table, lounge chair, bed, television, thick drapes, and a bathroom. She shrugged, took her makeup case to the bathroom, and closed the door to freshen up. Leaning against the sink, she stared at her reflection in the mirror. *I can do this. There's nothing to be afraid of.* She wanted to admit to herself once again that she was in love with him, but there was that fear factor again. She gave it a name. She was afraid of him leaving her for someone else the way Harvey had done. She washed her hands, dried them on the towel and bit into her lower lip. *I really do need to stop comparing him to my ex-husband.*

"Would you like to go for a walk then dinner, or the reverse?" he shouted through the door.

"Doesn't matter. Whatever you wish," she said, coming through the door.

"Are you comfortable with me being with you?" he asked, not sure what she was feeling right now. He got off the bed and pulled her to him.

"Yes," she looked into his eyes and smiled. "Yes, plus if you didn't come with me, you'd have missed me too much."

His face shadowed hers and in answer, his moist lips touched her waiting mouth. His tongue traced the soft fullness of her lips sending the pit of her stomach into a wild swirl.

His loins went into a scorching tremor and easing his body a little from her, he moaned as his mouth covered hers hungrily.

Her arms went quickly to his neck, her hands pulling his head more toward her.

"Alice," he whispered against her cheek, his hot mouth once again claiming hers.

"Yes," she replied as he lifted her and took two steps back to the bed.

Slowly he removed his lips from her mouth and lowered her to the bed. Lying beside her, he reclaimed her lips, crushing her to him. His kiss was gentle and taunting making every fiber of her body want him.

"You're playing with me," she said, releasing her lips hesitantly from his.

"No." His lips brushed against hers as he spoke.

"How about that walk?" she asked, still desiring him and not knowing why she was prolonging the agony of wanting his body naked against her. The thought made her breast tingle against the fabric of her bra, and she bit into her lip and raised herself from her lying position.

Again, he felt her hesitation and attributed it to the argument she'd had with Harvey, but until she said those three little words or made the first move to make love, he felt obliged to keep his promise to himself. "Okay," he said, sitting up beside her. He needed a few minutes for his loins to cool. "How about that walk?"

She nodded.

"Give me a few minutes." He got up and walked to the bathroom. Splashing cool water on his face, he stood and looked at his reflection in the mirror. *Easy boy, she'll say the words when she's ready.* He walked back out to her, refreshed. She was still sitting where he'd left her, now, with a coat in her hand. He held it while she slipped her hands into the sleeves then held her hand and left the room.

They walked through the lobby to the Park Avenue exit and toward Fifth Avenue. A burst of cold air whipped through her, reminding her it was still winter, and she shivered. He was dressed in a short leather coat over a blue turtle neck. No gloves, he wanted to hold her hand. "Are you warm enough?" he asked.

She nodded.

They walked hand in hand on Fifth Avenue until they got to Tiffany's. She stopped and gazed into the window as she had done at other jewelry stores, but this was different. This time she paid special attention to an exquisite blood-red ruby platinum ring. His eyes followed hers.

"That's a very beautiful ring," he said. "Do you like it?"

She shrugged. "Who wouldn't? As you said, it's very beautiful." She smiled up at him and began walking away.

"Wait here for me," he said, letting go of her hand.

"Where are you going?"

"I need to use the rest room," he whispered while stepping into the revolving door at Tiffany's.

"I'll be right here." She said, reaching into her pocket for her gloves. Waiting, she turned toward the opposite side of the street and shook her head as she saw the woman who had come between her and Harvey. She was with another man. She laughed to herself and stood staring at the woman until she was gobbled up by the constant moving foot traffic.

Andrew walked out of the store and placed a warm loving arm around her shoulder. She held onto his hand. "That was fast," she said keeping in stride with him.

He smiled down at her but said nothing.

"I just saw Doris walking in the opposite direction."

"Who's Doris?" He asked.

"Oh, sorry. Doris is the woman I saw Harvey kissing the night I left him." She bit into her lip and made a face remembering she had never really told him exactly why she'd left Harvey."

"Really! You actually witnessed the act?"

She nodded.

"I'm sorry you had to see all that. I suppose when you hear it, you can dismiss it as hearsay, but seeing it is a completely different thing."

"Yes, and thankfully, I'm over it."

He pulled her closer to him and kissed the top of her head. "You are such a lady."

She sighed and pulled her coat more snug around her.

He noticed. "We can go back to the hotel and eat, you know. They have three fine restaurants there."

She was freezing. The coat was warm, but not the silk top she wore even though she had snuggies underneath. "Okay, let's go back to the hotel." She pushed her arm under his coat around his waist.

He smiled. "Better?"

"Getting there. You are so warm."

"Just for you, my darling."

They hurried back to the hotel, and Alice was glad for the warmth that greeted her in the lobby. They headed downstairs to the Bull and Bear and had to wait a few minutes to be seated.

Andrew took her coat, pulled the chair out for her then set the coat over the back of her chair. He took off his coat and slung it on the back of his chair before he sat down. When the waiter came, he ordered a bottle of pinot then looked at her. "Is that all right?"

She nodded. "Yes, and I know exactly what I want," she said glancing at the menu.

The waiter stood beside her with pen and paper ready and she ordered the lobster with vegetables.

"I'll have the same," Andrew said.

The waiter left and came back within a few minutes with the bottle of wine, opened it and carefully poured it in both glasses.

After her first sip of wine, he gazed inquiringly at her and she nodded. "I like it."

"Good. Do you wish to tell me about that evening?"

"What evening?" She took another sip of her wine and felt the liquid slowly go down her throat through layers of her stomach.

His eyes met hers. "You don't have to talk about it if you don't want to."

"Oh, that evening, she said with dull enthusiasm. She shrugged. "Nothing to tell really. It's as I told you." But she told him anyway.

"That must have been awful for you." He said when she was finished. His eyes searched her face for a sign of hurt, but there was none. He came to the conclusion that she was really over it.

"It was," she said in a light, I-don't-care-anymore tone. "I'm better," she said, looking into his eyes.

He nodded. "I'm glad."

Their meal came and she was still in a talkative mood. "Have you heard from Willetta?" She sliced through the lobster meat that had been carefully taken out of the shell and placed a small amount in her mouth.

"Yes, she and William are in her favorite place."

She glanced up at him.

"Greece."

"Ahhh, yes." She took another sip of wine.

Andrew took a swallow of his wine and watched as she placed the glass on the table and fingered the rim with her slender index finger. He gulped. It had been too long since he'd made love to a woman. He pulled his eyes from the movement to her face.

She was looking at him with eyes that told him that she'd had enough to drink.

"I noticed from that day we spent together at your home that you're not a big drinker."

His eyes were like the azure seas of Negril and for a moment, she got lost in them.

"Alice?"

She smiled away from them. "Yes. Ahhh, no I'm not a big drinker. I get intoxicated very fast." She pushed the glass away from her. "I have to be fresh for tomorrow."

He nodded. He had a feeling that that would be her distraction until the meeting was over and everything was in the bag.

———

After dinner, with Andrew carrying both coats on his arm, they took the elevator back to their room. Silently, they entered the room and Alice was now very aware of the space they shared. They'd forgotten to turn the heat up, so now the room was cold enough for her to wrap her arms around herself.

Andrew hung the coats in the closet, turned up the thermostat and said, "I'm going to take a quick shower."

"Okay, I'll take one after you. Maybe that will warm me up quicker than my arms will."

He stood before her and wrapped his arms around her. "I can rectify that for you."

Yes you can. His body was just the right temperature, cozy warm, and she pushed her arms around his waist and rested her head on his chest. "This feels so nice, I don't want to move." *Wine plus the warmth of your body is all I need right now.*

"You don't have to. But if you allow me to do just one quick thing first, I promise you can stay in my arms all night."

The Upside of Down

She said nothing and watched him turn down the bed. He came back and scooped her up in his arms. She hugged his neck and didn't release her hold even when he placed her on the bed. He slipped in beside her. Using his feet, he pushed off his shoes, but it was a bit difficult to take her shoes off with his feet.

He heard her shoes fall to the carpeted floor and smiled as she snuggled in his arms. "Are you warm enough?" he asked as he pulled the comforter over them.

"Yes. Just hold me for a few minutes, then you can go take your shower."

He chuckled, turning onto his back, and her head lay comfortably in the crook of his arm. "For as long as you like." His hand caressed her shoulders on top of the comforter and he closed his eyes to the emotions that ran through him. He really needed to take that shower.

After a few minutes of being so close to him, the heat of his body, the closeness of his powerful thighs to hers, she took a deep breath and said, "You can take your shower now."

"Are you sure?" He kissed the top of her head.

"Yes."

He slid off the bed, tucked her in and went to the bathroom.

Alice watched him until he closed the door leaving only a crack and wondered if that was an invitation for her to join him. She wasn't going to. She heard the water running and in spite of herself envisioned him peeling of his clothes down to his underwear very slowly. She closed her eyes tightly to block the vision, but that didn't work. Her body reacted instinctively and she flung off the comforter and went to stand by the window. She unbuttoned her blouse slowly and stood staring out at concrete. The warmth of his body fresh in her mind, she could still smell his cologne. She closed her eyes and inhaled slowly and exhaled as she opened her eyes. *Is he really as genuine as he seems to be?* She wondered. There was no doubt she'd fallen for him, but old fears and uncertainty gnawed at her. She shook her head. It had taken her a while to fall in love with Harvey, but with Andrew—he was right—there was an instant attraction that she'd been fighting from the day they met.

When Andrew came out of the bathroom, Alice was still standing at the window. She caught a whiff of his aftershave as he came up behind her and slipped his arms around her waist. She wrapped her arms around his and leaned her head against his warm, naked chest. His damp curls tumbled to her face as he bent to kiss her cheek. She turned in his arms and her breath caught in her throat as she felt his nakedness against her.

"You're still not quite with me, are you?" he asked.

She tried to relax, smiled, reached up and touched his curls, then wrapped her arms around him and leaned her head against his chest. The beating of his heart in her ear only made things worse as a light electrical current moved from her breast to her inner thigh. She couldn't move away, that would either hurt his feelings or give her weakness away. She stood still and felt soft curls on her cheek as he once again bent and kissed her cheek.

He placed a finger under her chin and brought her face up so that their eyes met. "Alice, darling," he said. "Everything will go well tomorrow and I'll be right here waiting for you when you get back."

She nodded. "I know." She tried to look away.

He held her eyes, "But?"

"Oh, Andrew," she whispered. "I've never met anyone like you…"

"Dashing, debonair?" he teased. His eyes clung to hers, analyzing her reaction.

"I'm afraid of you." Coming back to her, she didn't want to say it like that. Her words sounded cruel and she stumbled to rephrase it. "I… I mean…" she drew her lips in with regret, staring wordlessly at the sight of his bewildered stare.

The buoyancy left his entire face as he guided her to the bed, sat down, and pulled her down beside him. "Why?" he pleaded.

Awkwardly, she cleared her throat, and avoided his eyes, staring into his naked chest adorned with sparse silky brown hair.

"Because I love you so much and I'm afraid that something's going to happen and you're going to change somehow."

He breathed as if he were taking his first breath. The words he'd waited so long to hear had finally been spoken but in the wrong context. He didn't want her to fear her love for him. He wanted it to be celebrated, strong and certain. "On my life and that of my grandmother, I will love and take care of you forever. I can't predict anyone's future, Alice, but I know that I can predict ours. I love you with all my heart and I know if you will let me, I will be yours forever."

Her eyes sought his. "I will let you."

"I'm a one-woman man, Alice. I am your man, no matter what. We can weather any storm. Anything, I promise and I never break my promises."

Gazing into his eyes, she believed him.

"Say those words again. I want to hear them everyday for the rest of our lives."

Her voice filled with entreaty, she voiced the words once again. "I love you with all my heart."

And when his lips came down hungrily onto hers, she knew that he knew and he knew that she knew because the kiss made every nerve in her body tingle.

His mouth took on a more demanding crush and she relaxed and allowed the sensation to engulf her entire body.

He slipped the blouse from her shoulders and her kiss became deeper and more demanding.

Then suddenly he stopped.

"What's the matter!" Her heart beat faster and her body grew hot and tingled with wanting as she grabbed his arms.

"I don't have protection," he said panicked. He didn't want to get her pregnant.

She gazed at him wondering if she should tell him it was okay. She wanted him to keep touching her, to keep the fire burning inside of her, but she said nothing. She had a feeling he'd not had another serious relationship since his wife and she certainly had not had anyone, but still she said nothing. She could feel the slippery tingling sensation inside her waiting to be sated, but she wanted this to be his decision.

Andrew looked at his watch. "There must be an open pharmacy somewhere in his city. Don't go anywhere. I'll be back." He got up and hurriedly slipped into his clothes, pulled his shoes and coat on, grabbed her shoulders and kissed her hard on the lips then left the room.

Alice took a deep breath, calmed herself and finished taking her clothes off. *I can control this,* she kept telling herself. *I will not finish without him.* She needed a slow, hot shower. She turned on the water to a setting as warm as she could stand it and stood with her back toward the water. If she made one wrong move and touched her breast, it would be all over. She imagined Andrew running out the door into the cold air down on Lexington Avenue. She smiled and ran the soap over her body then washed off and got out. Drying herself off, she slipped into the white hotel bathrobe behind the door, slipped back into bed and turned on the television.

⸺ ∞ ⸺

Andrew rushed out of the hotel after the concierge told him where to find a pharmacy. He took a cab to the first pharmacy. It was closed. He went to three other pharmacies, but they were also closed. He gave up. He was tired and drained. Frustrated, he stood in the middle of the street on Sixth Avenue and shouted, "Where is the rain when you need it?" Two minutes later, it began drizzling. He needed the rain to cool him off. "I can't get a break," he murmured. Then he turned his face to the skies. "Shoot me. Shoot me right now!"

The taxi man across the street heard him, laughed and said, "This is not the place for that, buddy. What do you need?"

Andrew looked in his direction and smiled as he crossed the street. "I need an open pharmacy."

"Get in."

He got into the taxi and the driver took him uptown to a Duane Reade all night pharmacy. As he pulled up he looked back and smiled at Andrew. "This is New York, son. You can always find an open store if you look hard enough. Do you want me to wait for you?"

"You're a life saver. Yes, please wait." He got out of the taxi and was back within five minutes.

"Where to?" the taxi driver asked.

"The Waldorf." He settled back with the precious stash in his pocket.

When they got to the hotel, he thanked the driver, gave him a big tip and ran into the hotel. But when he got back to the room, the television was on. Alice was fast asleep on her back with the covers resting on her thighs, the robe pulled away revealing a promise of what he could have had. His hungry eyes raked over her beautiful body and her peaceful, beautiful face. He sighed with resignation and gently pulled the comforter over her. He peeled the wet clothes from his body, slipped into his pajama bottom then just sat gently on the edge of the bed gazing at the woman he was so deeply in love with. She stirred, her eyes fluttered. "Andrew," she whispered.

"Shhh, go back to sleep," he said, slipping under the covers with her. When he was sure she was fast asleep, he reached over, searched into his jacket pocket and found the tiny box containing the ring he'd bought at Tiffany's. He gently slipped it onto the third finger of her left hand. She stirred again and pulled her hand under the covers. He pulled her into his arms and hoped she wouldn't freak out when she saw it. *What a night,* he smiled to himself. He fell asleep the way he'd dreamed of for the last few months, with her in his arms.

Chapter Nineteen

Enclosed in the warmth of Andrew's arms, Alice cast her eyes on the bright light of the clock sitting on the night stand; it was 6 a.m. Remembering the night before and what might have been, she glanced back to see him looking at her. She smiled. "Sorry about last night."

"It was my fault. I didn't want to take anything for granted and—" His voice was low and smooth as his loins fired with memories. He didn't move.

She silenced him with a single finger to his lips. "You could never take me for granted, that much I know about you." She moved closer to him and felt the hardness between his thighs that surprised and delighted her. She placed his warm hand on her taut, naked breast and he took a deep satisfied breath. Raised on one elbow, he teased her breast with a kiss and pulled it into his hot mouth.

"Mmmm," she groaned as a ripple of desire for his magnificent body raced through her. Sliding her hand down his naked side into the pajama bottom, onto his firm thigh, she hesitated.

"Don't be shy," he whispered. "I am yours to do with as you please," he murmured planting deep kisses against her neck. He pushed the robe and the comforter from her shoulder, then raised himself up and finished the job of slipping the robe entirely from her body as she eased out of it.

He pushed the last bit of clothing from him, laid on his side and guided her trembling hand toward the spot that she seemed to fear. "Touch me," he whispered.

She boldly encircled him with her fingers, tightening then releasing as he throbbed in her hand.

Andrew's eyes took in her body in one full sweep. "You're just as beautiful as I imagined." His mouth came down to touch her nipple once again with tantalizing possessiveness as his hand roamed over her smooth, soft body.

His tongue slowly licked her nipple sending currents of desire directly to her most intimate part. She shuddered and parted her thighs, allowing him to caress the part of her that became slick to his touch.

Needing a deeper caress, she arched into him. This was what she'd wanted and needed for so long. She needed to be loved, to be shown love, deep love.

Andrew stared down at the slim body by his side and into eyes that seemed so innocent, so trusting; eyes that told him how much she loved him. "I'll never hurt you."

"I love you."

"I need to hear that for the rest of my life," he said.

The expression of driven need on his golden features as he sustained eye contact made her feel more amorous and she felt her need build as his mouth recaptured hers. His hand moved down the length of her back then explored the soft lines of her waist and hips back to that area that sent her to a higher level of ecstasy.

Her body burned for him as she pressed into him and grabbed onto that part of him that throbbed once again and glided expertly until she felt him throb repeatedly. And just when she felt as if she couldn't hold on any longer, he reached over to the nightstand, slipped the condom on and lowered his taut body slowly onto hers penetrating that softness that held onto him as he inched deeper into her.

She gasped as he entered her and he didn't move for a few seconds. "Are you okay?" he whispered, the huskiness of want in his voice.

In response, she pulled him deeper into her as she raised her legs and arched to receive him. He moved slowly then caught a ready nipple between his lips and pulled gently sending a ripple sensation to her wet area that cried out for release as he went deeper.

And as pure pleasure radiated through her, she moved as one with him in sync. His chest moved against her nipples rousing a melting sweetness within her. Her thighs wrapped around his back, pinning him deep within her as he hit that spot that sent her to the heights of no return. When the peak of delight was reached and exploded in a downpour of fiery sensations, waves of ecstasy throbbed through her and she arched her back one more time pulling everything from him until he moaned with deep satisfaction and fell on top of her.

He quickly slid from her and pulled her damp body to him. "I love you. I can't say it enough." His mouth kissed her softly and she kissed him back with the raw intensity of her love for him.

She pushed the damp curl from his forehead and lay in his arms drowned in a floodtide of the liberation of her mind and body as contentment flowed between them.

"Do you want to have an early breakfast with me? Lunch is quite a ways off."

"Yes. Should we have room service?"

"I'll order it while you take a shower. What would you like?"

She took a deep breath, stretched both arms in front of her and saw the ring on her finger. She gasped. "Andrew! What did you do?" She sat up with a start and stared at the exquisite ruby ring on her finger. She turned and looked at him, her mouth still agape.

He sat beside her, trying to read if she was happy or freaked out. "I wanted you to know how serious I am about our relationship."

She kept staring at his face while her thumb spun the ring on her finger. "I... I... I don't know what to say." She bit into her lip.

"You know how I feel about you. I wanted our lovemaking to have a deeper meaning for us."

"But—" she was confused. Did this mean he considered them engaged? She was afraid to ask the question.

"I want to marry you Alice."

And the question was answered for her. "Now!" she asked.

He felt relieved that she wasn't upset or felt rushed. He chuckled and hugged her. "I love you so much." He gazed into her liquid brown eyes and wiped away a single tear. "I would marry you now if you'd let me."

"Oh, Andrew." She looked down at the ring once more then back at him. She didn't want to hurt him in any way. "Andrew, I'm a mother of two small children. I just got divorced—"

"I know, and two charming little ones at that."

"I also have a pesky ex-husband who won't seem to go away."

"Well, you can deal with him. I'll deal with everything else."

"We don't even know each other very well." Her voice was fragile and shaking.

He held her hand and caressed them with his thumb. "Alice, are you trying to talk me or you out of our engagement?"

"I don't know," she lowered her eyes to where he held her hand.

"Look, I know you have two glorious children. You like old movies with Cary Grant. You are a bit shy but cover it up very well. You hate confrontation. You're exquisitely beautiful, patient, and loving," he finished, a gentle softness to his voice as he tried to get her gaze back.

"And now you're waiting for me to say what I know about you?"

He nodded.

"You're kind, understanding and patient. You seem to love my children to death and would spoil them rotten if you got a chance. You love to protect me, and although you can't guarantee you'll love me forever, you do love me." She watched his face for his reaction.

"Everything true, except, I can guarantee that I'll love you forever." His hand now rested on her thigh. "Alice, nothing you can say or do will change the way I feel about you. I take relationships very seriously, and when we marry, it will definitely be forever, no matter what." There was a finality to his tone that made her eyes grow soft and teary.

She wondered if she should broach the subject of their color difference. He certainly didn't seem to give it a second thought. Until now, neither did she, but what will her mother say? Merl loved Harvey, not only because he seemed genuine in the beginning, but he was very kind to her. He'd actually helped her to buy the house she now lived in. She'd paid him back but never forgot that when she was in need he was there for her, no questions asked. For some reason, she'd loved the fact that her daughter had married within her own culture. Andrew was very British. Down to earth, white, handsome, white. She had to get that out of her head. Her mother was very broad minded. She left it at that and looked at Andrew looking at her. She made a face. "Will you ask me again in a few months?"

He smiled and nodded. "I know I just sprang this on you, and I also know you're still fragile from your divorce. So yes, I will ask you again."

She was about to take the ring from her finger and he stopped her. "Please, don't take it off. I will wait until you're ready to get married, but please don't give it back to me. Think of it as a promissory ring."

She laughed softly. "Isn't that what an engagement ring is?"

"Yes. We can be engaged for as long as you wish."

She loved him, there was no doubt of that, but she'd just gotten out of one marriage. She wasn't ready to rush into another just yet even if it was to this gorgeous, perfect specimen of a man. Looking into eyes that begged for understanding, she knew he would wait. She nodded. "I love it. You don't mind if sometimes I wear it on my right hand, do you?"

"When you introduce me to your mother, for instance?"

She laughed and nodded.

"No, as long as you wear it."

"Okay." She pulled the gown from between the twisted sheets on the bed and he helped her slip it on. She got out of bed and pulled the belt around her waist. "I would like scrambled egg whites, turkey bacon, tomato wedges, wheat toast and black tea for breakfast please."

His long legs fell to the floor and he pulled her shamelessly back to his naked body. "Worked up quite an appetite, but what about your breakfast meeting?"

"It's not a breakfast meeting. I'm meeting them in their office." She tried not to look at his body as he hugged her and laughed.

"You can look at me you know. This is all yours."

"You have no shame." She giggled as he pulled her back into the bed and began kissing her from mouth to shoulder, moving to her breast. She was once again ready to be made love to and his body grew hard.

"Not with you, my love." His big body was on top of her and she moved her legs apart to welcome him back into her body.

Once again, spent and happy, he laid with her in his arms, glanced at the clock and pushed her toward the bathroom. This time she wore nothing as her inhibitions fell to the floor just like the robe. He gazed at her, shook his head and took a deep breath. "You are beautiful. I could stay locked in a room with you forever."

She giggled, rushed into the bathroom and closed the door while he ordered room service.

Andrew ordered room service then slipped into the longer robe hanging in the closet and stood at the window watching the rain fall. He thought of calling his mother and wondered what she would say about the union. She would probably be very happy for him. Even though she didn't know the real reason why he divorced his ex-wife, she'd once remarked that she was tired of seeing his chin to the floor. *Find yourself a nice girl and try it again,* she'd told him. *They say three times is the charm but you've learned a lot from the first one, you certainly won't make the same mistake twice.* How right she was. Alice was the exact opposite of his ex-wife. There was one thing they both had in common: they were both divorced and were not destined to make the same mistake twice; they were too smart and in love for that. Frankly, he didn't think his first wife loved him. She'd married him because she thought he was rich. The rich part came later but she'll never know that.

He didn't know how long he stood staring out the window, but turned when Alice tapped him on the shoulder. She'd slipped back into the robe. Her brown hair hung down to her shoulders. She wore very light make-up, and to him, she didn't need anything else, not even the lipstick she had not applied yet.

He scooped her up in his arms and buried his face in her neck. "I'm such a lucky man," he whispered in her ear.

"I have a temper, you know."

"You can't scare me off, mi lady. Love really conquers all."

"But there's one thing we have in common that I hope will never go away."

He held her at arms length. "Pray tell."

"We are both hopeless romantics."

"I like that."

There was a soft knock on the door. "Room service."

Andrew let him in and advised him where to set up breakfast. When he left and they sat down to eat, she poured him coffee and he poured her tea. "Would you like to stay another night?" he asked.

"In New York?"

"Uh huh." He buttered toast and placed it on her plate.

"Well, we did plan to go home tomorrow. If I don't get the contract this morning, I plan to take them out to dinner this evening."

He smiled. "Good girl." She'd forgotten that when she got the contract, they'd go back home by way of Paris. He'd remind her when she got back. One thing at a time. Get the contract, then start making arrangements for the product launch.

Alice ate a little bit of everything, excused herself and got dressed in a light blue pants suit over white silk blouse and black pumps. She wore pale mauve lip gloss and an understated yellow-gold diamond earring in her ear. She wore the ring on her left hand, just where Andrew had placed it. Deveraux Incorporated was not more than twenty minutes across town, but factoring in traffic, she would rather be too early then late. "Wish me luck," she said, standing before him with everything she needed to make the presentation in hand, plus her purse.

"You don't need luck, darling. And may I say, you look gorgeous. Now, go and knock them dead." He got up and hugged her tight.

"Thank you, but you can say all that because you're in love with me."

"Yes, I can, but nevertheless, it's the truth. I'll be right here waiting for you."

She nodded, kissed his cheek and walked to the door, then She turned. "I'll have my cell phone off, but you can always leave a message. I'll pick up my messages after the meeting."

He opened the door for her, kissed her again and watched her walk away until she rounded the corner to take the elevator.

Outside, Alice got an umbrella from the bellman and got into the taxi that had just pulled up. She gave him the address then settled back for the ride. She'd timed it right. Traffic was never light in New York City unless it was maybe three in the morning, and when the taxi pulled up at Liberty Plaza, she had ten minutes to spare. That's the way she liked it. She got out of the taxi and walked up the steps to the revolving door of the building that she'd left more than three months ago. She smiled. She'd worked at this address for more than five years, but was only familiar with the twenty-first floor. Today she'd be going to the twenty-fifth floor in a capacity to make her or break her. She pressed the elevator button, straightened her shoulders, took a deep breath, stepped in and exhaled. *You've got everything covered, Alice.*

Yes, she did. When she got off the elevator, in front of her she read the name, *Deveraux Inc. A Cosmetic Corporation.* She pushed the door and stepped in. She spoke to the receptionist who told her Mrs. Deveraux would be with her in a few minutes.

She sat and remembered Andrew's words. *You don't need luck.* She stood when a neatly dressed, petite woman of color smiled and came toward her with an outstretched arm. "Mrs. Vaze. We meet at last."

Alice took the woman's warm hand in hers and smiled. "I'm sure it was well worth the wait."

"Come into the boardroom. There are some people you should meet."

Alice had only expected Maloney Deveraux, but in the small conference room fitted with twelve chairs and a large highly polished table, she was introduced to three other people, including the woman's daughter. Maloney was divorced but was trying to keep it a secret, even with a twenty-six year old daughter.

"I must apologize for springing my daughter and two sisters on you, Mrs. Vaze, but they are my board members and I thought it imperative that they be present. We are very informal people here, so please, call me Maloney." Her small mouth smiled and she pushed a strand of gray hair away from her face.

Alice noticed that the woman's complexion was flawless, but she also noted that she wore a lot of make-up to keep that flawless look. "Of course, and please call me Alice." She sat beside Maloney Deveraux's beautiful daughter, Tiffany. Informal or not, no one wore T-shirt and blue jeans.

Tiffany was quite slender with pouty lips. She wore her black hair shoulder length, and very little make-up. The two sisters, Eva and Jennifer, were a bit on the heavy side, but dressed like plus-size models. It was apparent that they took pride in the way they looked.

Tea, bagels and donuts were served, but Alice only had tea. Maloney told her about the company and what she expected of Frank's agency. The company was very young, only two years old. They expected Frank's to take them globally.

"We will do nothing less than global," Alice said, asking for copies to be made of her written proposal. She handed the six-page document to the administrative assistant, then pulled out the drawings she'd made and placed it on the easel. She waited for the pages to be returned to her, gave a copy to each member, and made her pitch. She told them exactly what her firm would and could do for the company. She also mentioned that she used their cosmetics.

When she finished her presentation, Alice looked at faces that seemed pleased, but Maloney was also looking at another advertising firm.

"I like you, Alice, and I love your presentation. If we decide to go with your firm, will you be working alone? I only ask because sometimes people work as partners in some firms."

"No, one other person will be working with me, but I'll be the lead person."

Maloney leaned toward her. "Between you and I, is he black or white? Man or woman?"

Alice smiled. "White and male."

Eva, the more eccentric one, clapped her hands and laughed. "Yes, that would be perfect."

Maloney, cast a foreboding look her way, then turned to Alice and smiled. "Let us talk amongst ourselves and get back to you very soon, Alice."

Alice looked at the faces of each woman in the room, especially Maloney, and knew that she had a chance. "Of course. It was very nice meeting everyone and I hope this will not be the last time we see each other." She gathered her things and shook everyone's hand. But then she put plan B into action. "If you don't mind, would it be possible for us to have dinner this evening at my hotel? Mr. Benton will be in town and you can meet him then. We can further go over any questions you may have."

Maloney looked at Alice and smiled, then checked her appointment book. She tapped her long fingernail on the table then nodded. "Yes, let's do that. I will be free at seven-thirty."

"Okay, we can meet at the Bull and Bear at seven-thirty."

Maloney nodded and shook Alice's hand once more.

Before she got to the elevator, Alice turned on her cell phone. Whether she got the account or not, she'd done an extremely good job. She was not nervous, but she'd given a damn good presentation.

Chapter Twenty

It was still raining when she got outside and hailed a cab. She gave the driver her address and sat back. In her mind, she went over everything that was said in the meeting. Everyone seemed to hang onto every word she spoke. They asked the appropriate questions and got straight answers.

When she got to the hotel, she paid the driver and walked through the pouring rain without even opening the umbrella. Then in the elevator, what she'd done hit her. She'd committed Andrew without his consent. He had his own accounts. Would he work with her on this one? He'd said more than once that this was her baby. She bit into her lip and took a very deep breath. She glanced at the ring on her finger, and pushed it around with her thumb.

The elevator stopped on her floor and she got off. Sliding her key in the slot, she opened the door to see champagne in a silver bucket and two flutes. Andrew was sitting at the small writing desk, working. He got up when she entered, smiled widely and hugged her. "The account is yours?"

She shook her head. "Not yet, but I placed plan B into action. We're having dinner with Maloney this evening at seven-thirty." She bit her lower lip and watched his face.

"We," he said smiling.

"Yes." She threw her purse on the bed and placed her briefcase on the floor.

He helped her off with her coat and noticed that she wasn't very happy. "Okay, what's wrong?"

She pulled him to the bed, and sat. Holding his hand, she looked into his eyes. "You did say that whatever happens we're in it together, right."

He nodded slowly.

"I did a bad thing today."

He chuckled. "No, you could never."

She sighed. "They asked me if anyone would be working on the campaign with me and I panicked." Her voice sounded tired as she downplayed her excitement.

"Yes," he encouraged.

"I told them that you would be working with me." She bit into her lip and looked into clear green, laughing eyes.

"So what's the problem? You know I will."

She jumped from her perch on the bed and hugged him. "Oh, Andrew. I was afraid I'd overstepped. You have your own accounts and I…"

He hugged her and nuzzled her neck. "You must never be afraid of what I may think, because when it comes to you, I'm always at your side. Plus, you've worked on a few of my accounts with me."

"I know, but this is my very first one and I didn't want to assume."

"You're not assuming anything when it comes to me. We're one, even if we're not yet wed."

She sat back on the bed and held his gaze. "And that's where the *we* comes in."

"It's your account, darling. You have to get over your shyness. You will get this account. I'll be silent at dinner unless I'm asked a direct question. As I say, this is your account." He reached over, picked up the bottle of champagne and poured it into the flutes. He gave her one and held up his. "You may think this is premature, but it's not. To you. May this be the first in many accounts that you will acquire."

She raised her flute and took a sip. "Thank you."

"You know, I was going to call Danielle, but a little voice inside, stopped me."

"Oh, Andrew," she placed a hand over her face.

He gently pulled it away and kissed her lips.

She laughed.

He caught her around the waist and pulled her to him. "You have no idea how happy I am just because you're in my life."

"Me too," she said.

"Did you really think I'd be upset about working with you on this account?" he asked, peering into her face.

"No. Yes. I don't know."

"I'd be upset if you didn't ask me; maybe not upset if you wanted to go it alone, but a little hurt if you'd asked someone else."

"Trust me; no one could fill that slot but you."

He nodded then chuckled. "Oh, I forgot to tell you that Danielle Frank is half black. Ben's wife is African American." He saw the surprise in her eyes.

Alice blinked, then focused on him. "And you chose now to tell me?" her voice rose an octave. She shook her head and moved away from him as the wheels in her head turned. When she got the account, maybe she could use both Maloney's daughter and Danielle.

"Sorry. How can I make it up to you?" Two deep lines appeared between his eyes.

"I don't want to go to Paris, but maybe we could get her to come home for a little while. I could speak with her via Skype. I could take a peek at her complexion before asking her to do this. What's my excuse to call?" she cleared her throat and looked at his smiling face.

"No excuse. She's a friend of mine so, I'll call her with you. It will be a social call to begin with, then just ease into business."

She laughed.

"What?"

"We're talking as if I've already procured the account."

"But you will, darling. I'm sure before we leave here tomorrow, you'll have a signed contract in hand."

"I know I've said this before but it bears repeating, you're so good for me."

"And you for me."

Alice called down and made the dinner reservation for three at seven-thirty.

Alice dressed in a simple black dress and Andrew in a white shirt under blue blazer and navy blue pants, they arrived at the restaurant a little before the appointed time, but waited to be seated. Maloney was right on time. Alice introduced them and they sat down and ordered wine. Maloney was in a very talkative mood after a few sips of wine. She smiled and looked at Alice. "My dear, my sisters were very impressed with you." She looked at Andrew then back at Alice. "My sisters would be very upset if I didn't ask this question. Are you by any chance from the West Indies?"

Alice smiled. "Yes, I am. I'm from Jamaica."

She laughed. "That's what Eva said." She took another sip of her wine. "Well, we went over all that you'd said at the meeting this morning and would like to give your company the account on one condition."

Alice glanced at Andrew the same time he glanced at her.

"As you agreed, we want a big to do. We want people to wake up and know that there's a product out there that's plant-based and good for their skin, and we want your face on our product." She kept looking at Alice.

"Me?" Alice said in a squeaky voice.

"Yes, dear. You have the type of skin that says here's a woman with a flawless complexion who's not afraid to use our product."

"But wouldn't you rather have a professional model, or your daughter for instance, she…"

"No dear, we want you."

The waiter came over and they placed their dinner order.

"I have been asking my daughter since the inception of our product to be our spokes-model, but she's painfully shy and refuses," Maloney continued. She looked at Andrew. "Don't you agree, Andrew?"

Andrew looked at Alice and chose his words carefully. "I do agree that she has a very convincing complexion, but that will be her decision."

Alice's desire to have this account made her nod. "Okay, but I think there should be more than one face to launch your product. There are different degrees of color to African Americans and I think we should take advantage of that."

Maloney nodded enthusiastically. "I agree, as long as you're one of them."

"Yes," Alice said again.

"Then where do I sign?" Maloney said with a wide smile. "I don't think we'll regret this alliance."

Alice pulled out the contract and handed it to Maloney. She had a feeling the woman had made up her mind before she got there.

As Maloney signed the contract, Andrew grinned. He'd had no doubt that Alice would have gotten the contract, and was glad that he'd come to give her, if nothing more, moral support.

"Ever since I was a little girl I wanted to do this," Maloney said. "We started off with a beauty parlor. We created our own hair care products. When I got divorced, I thought the dream would die along with my marriage, but my sisters stood by me and, well, here I am, with the help of God, holding strong. My daughter and I will be in South Beach next week on vacation. She's never been to Florida and I think she's too old for Disney World but not for South Beach." She laughed.

"Please let us know the exact date when you'll be there and we can have dinner together again," Andrew said. He looked at Alice.

"Of course."

"I'm toying with the idea of creating a fragrance. I want something unique made from flowers. What do you think, Alice?"

"Yes, that would be wonderful. We can help with that, too."

Maloney nodded. "I'm very happy with the decision we've made."

"Welcome to the family," Alice said.

"Thank you, I think we're going to have a lot of fun."

When dinner arrived, they talked some more; Alice about her childhood in Jamaica and Maloney of hers growing up in the San Fernando Valley in California.

Andrew was more fascinated with Alice's childhood than Maloney's but only he knew that.

———

The next morning, Alice and Andrew had breakfast in their hotel room and got ready to leave for home.

"We need to come back to New York just for fun," he said, looking around to make sure they weren't leaving anything behind. He opened the door for her. "We'll wait until it gets warm, then come back. What do you say?"

"I say yes. This campaign will take root and grow in a few months. Then we'll have time again."

———

There was one thing Andrew couldn't get out of his mind, and thought he had to be upfront with Alice; so, on the plane he asked her again about Alvin. "Did you ever talk to this Alvin fellow when you were in college?"

He took her off guard. She'd been thinking of how she'd handle the account to make it the best, and didn't quite hear him.

"Alice," he said, gently touching her hand.

"Yes."

"I wanted to know about Alvin."

"Oh, we went to the same university, that's all. I don't think we said two words to each other while we were in school. But when I saw him outside my hotel when I came to Florida for the first time, he told me that I'd broken his heart because he'd been in love with me in college but couldn't approach me. I thought that was the most ridiculous thing I'd ever heard." Thinking of Alvin, her voice was shakier than she would have liked. As a matter of fact, she would have been more comfortable if just the mention of his name didn't send fear down her spine.

"Well, I went a bit further than just leaving him alone when I dropped you off at your mother's house that evening."

She looked up at him. "What do you mean, Andrew?"

"I called a friend of mine at the Ft. Lauderdale police station and asked him to run a background check on the guy. He's been to prison for fraud, Alice."

Her mouth fell open as she stared at him dumbfounded. "What!"

"I didn't do anything. I just told my friend that he'd applied for a job with Frank's. I'm sorry, Alice, but I had to know if this guy was dangerous or violent. Turns out he's just a two-bit con artist." His fingers intertwined with hers.

She turned her head and looked out the window at the dark ugly clouds that were forming. Then she looked back at him. "You know, you always want to think that the people you go to school with at least landed a respectful job." She shook her head. "I know, I may be the bleeding heart here, but that's just who I am. I didn't trust him, I feared him."

"There's no need for you to fear him, or have anything to do with him anymore."

"I know." She leaned her head against his shoulder, and in a few minutes she was back thinking of her account. She had no time for people who didn't care about themselves.

Chapter Twenty One

At work the next day, Alice began working on the campaign to launch Deveraux's products. She spoke with Danielle via Skype in the conference room. And just one look at her beautiful, milk chocolate complexion and pretty face decided that she wanted her for the campaign. They talked for an hour, during which Alice had to almost beg her to be a part of this for the company's sake, for her mother's sake, for her father's sake. She didn't know which one worked; maybe it was when Andrew said, "Do it for us, Danny. And don't you think it's time you buried the hatchet and talked with your parents? They miss you terribly, you know."

She laughed. "I'll do it for you guys. And Andrew?"

"Yes."

"Begging doesn't suit you." She took a pause and looked at the two people in the small space. "Who does the account belong to?"

"Me," Alice said.

She nodded. "I see. This will seal the deal. Are you guys an item?… Hold on before you answer." She hurried to say, "I only ask this because I once had the biggest crush on Andrew."

"Had?" Andrew said with mock hurt, holding Alice's hand and laughing.

"Yes. I think I'm over you. I met a special guy."

"Congratulations, and yes, Alice and I are an item."

Alice looked up at his perfectly beaming face and shook her head. "I thought we were keeping it a secret."

"Ahhh, we're only telling her," he said sheepishly with a slight stutter as he looked from one woman to the next.

"Guys, this is a two-way video and audio. I can hear you." Danielle laughed out loud and so did Alice when she covered her face with her hands.

"I'll come home in a few weeks. Will that be soon enough?" They both said, "Yes," together.

When they'd disconnected from Danielle, Andrew turned to Alice and asked. "When do I get to meet your mother and sister?"

She didn't look at him. "Ahhh, when would you like to meet them?"

"Whenever you say. We have all the appropriate wheels turning on your project so you don't have to work so hard right now, certainly not on weekends. I'm free any Saturday or Sunday."

"I'll let you know." This was one time when the ring would definitely move from her left hand to her right hand and stay there for a while. She'd been playing around with the ring at work, moving it from her left hand to her right thinking no one would think anything of it. But Andrew had noticed each time he saw it on her right hand.

Hopefully the children wouldn't talk too much about him having breakfast at the house every morning. She picked up her paperwork and hugged it to her chest. "I need to work on these."

"I know," he said. He was sitting on the edge of the desk and noticed that she'd put up a protective wall between them. He cocked his head to one side. "Everything all right?"

She nodded. "Everything's wonderful."

"Good." He got off the desk and opened the door, then walked through with her.

Andrew went into Ben's office and Alice went to her office. She placed the paperwork on her desk, sat down and dialed Nikki's number on her cell. She had not spoken to her in a while. She certainly didn't know anything about Andrew. Nikki answered on the second ring. "Hey lady," she said.

Alice laughed. "Don't start cursing because I haven't called."

"I would never do that. You just started a new life, so I thought you'd be very busy with work, the children and settling in."

"Yes, I have been." She sighed and leaned back in her chair. "I met someone."

Nikki was silent for a few seconds.

"Was that too fast? I mean—I met him before I left New York."

"And?"

"Well, we work together." She stuck a fingernail in her teeth.

"Keep going. This guy must be very special for you to want to tell me about him."

"Yeah. He stuck a ring on my finger."

Nikki gasped. "Alice. Wow! Does he know everything there is to know about your current situation?"

"Yeah, pretty much. You remember me talking about Willetta Benton, the woman who worked for me a long time ago and now works for the airlines?"

"Mmmm. I think so."

"Andrew is her brother. Nik, he's a great guy, the kind every woman dreams about. Sometimes I think he's too good to be true."

"I didn't hear handsome in there."

"Gorgeous would be the word I'd use to describe him."

"Okay, so what's the problem? He wants to meet the family?"

Alice laughed. "Yeah. And he's white. Should that bother me? I never dated a white man before."

"Oh, come on Lise. Your grandfather was a white man, married to a black woman. We Islanders are so mixed up when it comes to color and culture that his being white shouldn't be a concern for you or Mom."

She smiled. Nikki could always set her straight on matters of that nature.

"How does he get on with the children? I'm assuming he's already met them?"

"Yes he has, and Alia is nuts about him. Phillip is cautious. But he adores them both."

"Good, then it's time he met your sister from different parents. You're still coming home end of spring, right?"

"Yes."

"Then introduce him to Mom. Tell him that I have to give my stamp of approval before he even thinks of marching down the aisle with you, and…" She heard her name over the PA system. "I have to go. Give everyone my love and I'll call you in a couple days."

"Thanks, Nik. Go save lives. Love you."

"Love you too, sis. Hey what about Alvin?"

"Nightmare, mistake, horror. Talk with you later."

Alice hung up and began working. For some reason she wanted to get involved in every facet of this account. She began calling buyers from the major department stores: Nordstrom, Neiman Marcus, Bloomingdale's, but mostly, she wanted Nordstrom and Neiman. She set an appointment to talk to the buyer at Neiman Marcus for the next week. Nordstrom would get back to her.

She'd noticed that these stores didn't carry any straight line for people of color and thought that needed to be rectified. She herself used a doctor's brand exclusively, which Sephora carried; but on occasion, she would buy a compact of a different brand from Nordstrom or Neiman, which brought to mind another store. She called Sephora and set up an appointment to talk with the buyer; this too would be over the phone.

Sitting back, she thought awhile about dinner with her mother. She knew Gen would be very happy to meet Andrew, but she cared more for her mother's feelings and opinion then Gen's in this matter. She dialed her mother's number, Merl answered. "Mom, how are you?"

Merl laughed. "I'm fine, little one; just taking a nap to get ready for work at four."

"Okay, I'll make this quick. Are you working on Saturday or Sunday?"

"Saturday, but not Sunday, why?"

"I would like to bring a friend of mine over to meet you. How does dinner at your place sound? I'll have Delia come over and cook."

"Sounds fine, but your sister can cook. Poor Delia has the children to run her ragged every day, and I don't want to add to it by having her cook for us. Will this be a man or woman?"

"Does it matter?" Alice squinted and made a face when her voice squeaked.

"Ahhh, so it is a man. You young people move so fast these days, I can't keep up."

"It's not like that, Mom. It's someone I work with, but he's pretty special."

"You know I only want you to be happy, little one."

"Yes, Mom. I know."

"So bring him over. What does he like to eat?"

"Anything Jamaican, but let's not traumatize him with goat's head soup." She laughed.

Merl cracked up. "Who drinks that stuff? Your sister cannot stand it. The meat, yes, the head, no." She was still laughing.

"Okay, Mom, thanks for this. He's really a very nice guy."

"He must be for you to bring him to meet us."

"I'll see you on Sunday at about four?"

"Yes, four will be good. God bless you, Lise. Be careful, will you?"

"Yes, Mom. I love you. Oh, Nikki sends her love."

"Right back at her when you speak again. Love you loads, little one. See you soon."

"See you soon, Mom."

She dialed Andrew's number and as soon as he picked up, she said, "How does Sunday at four for dinner with Mom sound?"

"Sounds like a date. Are you sure?"

"What kind of a question is that? You wanted to meet my mother and now you ask if I'm sure. Do you want to back out?" she blurted, scarcely aware of her own tone of voice.

"Absolutely not." His voice lulled her into a relaxed mood. "But in my office you seemed a bit preoccupied when I asked."

"No, it's just that the only man who'd ever met my mother is Harvey. I don't know what she'll think."

"Alice, you respect your mother a lot and even though I haven't met her yet, I respect her too. But when the door closes at the end of the day, it's our lives and what we do with it that really matters."

She smiled at his words. "I know. I told her you were a very nice person."

"It matters a lot what you think of me," he said in a serious, committed tone.

"I know and I love you for that. There are three special people in my life that you have to meet. One is my very best friend. Then there's my mother and sister, Gen. I don't have a lot of friends because I take friendship very seriously." She chuckled. "I don't want to sound like a nudge, but I can't stand people who say they'll call me back and never do. I think it's ill-mannered, and I don't have time for people who have no manners."

He laughed. "Nikki would be the very best friend, and the ones without manners will be the ones I never meet?"

"Yes."

"Well, for me, you've already met my sister so my mother is next."

She shuddered. It was one thing for him to meet her mother but a whole nother thing for her to meet his mother. "Yes, but things are a bit too hectic for us to travel to England right now."

"I can bring her here."

She took a quick breath of astonishment. Things were moving a mile a minute. She couldn't handle it. "Andrew, can we wait awhile for me to meet your mother?"

He chuckled. He had a feeling this would be her reaction. "Of course, my darling. Just tell me when you're ready."

She gave a sigh of relief. She may never be ready for that one. "Of course. Okay, I have to go. See you in a few."

"Okay." Even when he heard the click on the other end of the line, Andrew still held the receiver in his hand. He knew she was still nervous about the Deveraux account. He shook his head. She had nothing to be nervous about, but another thing he'd noticed was that she was a perfectionist. He knew she would never fail. Unfortunately, she still thought of her marriage as one thing she'd failed at.

As soon as she hung up from Andrew, Alice got a call from the children's school; Phillip fell of the monkey bars. Before the teacher finished her sentence, Alice said, "I'll be right there." She grabbed her purse and was out the door. "My son had a little accident at school. I have to go," she said. "Will you let Andrew know? Tell him it's nothing serious. He fell off a monkey bars."

"Hope it's nothing too serious," Lee Ann said to thin air as Alice ran down the hallway.

Alice got into her car, backed out of the overcrowded parking lot and sped across town to the children's school, which was not too far from home.

The first thing she saw when she entered the nurse's office was the still bleeding swollen lip of her son. Ignoring the fact that she wore a white silk blouse, she bent and gathered him into her arms. "Are you all right? Are you badly hurt?" she asked, crushing him to her.

Phillip laughed. "Mom, look, I have a fat lip."

Easing him away a bit, she looked at him trying not to laugh. She shook her head. "Doesn't it hurt a lot?"

He shook his head. "No, I didn't even chip a tooth. My teacher said I was lucky I landed in the sand."

"You're such a big boy." She took the ice pack from him and held it to his lip, then turned to the teacher. "Sorry I burst in like that. I think I'm taking it harder than he is. He's never been hurt before." She forced a smile as she examined the small cut on his lip.

"I can see that," Lillian Johnson said. "It's not as bad as it seems. He's just a bleeder, but he took it all in stride. He didn't even cry." She glanced down at Phillip.

Phillip nodded and tried to smile as his mother handed him back the ice pack and stood to talk with Lillian.

"I think I'll take him home for the rest of the day."

Lillian nodded. "I'll get his sister for you."

"Thank you." Alice picked up Phillip in her arms. When she'd enrolled the children in school and met the red-headed, petite Lillian, she wanted to ask if she was in an accident and why she walked with a limp. But as she watched her walk away, she noticed that the limp was less pronounced. She concluded that it might have been an accident after all. She kept holding the ice pack to Phillip's lip while he rested his head on her shoulder. Her cell rang, but she ignored it.

As Alia appeared with her bag and Lillian with Phillip's, she thanked her. "I'm sure he'll be better tomorrow. Are they doing well in school?"

"They are both very bright children," Lillian said, then added, "and extremely mannerly."

"Thank you, Lillian."

Lillian touched Phillip's arm. "Feel better and I'll see you tomorrow."

He nodded.

Belting the children into their car seat, Alice kissed them both then slid in behind the wheel.

"Why are you bleeding?" Alia asked her brother.

"I fell off the monkey bars."

"Does it hurt?"

"A little, but I held on longer than the other boys."

Alia laughed. "Mom, I never fall off the monkey bar because I never climb it. It's too high for me."

"Good girl," Alice said, rolling out of the parking lot. She glanced back at Phillip. He was still holding the ice pack to his lip. "I'll put you in your pajamas and you can relax on the couch with Alia and watch television, okay."

"Okay, Mom."

When she opened the garage door, Delia opened the washroom door. Before asking why Alice was home so early, she saw Phillip holding the ice pack to his lip. "What happened? Why didn't you call me?" she opened the door and took Phillip in her arms.

"It's not too bad, Delia. He fell off the monkey bars." Alice unbuckled Alia and walked through the open door.

"I could have picked them up," Delia said over her shoulder.

"It's all right. I can work from home for the rest of the day. I feel better being near him right now even though his lip doesn't need stitches."

"Okay, I'll give them a bath and get their pajamas on." She glanced over her shoulder as she walked down the hallway to the children's room. "Did you have lunch, Miss Alice?"

"No, I'll make myself a sandwich, then work from my office." She placed her purse on the table and answered the constant ringing cell. "Hi, Andrew."

"Is he all right? What happened?"

She smiled. "Thanks for the concern, but the way he put it, he stayed on the monkey bar longer than the other boys. He'll be fine, just a fat lip. I'll work from home for the rest of the day." She kicked off her shoes, picked them up then walked to her bedroom.

"Thank heavens. I can work from home with you," he offered.

"That's not necessary, Andrew. I have a few phone calls to make."

"Then I'll leave early."

There was something warm and enchanting in his concern for her family that made her smile. "Thanks, Andrew. I'll have Delia make something special for dinner. See you later then."

"Okay. Don't work too hard."

"I won't." She hung up, took off her suit and slipped into something comfortable. She peeked in on the children in the tub. Delia had smeared Vaseline on Phillip's lip with special instructions for him not to lick or touch his lip.

After helping to dry them off and put on their pajamas, Alice tucked them into blankets on the couch in the family room.

The sun had deserted the skies and in its place gray clouds threatened rain. It had cooled off quite a bit and the wind picked up. The cold front had made it. And while Delia made a big pot of Milo, Alice went into her office to work. The first thing she did was make reservations for dinner at Mitu on Las Olas Boulevard for the Deverauxs, herself, and Andrew for the following week.

She leaned back in her chair when the rain began pounding the roof. Delia came in with a chicken sandwich and a mug of Milo.

"Perfect day for hot Milo and sitting in front of the fireplace," Delia said.

"Or hot Milo and watching or listening to the rain." She took the mug from Delia and brought it to her lips. "Andrew will be having dinner with us this evening." She peered at her over the mug.

"He eats anything we put before him, but do you know what his favorite food is?" Delia asked.

"Is that your round about way of asking how much I know about him?" she smiled.

"No. I know you like him a lot, so you must know his likes and dislikes." She shrugged. "I just wanted to know if there is anything special that he likes."

Alice took a breath and threw her feet on top of the desk. "I know he likes French food. But why don't we try making him an honorary Jamaican. We'll all be having dinner at Mom's on Sunday and I told her he likes Jamaican food, which he does. So let's make him something Jamaican. Do we have any snappers?"

"Yes. Do you want me to make bammy and fried fish?"

"Yes, and some pumpkin soup." She glanced outside at the pouring rain. "Seems the perfect day for it."

"Will do. Dinner will be ready by six."

"Okay. Thanks Delia. You're a godsend."

Delia looked at her. "I know. I'm making sure you can never do without me."

"That's a given. How was your visit with your friend the other day?"

Delia sat in the chair against the wall and wrinkled her nose. "I don't know. Maybe it's me, but she seemed a bit jealous when I described my life with you guys. She said being a domestic isn't something to boast about. I told her I didn't think of myself as a domestic but an integral part of the family." She looked directly into Alice's eyes. "After all, you've never treated me any other way."

Alice nodded, smiled, placed her mug on the desk and got up to give her a very meaningful hug. "No, Delia, we've never treated you any other way. You are my family. We've been through divorce and we're still together." She pushed away from her and looked into her eyes. "I feel so honored that you said that."

Delia shrugged. "We've always been that, right?"

"Yes, we have."

Delia threw a smile at her then walked out of the office.

Chapter Twenty Two

Andrew came home to Alice straight from the office, his hair dripping wet from the rain. "How is he?" he said, coming through the door and kissing her cheek.

She saw the lines of concern on his brows, heard it in his voice and marveled at how much he genuinely loved and cared for her children. "He's fine, really. They're watching television." She pointed to the family room where the children lay on the couch with Tee Tee very close by.

He walked into the family room while Alice went to get a towel to dry his hair. When she walked back into the room, for the first time she saw her son on Andrew's knee. She smiled and ran the towel through Andrew's hair pulling the band from it. *This is good*, she thought, *very good*.

Delia handed him a cup of hot Milo which he'd never had before. He lifted it to his mouth without asking what it was. Both Delia and Alice watched his reaction. He nodded. "This is very good. It has a chocolaty taste. What is it?"

"It's Milo, a Caribbean drink," Alice said. "We all love it, especially when it gets cold or rains like it's doing now."

Delia went back to the kitchen.

"Something smells wonderful," he said, placing the mug on the coffee table and leaning back with Phillip still on his knee.

"How are you feeling?" He looked to see his lip not as swollen as he thought it would have been.

"Better," Phillip said.

Alia placed herself on Andrew's lap and leaned her head against his shoulder. *Daddy's home,* he thought to himself. He'd longed for the day when Phillip would warm up to him. He now felt like he fit into this little family. He leaned back with the children and Alice went back to her office to finish up her work, soon to return with her mug in hand to be with them.

In less than an hour, Delia announced that dinner was on the table. The children's fish was free of bones, but the others' included heads and bones, just the way it should be. Instead of frying the bammy in a lot of oil, Delia had coated it with olive oil and placed it in the oven on a baking sheet until it was brown and crisp. She'd used red peppers, onions, garlic, vinegar, scotch bonnet and a little oil to do the escoviche. The plantains were also done in the oven.

"You're gonna love this, Uncle Andrew," Phillip said when Alice placed a few pieces of plantains on his plate.

The children's meals usually didn't contain any kind of pepper, but the adults' did. There's no way one could make an authentic Jamaican escoviched fish without scotch bonnet pepper. Alice watched Andrew in amazement as he ate the spicy food without even getting red faced.

And as a reward for enjoying this spicy authentic Jamaican dish, Andrew enjoyed a generous helping of potato- cornmeal pudding.

Delia removed the dishes from the table and went to put the children to bed. After Alice and Andrew placed the dishes in the dishwasher, they stood on the patio each with a snifter of Disaronno liqueur. The rain had stopped, but the wind still shuffled the leaves on the trees enough to be heard. Seemingly, a million frogs croaked in the lake and the smell of jasmine permeated the air. "I really do love the smell of jasmines," Andrew said, as he took Alice's hand and they made their way through the gate, out of the patio area toward the lake.

"Glad you like it. I planted them just for you." Her voice held a hint of laughter.

"You planted this before we found each other," he said while placing a hand around her shoulder and guiding her to the side of the house where the children couldn't look out their window and see him kiss their mother. He set both snifters on the slate picnic table and kissed her upturned lips. "I've waited all day to do this," he said, kissing her nose then a gentle lingering kiss to her waiting mouth.

A tingling of excitement raced through her as his fingers trailed sensuously down her arm. They'd made love only once or maybe four times within a twelve-hour period but now she wanted to feel his body naked on hers once again.

His lips traced down to her neck and she felt the heady sensation that traveled to her inner thighs. "Stay with me tonight," she whispered breathlessly.

"The children," he replied nibbling on her earlobe. "Come home with me. I'll bring you back before they awake."

Somehow his plan was sounder than hers. They wouldn't have to whisper or be careful with sounds or movements at his home.

"Okay," she breathed but wasn't sure if she could last that long. She dragged him inside and called to Delia. "Delia, we're going out for a while. Don't wait up."

"Okay." Delia called back.

Alice picked up her purse and Andrew followed her. The pleasure he felt at how focused she was radiated outward as he quickly opened her door and ran around to the driver's side.

The old Volvo had not been driven that fast in a very long time and when they got off the freeway, Alice turned to him and said, "You need a new car. This car is for an old person."

She watched him grimace but said nothing as he nodded. His fingers gently massaged hers and she inched closer to him, causing her dress to creep up onto her thighs.

With just one glance, Andrew took a deep breath and slowly exhaled as his foot pressed down on the accelerator. If he got a speeding ticket now, it would be worth the reward.

When they finally got to his place, he hurriedly parked. Alice didn't wait for him to open her door. They raced to the elevator, which showed it was on the tenth floor. So they raced up the stairs and were quite out of breath by the time they got to his floor. Inside, they both leaned against the closed door and burst out laughing. "How about a glass of wine?" Andrew asked.

She nodded and sat on the stool. They recovered fast from the run up the stairs, and when Andrew stood before her and handed her the glass, his hand gently caressed her thigh, sending her once more into heightened ecstasy. And as he aroused her passion, his own grew stronger. The wine forgotten on the counter, he picked her up and took her to the bedroom. Laying her gently on the bed, passion took over, and she grabbed his collar and pulled him to her.

His lips caught hers and began a gentle massage that sent currents of desire through her as his tongue slipped between her half-open lips.

She began unbuttoning his shirt and reluctantly he tore his lips from hers and pulled the shirt over his head. Quickly but gently he undressed her as if he'd been doing it all his life and within minutes they lay naked touching each other in places that sent their arousal to a height so great, neither could wait. There wasn't any time for foreplay; they were to the brink of pain. Andrew's hand gently traveled over her ripened nipples, and his hot mouth covered and gently pulled as he lowered his body over her and entered her with a force that made her cry out. "Did I hurt you?" he asked, alarmed.

"No." Alice breathed lightly between parted lips when he immediately found that spot that sent her emotions into overdrive. She looped her legs behind him and pulled him into her as together they found that tempo that bound their bodies together. The blood pounded in her brain and her entire body shivered as she was drawn to a passion even greater than before. Her cry for release was answered as his lips claimed hers. The gentle massaging of that sweet spot took her higher as the turbulence of his passion swirled around her sweetly, giving her that release she so craved.

She returned the favor by clamping down on his manhood as he moved inside her and felt him shudder and moan with delight.

He quickly slid off her and she could hear his heart beat when he gathered her into his arms. Wet together, they lay savoring the feeling of satisfaction they'd given each other.

Too late! They both remembered they'd not used protection and Alice had not used the pill in years. "It's all right," she told him.

"Are you sure?" he asked, concern for her well-being clearly expressed on his face.

She nodded. "Yes, it'll be all right," she said, remembering how difficult it was for her to get pregnant with the twins.

She pulled closer into him and kissed his lips as he turned toward her and smiled. He would marry her in a heartbeat.

But for Alice, she had no intentions of rushing into another marriage right now, even though she was head-over- heels in love with Andrew. With her head on his chest listening to the thumping of his heart, she closed her eyes in the safety of his warmth. His naked body so close to her, his long fingers caressing her cheek, she succumbed to the numbed sleep of the satisfied lover.

At midnight, still in Andrew's arms, Alice turned on her back and looked up at the ceiling. Remembering their passionate lovemaking and the rush to get to his house, she smiled pleasantly. Turning to look at his face, her breast crushed against the hardness of his chest, awakening desires she wanted to fight against. She didn't want him to think she was a nymphomaniac or something.

But gazing into those green eyes, she knew he was as awake as she was. She ran her hand along his flat belly to... yes, he was awake and shared her same desire.

"Hi, had a good sleep?" he said, his big body turned fully toward her.

Feeling the hardness against her thighs, she took a deep breath. "Yes."

Skin to skin, once again they were one as his hand wandered over her silken body to that soft wet spot that called out for him. He slowly slid on top of her and she welcomed him into her body once more. She quickly matched his movement as the real world spun and careened on its axis. His strokes were long and purposeful, and she pulled him deeper into her body back to that sweet spot which he massaged until she cried out with pure delight as he brought her to that divine ecstasy that made her shudder with satisfaction. She closed hard around him and felt him shudder against her in a moment of uncontrolled passion.

He quickly rolled off her, once again pulled her into his arms and covered her mouth in a long hungry kiss. Parting, she whispered, "I love you so much, it scares me."

He looked into her eyes. "Please don't be scared. I didn't think my love for you could grow any more, but each day it grows more and more. Love me without fear, Alice because I won't hurt you or let you go."

She smiled and wanted to believe every word he spoke. She nodded.

His long legs touched the floor, and he gathered her in his arms. She clung to his damp neck as he took her to the bathroom for a refreshing cool shower. He pinned up her hair so it wouldn't get wet and bent to accommodate her height as she shampooed his hair. "This is the second time you've done that," he said with a chuckle.

"It's the second time we've made love, and I love doing this," she said, making sure the soap didn't get into his eyes.

"This was very exciting."

"What?" she asked knowing fully well what he meant.

"This rushing to make love thing. I thought I'd never make it."

"Especially having to run up the stairs." She laughed rinsing the shampoo from his hair.

He ran the soap over her body, rinsed her off then himself and towel-dried them both.

They dressed and leisurely took the elevator, sauntered across the street to the beach and walked barefoot on the cool sand. "Are you cold?" he asked as she pushed her hand inside his sweater.

"No, I just love the feel of your skin."

"Careful, we don't want to rush back upstairs, do we?"

She looked up at him in wonderment. "Really?"

"I can never get enough of your brain or your body." His arm around her shoulder, he gave a gentle squeeze. "You make me feel like a teenager again."

"And you me." She wasn't kidding. She couldn't remember making love twice in one night or in the case of their first time, four times in a twelve-hour period. She held on to him as they walked in the quiet darkness of the night with only the gentle, mysterious ocean lapping at their feet.

When they crossed the street and got into his car, he cringed when she repeated, "We really have to get rid of this car; time to update."

He swallowed and nodded. He'd had the Volvo for more than twelve years, got it tuned up every year and didn't even think of trading her in, but if Alice said he should, then that's exactly what he'd do. Plus, it still had memories of his wife that he needed to let go of.

"Will you miss it a lot?" she asked, watching the shadows cross his face at the thought of letting go of his car.

He shook his head. "It's time," he said without elaboration.

"How about Saturday?"

"Yes."

"What should we look for?"

"You choose."

"BMW, Porsche, Mercedes."

"You choose," he repeated thinking she would choose BMW like her own car.

"Porsche," she said, looking straight ahead at the passing cars.

He nodded. "Any particular model?"

"They now have a four-door sedan; Panamera, I think."

"Okay."

"Why are you agreeing to everything I suggest?" she asked turning with a quizzical look on her face.

"I love you and want to please you."

"But this is not for me, it's for you."

"I know." He grinned.

When Andrew dropped her home, they were very quiet in order not to wake anyone. He kissed her at the door and she hugged him. "Don't worry; I'll make the parting very painless."

— ∞ —

Alice was true to her word when they went to the Porsche dealer to buy Andrew's new car. All he had to do was pay for it. She wasn't surprised when he paid cash for the car. But she was surprised when he insisted that her name be added to the ownership papers. All her protest fell on deaf ears. She finally gave up and signed with him.

On Sunday, at her mother's house, Andrew was welcomed with open arms, after the children, of course. When Delia and the children walked into the living room, Merl now paid attention to her new guest.

"Finally we meet," Andrew said, bending to hug the plump five-foot-one inch mother of his fiancée.

Merl was about to say, *I wish I could say I've heard a lot about you*, but thought it would be in bad taste. "It's wonderful to meet you," Merl said moving away from the door to allow the couple entry. She got the impression from Alice that this was just a special friend from the office but Andrew seemed more than just a casual friend. When she hugged her daughter, she whispered, "Is there anything I should know about?"

Alice shook her head and headed inside with her hand around her mother's shoulder.

Coming out of the kitchen, Genevieve cleared her throat. Andrew turned and greeted her warmly. "I know who you are," he said hugging her.

Gen snickered and looked at her sister with amusement. "You know, Alice hasn't really told us anything about you." She looked up at Andrew and smiled devilishly.

Andrew cast an innocent look in Alice's direction. "Am I in trouble?"

She shrugged. "I suppose we'll find out by the end of dinner."

He was keenly aware of both women's scrutiny. Alice had not really told them anything about him.

Merl invited them onto the patio to sit and chat before dinner. She offered Andrew and Alice a drink of wine then sat and looked at Andrew.

No one had paid much attention to the ring on Alice's right hand. To them it was just a ring; if they noticed it at all.

Sitting on her mother's lap, Alia caressed the ring on her finger and Alice talked about how cool and wet the weather had been the past few days.

Gen came to the door. "My food does not taste very good cold, so, dinner is served." She stood aside and beckoned with her hand to make sure they knew she was serious.

At the table, Gen made sure she placed Andrew between her and Merl, then gave Alice a winning smile.

As they ate, Alice could tell that Andrew was winning Gen over with his charm and wit. But although Merl was very charming toward him, she wondered what her mother's true feelings were.

"So, Andrew, how long have you been in this country?" Merl asked, noting his crisp British accent. She also wanted to make sure her daughter had not chosen a friend who wanted his green card.

Andrew placed his utensils on the side of his plate and caressed his chin. "I was actually born in New York. My parents moved to London when I was only a baby. My sister and I came back to live in the States after college."

Hmmm, Alice had not known that.

"Does your mother live in London?" Gen asked.

"Yes, but she visits the States at least once or twice per year. She has a lot of friends here."

"Do you spend a lot of time in London with your mother then?" Gen asked again.

Janice Angelique

"I try to be with her on the holidays, you know, Christmas, Easter."

"Any brothers?"

"No, just my sister."

And then came the big question that Alice knew Gen, not her mother, would have asked.

"Ever been married, Andrew?" Gen asked, casually cutting into her curried chicken.

"Yes. I am divorced." He glanced at Alice and she gave him a you-asked-for-it look.

Gen nodded at his answer. "Don't you like my cooking?" she asked.

He didn't miss a beat. "Of course, it's delicious." He picked up his utensils and began eating the gravy- slathered rice and peas.

Alice snickered, still looking in her plate, and cleared her throat. "Well, Andrew, I guess you're in the clear," she said, glancing from her mother to her sister.

And for the first time, Merl noticed the ring on her daughter's finger. She was about to comment on its beauty when Alice realized what her question would be.

"Mother, we have to talk later this evening," she said, cutting her off at the pass, so to speak, and looking at her under her lashes.

Merl nodded slowly.

When dinner was over, they enjoyed tea on the patio. Knowing how much her mother loved to sing, and how much everyone, including herself, loved to listen to her, Alice smiled. "Mom."

"Yes, dear."

"Sing for us."

Merl smiled. "Andrew doesn't want to hear an old woman mangle notes, dear."

Alice glanced at Gen and they both laughed. "You mangle a note? Never!" Alice said.

Merl shook her head. "Acapella?"

"I'll play for you, Mom," Andrew said, remembering that he'd seen a piano somewhere in the house. "Just point me to the piano and tell me what key you wish to sing in."

Gen glanced at her mother, then at Alice, who shrugged.

They walked to the living room. Merl chose "Through The Eyes Of Love," a song dear to her heart.

At the sound of her voice, Andrew's eyes lit up as his fingers gracefully slid across the black and white keys. When Merl took the high note, he literally got goose bumps.

Merl finished singing and he stood and applauded. "You have the most beautiful voice I've ever heard," he said, hugging her.

"You make an old lady feel very good," Merl replied, laughing.

"Your boyfriend is a good hugger," Gen whispered to Alice.

"Shush."

Gen noted that Alice didn't deny that he was her boyfriend. If she was trying to hide something, she'd failed.

"It's true, you have a very powerful voice, Mom," Alice said. She looked at Andrew, who was still shaking his head.

"Magnificent," he said.

It was after six when Alice decided that she had to go home, but before she left, she helped her sister and Delia clear the table and put the dishes into the dishwasher, leaving Andrew and her mother alone to talk for a while. She hoped Merl had not asked what his intentions were.

"I don't think you'll get to know him in just one evening, Mom, so, we'll be back soon." She kissed her mother's and sister's cheeks. "I'll call you guys later," she said, waving as she walked out to Andrew's brand new Porsche.

When they got to her home, Andrew helped with the sleeping children and stayed for a while sipping cognac with Alice on the patio. "Alone at last," he said, pressing his hand into Alice's. "How did I do? Do you think your mother and sister like me?"

"They absolutely love you."

"How do you know that?"

"Because, if they didn't, they wouldn't have asked you all those questions." She laughed.

He drained his glass.

"Are you leaving?"

"Yes, I have to talk to Benjamin. He left a message for me to call him as soon as I get home. By the way, when is the dinner meeting with Maloney?"

"On Tuesday at 7:30."

"I'll mark it on my calendar."

"Thank you for a wonderful weekend," she said.

"No, thank you. You took me to heaven's door. Talked me into buying a new car and... introduced me to your family. What more can I ask for?"

She smiled. "There's one more for you to meet."

"I know. Nikki."

She nodded.

He pulled her into his arms and kissed her hard.

"Wow!" her eyes fluttered. "A kiss like that will drive a woman insane."

"Should I do it again?"

"Yes, please." Her face upturned, her lips still warm and moist, she gave herself freely to the passion of his kiss.

They parted just in time to see Alia come onto the patio. Andrew smiled and lifted her in his arms. "I will see you in the morning," he said to her, then placed her back on her feet.

Alice held Alia's hand and walked Andrew to the door. "See you in the morning?" he said to Alice before leaving.

"Yes."

He walked through the door and she closed it behind him. She stood looking at the closed door until Alia touched the ring on her finger and said, "Mama, I love your new ring."

She smiled at her. "Thank you, honey. Now it's time for you to go to sleep." She picked her up and kissed her.

"Are you going to marry Uncle Andrew?"

It was not as if she didn't expect the question. The children had never seen a man come and go so often in their home except for their father, but she was not quite prepared for it so soon. "Not right now, sweetie."

"Later?"

"Much later. You like Uncle Andrew, don't you?"

"Yes, is he gonna be our new daddy?"

"Do you want him to be?"

Alia shrugged and Alice didn't continue the conversation, but placed her daughter in bed. With a kiss on her cheek and one on Phillip's cheek, she turned off the light and closed the door.

She walked into her bedroom to a ringing phone. She picked up the receiver. "Hello, Mother."

"Hello, darling. It was so nice meeting your fiancée today."

Alice didn't answer for a few seconds. "Why do you call him my fiancée?"

"Alice, I've been your mother since before you were born. I saw the way you both looked at each other. I think that man would go to the ends of the earth for you. Plus, although you wear the ring on your right hand, I know you'd never buy such an expensive ring for yourself."

"Oh Mom," she breathed. "You don't think we're moving too fast?"

Merl took a deep breath. "So you're really divorced?"

"Mom, I was divorced for a very long time before I actually signed the papers."

"I'm sorry. I really liked Harvey, but I can tell that Andrew loves you."

"You don't mind that he's white?"

Merl chuckled. "No. I don't mind. I would be slapping my father in the face if I said I did. Does Andrew make you happy?"

"Very happy, Mom. And as far as Harvey is concerned, I think I already told you that I'm the one who divorced him. There's no reason why you can't still like him."

"I know. So when will we see you again?"

"Maybe on the weekend or one day in the week. But it goes two ways you know, Mom. You can visit too. The children will be happy to see more of their grandmother."

"Yeah, I'll work on that. Take care and be happy, my darling."

"You too, Mom. I love you very much."

"I love you too, little one—Oh, wait, your sister wants to say hi."

When Gen came to the phone, her first words were, "Couldn't you have found a black man anywhere in Miami?"

She wasn't very surprised. "The heart wants what the heart wants, my sweet sister. Do you love him any less?"

"I wish I could say yes, but he's gorgeous."

"So it's jealousy?"

"Absolutely."

"I love you, too, big sis. Talk with you later." Alice hung up the phone, pulled the covers to her chin and lie there gazing at the ceiling. Her mother and sister loved him, but still deep down she feared the relationship. She reached across and turned off the light. Tonight, she didn't even turn on the television to put her to sleep.

Chapter Twenty Three

M onday morning, Alice drove in with Andrew. All morning she locked herself in her office working hard on the Deveraux account. She wanted to have everything ready for the woman. At 1 p.m., she had lunch with the Neiman's buyer who was in town for just one day.

On Tuesday evening, while Alice went over all the information she'd gathered with the help of the other departments, Andrew walked into her office. "Are you ready?" He leaned across the desk and kissed her.

"You keep doing that with the door open and someone is bound to see us."

"Will that be such a bad thing? I'm bursting to tell everyone."

She laughed as he walked back and closed the door. He sat cross-legged before her and gazed at her smiling face. "What?"

"My mother thinks we're engaged."

His face lit up as he uncrossed his legs and leaned in. "Does she approve? What did she say?"

"You sound like a little boy."

He leaned back and deepened his voice. "What is her opinion?"

She laughed. A part of her reveled in his open admiration of her, but still a part of her wanted to blindside her with caution.

"She likes you Andrew." It was hard to be cautious with him so close to her. She wanted so much to relinquish the feeling of dread. She shook her head. *Divorce really messes you up. And this too shall pass.*

"What's wrong?"

Swimming through a haze of feelings and desires, she brightened just for him. "Nothing. I just want everything with the account to go well."

"It will. Don't worry about a thing. I have all the confidence in you."

She'd been working so hard at this thing, everything had to be great. She in no way would let him know that that was not what she was really worried about. She glanced at her watch, got up from behind her desk and fell into his open arms. He crushed her to him. "I know failure is not an option with you. Let's go have a good time." He let go of her and held her hand.

At the door, she looked at him and smiled as she let go of his hand.

He shook his head. "One day soon, you'll not let go ever."

She nodded. "You're right, but for now…"

He took a deep breath and exhaled. "I understand. No rush."

They met Mary and Brenda, account executives, who were on their way out. Mary smiled and held out her hand to Alice. "Congratulations on landing the Deveraux account."

Alice took the hand offered, and looked into the woman's eyes, noting that she didn't mean a word of what she'd said. "Thank you." She let go.

Mary looked at Andrew. "Nice car. Maybe one day I'll get a ride."

Andrew smiled and continued walking with Alice.

If Alice had looked back, she would have come face to face with the daggers being thrown at her by Mary; not that it would have mattered.

With one single file in her hand, Alice got into Andrew's car and they drove onto Las Olas. Maloney and her daughter had not gotten to the restaurant when they got there, but arrived five minutes later.

"We came in last night," Maloney said as soon as she sat down. "This is my first trip to South Beach and I have to say, I love it here. We're staying at the most beautiful hotel."

"Why didn't you let us know. We would have met you in there," Alice said.

"Oh no, we wanted to come here." She looked at Tiffany then back at Alice. "I don't know what you said to Tiffany, but she's really looking forward to working with you. So, as I understand it, there will be three faces representing the line. One I haven't seen yet, and you two." She nodded. "I like this. I like it a lot."

Alice opened the file and pulled out a picture of Danielle. "This is the other face." She watched Maloney's face light up and glanced quickly at Andrew.

"This is wonderful. Three shades of black. I'm so glad I picked you to represent us."

"Me too," Alice said, going over everything for the campaign. "Danielle will be here next week. How is the perfume coming?"

Maloney pulled a small vial from her purse and gave it to Alice.

"May I?" she said.

"Of course," Maloney said.

Alice dabbed a little on the inside of her wrist before passing it to Andrew.

After a few seconds, she sniffed it.

Andrew nodded.

"What do you think?" Maloney asked.

"It's beautiful, soft and breezy. I don't think I've ever smelled anything like it," Alice said. She didn't have to sniff it again to know she really liked it.

Andrew kept looking at her from the moment Maloney and her daughter sat at the table. He saw the confidence in her grow to a very relaxing position. Smiling secretly, he wondered if she knew how confident she was every time she headed a meeting or met someone. Her confidence made her so much more beautiful that sitting there, he fell in love with her all over again.

They drank wine, ordered dinner and sat chatting for more than two hours through dessert and cognac. Everyone felt so much at ease, Andrew ended up driving Maloney and Tiffany back to South Beach.

Tiffany would be back in a week to begin the photo shoot with Danielle and Alice.

"I would want only you on any product I develop," Andrew said to Alice on their way back home.

"What would it be?"

"I have no idea, but I would want you on it. You have a way about you of putting people at ease and making them believe that the impossible is always possible."

She stirred uneasily in the seat next to him, then took a deep breath. "I can't help thinking of Mary and the way she looked at me this evening."

He glanced at her. "I'm surprised you're talking about her."

"Why?"

"Because although you don't want them to know we're engaged, you don't seem to care for anyone at the office except for Lee Ann and Ben."

She shrugged. "I was never a social butterfly, Andrew. I got along well with the people who worked for me in New York. There's a rivalry here that doesn't sit very well with me."

"It's no excuse, but sometimes that's how it is in the advertising world."

"But you're not like that." She looked at his face.

He shrugged. "No, I'm not. I think I'm a bit like you. I hate rivalry."

"You get on very well with your sister."

He laughed. "And you with yours."

She nodded. "I guess you're right. We are alike."

He clasped her hand in his, brought it to his lips and kissed it. "It took you long enough to see it."

She smiled and nodded.

When they got to Alice's house, the children were fast asleep. But Andrew just had to peek in and kiss them goodnight.

"Thanks for being with me tonight. Having you there really helped," she said when he walked to the door.

"I doubt my presence made a difference, but just being there with you made my day."

"You have no idea, do you?"

"You're a very confident woman, Alice."

"Thank you." She reached up and kissed his lips. "I love you."

"I love you," he said, hugging her and burying his face in her neck. He let go and stepped through the door. "I'll see you tomorrow."

"Yes." The launch would be in three weeks. The invitations were sent, the catering arranged. The event would be held in the ballroom of the Ritz Carlton on A1A. She'd pulled out all the stops for this one.

For the rest of the week and into the next week, Alice worked harder than she ever had in her life. She begged her children's forgiveness and told them she'd make it up to them once the craziness was over. Her social life would have gone down the drain if Andrew had not worked side by side with her. She bounced ideas off him and he helped her come up with things that proved vital to the launch.

Chapter Twenty Four

Alice had coordinated dinner at her house with Ben and his wife for the same day when Danielle would come in from Paris.

Dinner was at seven-thirty, and Danielle's flight would come in at six. With baggage and everything, both Alice and Andrew thought he'd get her to Alice's house by seven if there was no delay. The Franks were very prompt and would come to Alice's for drinks first, and dinner would be on the table at seven-thirty. She hoped they had strong hearts.

Alice was dressed in a long blue blouse over a long white skirt, with a blue belt at her waist and black sandals. When she opened the door for the Franks, the first thing Ben said was, "I thought Andrew would be here." He introduced his wife; a woman Alice thought would have had a very light complexion. Instead, her complexion was darker than Alice's, but cool. She was an inch or so taller than Ben, even in low heels, but very pretty and talkative.

"Andrew is running just a few minutes late. He had an errand to run for me."

Delia came out for everyone's drink request and in a few minutes came back with them. Scotch on the rocks and red wine. They stepped out on the patio and Ben commented on almost all the trees in her yard.

She didn't want to talk about work just yet and hoped Andrew would hurry up. She was running out of trees and roses.

"You have to come to our house for dinner, Alice," Michelle Frank said. "I would love to show off my prize- winning roses. When I began planting roses my gardener told me they wouldn't thrive in this environment, but I ignored him and am glad I did because they're beautiful. I worry about them when it gets cold, but we're in South Florida, the cold never lasts long."

Alice nodded. "My gardener told me the same thing."

"We're a pair, aren't we?" Michelle laughed. Alice agreed.

It was fast approaching the time for Andrew to get there. The table was beautifully set and the children had already had their dinner.

Alice saw the light in her driveway and excused herself. The Franks stayed on the patio. Alice greeted Danielle as if they'd been friends for a long time. "So my parents don't know that I'm coming, I hear," Danielle said.

"Is that a bad thing?" Alice said with a quirky look on her face.

Danielle took a deep breath. "No, but do you mind if I do this on my own?"

"Not at all," Alice said. Both she and Andrew stood aside and watched Danielle walk to the patio.

"Daddy, Mommy," Danielle said.

Alice jumped as she saw and heard glasses shatter on the tile. Mrs. Frank was the first one to get up and rush toward her daughter, pulling her into her arms as if nothing had ever happened. Ben got to his feet and, realizing that his wife had no intentions of letting go of their daughter for a while, joined in the hug. Tears were being wiped away by both parents and Alice couldn't help choking up.

Alice held Andrew around his waist and wiped a tear from her cheek. "Are you crying?" he whispered.

"No, dust got into my eyes," she said awkwardly and cleared her throat.

"Oh," he crooned, hugging her to him. "You are such a softie."

When Delia came out with the first dish, she saw that dinner would be delayed. She turned around and went back to the kitchen.

Alice and Andrew went to the children's room keeping an eye through the window to make sure that they came out when the Franks began looking for them. It was more than half an hour later when that finally happened. They quickly made their way to the living room as the Franks walked in. "Well done, you two, well done," Ben said, his arm still wrapped around his daughter's waist. "You have no idea what you've done for us today. And there's no way we can thank you." He looked at Alice, then Andrew, not really knowing who the main character was in this homecoming.

Glancing out, Delia brought the meal to the table and made sure there was more than enough wine on the side board. And while her guests ate and drank heartily, Alice tried to size up the happiness meter of the Franks at their daughter's homecoming. She had no idea how long Danielle would stay or if Ben and Michelle would try and talk her into coming back home, but for now she was glad she and Andrew could have done this for them.

The petite, brown haired, gray-eyed young woman winked at Alice and mouthed, "Thank you."

Alice nodded, discreetly wanting very much to share the thanks with Andrew. After all, if it hadn't been for him, Danielle would not have been thought of at all.

They talked about the Deveraux account and the role Danielle would play. "It has been a long time since so much hoopla was made over an account," Ben said. "But it brought my daughter home, so I whole heartedly approve."

Alice smiled. *Good thing, because there's no way you could have stopped it even if you wanted to.* She threw a sly glance at Andrew.

Delia had outdone herself with dinner. She'd asked what the Franks liked and Alice knew Ben was allergic to shellfish, but loved salmon. Michelle loved Jamaican food but couldn't tolerate the hot spice, so Delia went ahead and made rice and peas, curried chicken, baked plantains, and broiled salmon with a sweet sauce, and sautéed vegetables.

At the end of a long and successful night when the Franks said their goodnights, Alice sent Delia to bed while she and Andrew cleared the table and took care of the dishes. They fell into the sofa and turned on the television, hot teas in hand like an old married couple. "That went well," Andrew said.

"Better than I thought it would. I'm glad we kept Danielle's homecoming a secret."

He nodded. And before he left, he begged her to acknowledge their engagement.

"After the launch," she promised.

"I know you never go back on your word, so I'm very excited."

He wasn't kidding. His smile was wide as he swept her up in his arms and twirled her around the family room.

The day of the launch was fast approaching. Tiffany Deveraux and Maloney were settled in a condo in South Beach, which had become their favorite place.

The photographers were busy snapping away hundreds of photographs of all three women. And even though Alice didn't really want to do this, her smile was radiant.

The cameras were rolling for the commercials, close ups and far shots. They'd chosen a remote spot in South Beach for the photo shoot.

They had two limousines shuttling the women and photographers back and forth from Parkland to Ft. Lauderdale to South Beach. At the end of each day, Alice was exhausted. If she'd known how hard it would have been, she would have insisted that Danielle and Tiffany be the only spokes-models for the line. She could have stayed in South Beach for the entire shoot, but her children were in school and she didn't want to spend a night away from them if she didn't have to. In her very busy days, Andrew was never far from her side.

For weeks after the photo shoot, Alice and the different departments pored over all the photographs and potential commercials. She spent long days and long nights at the office, and lots of flying back and forth from New York and Los Angeles to Ft. Lauderdale putting photos on bill boards. Danielle and Tiffany had even gone to Paris to promote the product there.

Weeks turned into months. Alice had never worked so hard in her life. The way she went at the account, she knew there'd be backlash from some in the office, mainly, Mary. She got reports from Lee Ann, who sometimes socialized with some of the women, that Mary was not a happy camper and questioned the way she was handling the account.

Alice had no time at all to give jealousy a second thought. Plus, she knew Lee Ann would speak on her behalf.

Finally the day of the launch arrived. Early in the morning, Andrew drove Alice to the hotel to make sure everything was as she wanted it. He could tell she was tired but still very radiant.

In a pale yellow suit, she entered the hotel ballroom with heels clicking on the tiled floors, extremely professional. Papers were shoved into her hands to be signed off on. Half she gave to Andrew. She inspected the food, the flowers, the stage, the entire setting. Andrew begged her to just take a few hours to rest but she was too wound up to sleep. "After tonight, I'll rest for a week," she told him.

The tickets were bought for them to all fly to Jamaica for a few days. The children would leave tonight; she and Andrew would join them tomorrow.

Morning ran into afternoon. Afternoon ran into evening. And it was show time.

In her hotel room, she slowly got dressed in a royal blue off-the-shoulder gown. She was all photo'd out. "If I have to have one more photograph taken, I'll scream," she said to Andrew. He was dressed in a black tux, his loose curly hair resting on his broad shoulders. Even though he'd told her he'd gotten a hair cut, it didn't look much like it. She smiled. "You look so handsome."

"Not to be compared to you," he said while handing her a blue box.

She looked at it then at him. "What is this?"

"It's customary when one is given a present, one opens same."

Holding the long box in her hand, she guessed what it was and was almost afraid to open it. She stared at the box until he knelt before her and slowly opened it. She gasped. "Andrew! You shouldn't." She was wrong. She thought it was a bracelet.

"Yes, I should." He took the blood-red ruby necklace from the box and placed it around her neck. While his fingers remained on her bare shoulders, tears burned her eyes and fell to her cheek as her fingers touched the forty ruby strand necklace with twenty-four karat gold inlay.

"Good thing this mascara is waterproof." She quickly dabbed at her tears. "Oh, Andrew; really. This must have cost a small fortune." Her fingers shook against the necklace.

"Nothing's too expensive for you. You've worked so hard on this account; I just wanted you to have this." He watched her switch the ring from her right hand to the third finger of her left hand. "Thank you."

Careful not to smear her lipstick, he touched his lips to hers, and gave her the crook of his arm. "Shall we go? I don't think it can start without you."

Alice walked out of the room on Andrew's arm and knocked on Tiffany and Danielle's door. All four took the elevator to the garage, then got into a waiting limousine just to go to the front of the hotel and walk the red carpet. Yes, there would be more photos taken, but Alice seemed to be renewed with Andrew by her side.

And as they alighted from the limousine and flash bulbs popped in their faces, Alice held fast to Andrew's hand, leaving a lot of their colleagues guessing what their relationship was.

Everything went off without a hitch. Commercials had been running for weeks on television and radio about the product, but this was special, different. The official commercial was previewed for the first time and photographs lined every wall with the faces of the spokes models for the Deveraux line. Cosmetic buyers from all the major department stores were in attendance and everyone was ready to place a counter in their store of the most sought after African-American line of cosmetics that almost everyone could wear.

Maloney was overjoyed at the success of the launch. Alice laughed when Eva whispered in her ear. "You've made us rich, rich, rich. How can we thank you?'

"Pay me," she whispered, grinning.

Jennifer laughed and, along with her sister, raised a glass to her. She raised her glass in kind. Maloney came to stand with them. "You are a miracle worker," she said. She looked at her sisters. "We've come a long way from beauty supply stores and beauty salons."

"We're like the Jeffersons; we've moved up thanks to Alice and Andrew," Jennifer said, looking around. "Where is he anyway?"

But before Alice could turn to look for Andrew, Mary Jones walked up to her and congratulated her. "May I speak with you in private," she said, a big smile on her face.

"Of course," Alice said, excusing herself.

They walked to a corner of the huge hall and Mary said something that Alice had not expected. "How did you do it?" she said patronizingly.

"Hard work."

"No, I mean how did you get Andrew and the old man to agree to all this? The company has never done this before." There wasn't a trace of a smile on her face. "Did you do something special? Because we all want to know what your secret is."

Mary got the point as Alice's face took on a stern expression. "As I told you Mary, it's all hard work. The company never did this before because no one took the initiative to ask either Andrew or Ben to go to this length."

"Is all this necessary?" she asked, her thin lips tight.

"Look around you at all the buyers that are here. There are even buyers from as far as France and the Caribbean."

"I'm gonna ask this right out because there's been speculation thrown around the office. Are you sleeping with Ben?" A thin smile spread across her large lips. She wanted to provoke Alice to frustration. She'd picked the wrong lady.

As shocked as she was at the question, Alice laughed as cold dignity created a mask of superiority. "No, Mary. I'm sleeping with Andrew." With her left hand, she touched her necklace. "But you know, as small as I think you and the others who think like you are, I have to give you all this advice. Hard work never hurt anyone. Getting an account and sitting on it won't get the results or the satisfaction that I get from my job."

Now who shuffled and backpedaled with embarrassment? "I didn't say you were sleeping with Ben, I said I heard..."

"And you took it upon yourself to tell me. One question before I go. Did you want this account?" Alice's fist balled at her side with anger.

Mary didn't answer right away, but looked away into the crowd of people. "Among other people."

"I see. Did you come tonight just to insult me?"

"No, I wanted to tell you that you've done a good..."

"Don't patronize me, Mary. I'm going to stop you right there." She'd been smiling the whole time, but now the smile vanished. "I hate hypocrites. We may work for the same company, but we don't have to be friends. We don't even have to say hello to each other. Now, if you don't mind. I see my fiancée looking this way."

"There's no need for you to tell Ben or Andrew..."

"Isn't there?" It was a neat threat that she was sure scared the pants off Mary. She walked away without a backward glance.

She held her smile and her head high as she walked over to where Andrew stood with Ben. No, she wouldn't say anything to either Ben or Andrew. She was a big girl. She'd handled it. Andrew raised his glass, she reciprocated.

"Congratulations," Ben said. "You're taking this company into the twenty-first century. Two more accounts will be waiting for you and Andrew when you get back from Jamaica. The word is out. Frank's is the place to get results."

Both Alice and Andrew laughed. She looked into his eyes and with pulse-pounding certainty, she knew she had her work cut out for her.

It was a long but productive night. And when Alice and Andrew left the party, it was still in full swing. They stole away back to their room, then left the hotel without being seen and got into Alice's car. Andrew drove them home.

"The children are already in Jamaica, so will you stay here tonight?"

"Yes," he said without hesitation. Knowing how tired and drained she was, he sat her down on her bed, took all the pins from her hair and brushed it, then unzipped her dress and slipped her nightgown over her head. He put her to bed, took off his clothes and slid in beside her. With his hand around her waist, she backed up into him until she felt his warm body against her. She smiled, held his hand and fell asleep.

He kissed the back of her neck. "I love you." He was looking forward to the few days with her in Jamaica.

Chapter Twenty Five

Sitting in the seat next to Alice on a plane bound for Kingston, Jamaica, Andrew felt exhilarated. Not only had Alice's first campaign gone extremely well, she'd brought Danielle home to her parents and was now wearing his ring on the third finger of her left hand. It was official. Although they had not told anyone, they were definitely engaged.

When the plane landed, Nikki was there to meet them. She'd pulled a few strings to rush them through customs. "Before you ask, the children are waiting in the car," Nikki said, hugging and kissing Alice on the cheek before focusing in on Andrew.

He smiled, extending his arm, but Nikki hugged him. "We need to have a long talk," she said in his ear.

He chuckled. "It's really great to meet you, Nikki," Andrew said before gathering the luggage.

"My car is parked at the curb; let's hurry before I get towed."

"You mean your pull only extends to customs officers?" Alice teased.

She nodded. "You'd be surprised how nice people can be when you deliver their babies." She motioned toward the white Mercedes.

The children came running out and were scooped up in arms by their mother and Andrew. "I missed you guys," Alice said before settling them back in their seats.

When everyone was settled in, Nikki turned to Alice and asked. "Same place?"

"Oh, yes please," Alice replied before turning to Andrew, who was sitting in the back seat. "Every time I come to Jamaica, the first place we go is the beach. Apart from the fact that it's the best in the world, there's a woman there by the name of Myrtle who makes the best of everything." She glanced at Delia. "Except for you, Delia. No one cooks as well as you."

"I know," Delia said with a smirk.

"She's so humble," Alice said laughing.

Making their way to Helshire Beach, Nikki escaped the airport traffic and made the roundabout onto Palisades Highway. Through a small part of Harbor View's middle-income area with small green lawns behind white picket fences, they sped past vendors selling fruits and vegetables in front of shops and supermarkets. She skirted pot holes left by the last hurricane, then drove through downtown Kingston and onto the causeway.

Andrew informed Nikki of his hotel reservation, but she'd hear nothing of it. "How are you going to learn about Jamaica and her people staying in a hotel?" she asked. "I have ample space at my home, so don't worry about it."

He smiled and nodded without insisting. "Are you sure? I don't want to inconvenience you in any way."

"Don't be silly. You staying in a hotel would be the inconvenience. I would have to drive by to pick you up everyday and drop you off. I bet Alice didn't know that you'd made reservations at a hotel." She glanced back at him through the rearview mirror and saw the smile on his face.

"As a matter of fact, she didn't. I made the reservations myself."

"Aha! I see. I know she would have told you not to." She glanced at Alice, who was sitting in the passenger seat and pinched her arm. "Right, Lise?"

Alice rubbed her arm. "Ahhh, right Nik." She broke into an open, friendly smile. Actually, she would not have stopped him from checking into a hotel unless Nikki had invited him to stay at her home with them.

When they got to Helshire, everyone including the children replaced their shoes with flip-flops while Andrew watched in silence at the ritual. "You have to take off your sneakers or have them ruined by salt water, Andrew. And try to roll up your pants leg, or get a pair of shorts out of your suitcase," Nikki said looking at him. "You did bring shorts with you, didn't you?"

He gave a tentative smile, took his suitcase out of the trunk, searched for his trunks and marched toward a building that said *Men*.

"Has he been here before?" Nikki asked. She hugged Alice once more. "It's so good to see you. I missed you."

"I missed you too, but talk about being busy. I thought I would have lost my mind these last few weeks. Actually, if it weren't for Andrew, I probably would have." She looked back at the men's room. "Don't tell him I said that."

It was ninety degrees with eighty percent humidity. The sweat poured down Alice's neck to her small bosom. She raised her left hand to wipe the sweat and Nikki held onto her hand. "You didn't have this when I was with you. Usually, the only thing you wear on that finger is your wedding ring that I'm assuming you've thrown away. So…"

Alice flinched and took a deep breath. "Can we talk about this later?"

"Absolutely. And don't think I'm going to forget about it."

"I know you won't," Alice snickered.

Andrew came back still wearing his shirt, but Alice had a hard time tearing her eyes from his thighs. It wasn't as if she'd never seen him in trunks or naked before, but every time she saw his powerful thighs she seemed to be hypnotized. Nikki gently pushed her shoulder. "Don't tell me you've never seen them before."

"Uh huh." She closed her mouth, cleared her throat, waited for Andrew to put his clothes in the car and walked on hot, white powdery sand toward Myrtle's little shed. The smell of frying fish and escoviched sauce permeated the air. The hot sun beating down on their bare shoulders and slow warm tropical breezes reminded them of where they were.

While the children and Delia went straight for the solace of the tepid water, Alice, Nikki and Andrew went to the shed. Alice wrapped her arm around the big, chocolate-colored woman with the ample bosom, missing front teeth and aroma of fish.

Myrtle recognized her instantly as if she'd seen her just the other day.

"Miss Alice, you're back."

"Yes, I am, Myrtle, and I brought a friend with me. I told him all about your food and he can't wait to taste it."

Myrtle cast a look at the big bronze god and smiled. "I hope he can take the spice."

Alice looked at Andrew. He nodded. "I can take it; don't be afraid to pour it on."

The women laughed. He'd had Delia's and her sister's cooking, but their spice was child's play to Myrtle's spicy food. "Okay, Myrtle," Alice said. "We want lobsters, fish, bammy and festival. Remember, I have the children so no spice at all on their fish."

"Two of them, right?"

"Yes, Myrtle. You do remember."

"I can never forget you, Miss Alice. Just sit in the usual spot and give me half an hour." She handed them sodas and coconut water.

They headed for the huge grape tree cluster and sat on blankets and towels that Nikki had brought. Alice leaned against a palm tree trunk and breathed. For a long time no one spoke. They just sat there basking in the shade, watching the waves undulate onto shore... except for the children, who were giddily laughing and playing tag with the tide just like the sandpipers.

Chapter Twenty Six

Andrew stuck his sun shades on and they were so dark, no one knew if he was awake or asleep. He shifted his body slightly to fit more comfortably into the tree trunk.

Alice laughed. "I thought you were sleeping."

"No, I'm watching the children and the ocean. This is great. Thanks for inviting me."

"You're welcome. I have to repeat this though; you would have missed me."

"I probably would have followed you."

Nikki laughed and looked at them. "Okay, you know that I'm right here and can hear everything you say. So is anyone going to tell me exactly what's going on?"

They said nothing until Andrew touched Alice's hand and said, "You didn't tell her?" His dark brows arched mischievously.

"I just put the ring on last night, Andrew," she said, wishing he hadn't said anything.

Leisurely, he stretched his long legs leaving her to shuffle along. She wasn't ready to tell Nikki, but he'd dropped everything in her lap.

"I'm waiting," Nikki said, looking from one to the other.

"I accepted Andrew's engagement proposal last night." She looked away from Nikki and smoothed her brow with both hands.

"Congratulations, but I still have to approve this union." She looked over at Andrew. "And you and I have to have the talk, Andrew."

He lifted the glasses from his eyes, looked at her and grinned. "I think I knew that."

Delia and the children made their way to them just as Myrtle's help brought the food over. They were all famished. Alice watched Andrew as he ate the spicy food and marveled. "Not many white people can tolerate this kind of heat," she said.

"Who told you I was white," he said, his infectious grin setting the tone as everyone laughed, even the children.

No one challenged him; they were all too in love with him. Even Nikki, who was trying her best to be removed, showed signs of instantly liking Andrew. What was there not to like?

After they'd finished their sumptuous meal, they stretched languidly on the blanket, not caring that the tide had risen and was coming much farther onto shore. "I would like to come back here and eat Myrtle's food before we leave, Alice," Andrew said while putting on the dark glasses.

This time everyone knew he was about to fall asleep. And as he began breathing deeply and the children went back to play, Nikki whispered, "I thought you would have waited until I met the guy before accepting his ring."

"Well, now that you've met him, what do you think?"

"You sure know how to choose the gorgeous ones. Not that Harvey was this good looking, but…" She glanced over at Andrew. "Wow, he's handsome, but can he cut the mustard?"

"Oh, Nik, you're a tough one."

"Lise, you thought Harvey walked on water. You were so in love with the guy, you gave him the benefit of the doubt more times than I can count on both hands."

"Diplomacy is lost on you, isn't it?"

"You know me. You're the same when it comes to me. I just don't want you to get hurt again."

"I know. Believe me, I think about it all the time, but he's not Harvey. They're like night and day."

"You really love this guy, don't you?" she kept staring at Alice.

Alice took a deep breath and nodded.

"Then what else can I say? But I still have to threaten him. I didn't do it with Harvey and look what happened."

Alice laughed, reached across and hugged her friend. "I love you."

"I know, and I love you too. I wish you guys were staying longer. We could go to the North Coast tomorrow, but you'll be back in a few months, right?"

"Right."

"We have to talk more." She glanced back at Alice and smiled as two dimples appeared on her cheeks. "You're okay, right? I mean… I know you've been busy, but how are you really?"

Alice looked at her friend's pixie-like hair cut, brown eyes, small mouth and fair skin. "I'm good."

"Really?"

"Yes."

"Because of him?" she pointed to Andrew.

"Partially."

Nikki nodded, then whispered, "What happened with Alvin?"

Alice laughed. "Let's take a walk."

They began walking on the beach and Nikki anxiously asked. "So, was I right about him?"

"And then some," Alice replied. "I had to actually threaten to call the police for him to leave me alone."

"What! Why?" Nikki stopped and folded her arms across her chest. "How did it come to that?"

"I invited him out to dinner one evening…"

"You what? I can't believe you'd do that."

"Okay, I know, but just listen. I think he wanted someone to hang onto. You know; someone who would be his sugar-mama so to speak. But the best or worst part was, Andrew had him investigated and found out he'd gone to prison for real-estate fraud." She shook her head. "I'm really so disappointed in him."

They began walking again. Nikki shook her head. "That's a shame. The way he acted in school, I thought he'd have made something of himself. I didn't have any classes with him so maybe he wasn't as smart as we are making him out to be."

Alice shrugged. "Maybe not."

"But nevertheless, I knew there was something not right with him. I had no idea it was that bad. So he summed you up; thought you had money, and wanted to hook his buggy to your horse."

Alice laughed. "In a nut shell, I guess. Where on earth did you get that line?"

"Hey, I work among people from different backgrounds. I hear things, if it's funny, I repeat it." She shrugged.

Alice thought it best not to go into the fact that Alvin had begun stalking her. She was sure Nikki would freak out at that."

They walked for another few minutes then turned back.

They'd stayed at the beach all day until the sun began its descent. Everyone slept, but Andrew had slept the longest. "I must have been more tired than I thought," he said, stretching and winking at her.

"It's okay; you worked on that campaign just as hard as I did. You just allowed me to take the bows."

"No, you worked harder, and were very stressed. I'm only glad you allowed me to help." He reached over and kissed her forehead, only because Phillip was looking up at him from where he laid his head on his chest.

"Can we go back and swim in the water?" Phillip asked, looking into Andrew's face.

"It's all right with me if it's okay with your mom."

Alice nodded.

Phillip hopped to his feet and took hold of Andrew's hand. "I think I'm being summoned," Andrew said with a big grin on his face.

A few minutes after swimming with Phillip, Andrew left him and Alia to start a sand castle promising to come back and help.

Noticing that Nikki wasn't with Alice, he sat beside her. "When will you tell the children we're engaged?"

She smiled. "When I get a chance." She sat up and looked into his eyes. "It's important to you that they are okay with this?"

He nodded.

"Well, I know Alia loves you to death, it's only Phillip that you have to work on."

Just then Phillip came back for him. "Come on, Uncle Andrew, help us finish the castle."

Andrew grinned. "I can't get enough of them calling me uncle." He allowed Phillip to drag him along.

Alice laughed.

The red sunset glistened off the ocean so beautifully, Alice smiled. Sometimes she missed Jamaica and Nikki, and this. Yes, she was glad Andrew was in her life.

Nikki sat down and placed her arm around her. "Are you ready? We have a party to attend tonight."

She looked at Nikki and laughed. "Now you tell me that?"

"Yeah, did you have another date?"

"No, but, I wanted to relax."

"You can relax tomorrow. Tonight we dance."

She took a deep breath. "All right, I'm game."

Alice called to the children, Delia and Andrew. They gathered up their belongings, said goodbye to Myrtle, and headed out.

Leaving Helshire, they drove until they got to Trafalgar Road, then onto Hope Road, and headed to Grosvernor Terrace, where Nikki lived.

It was still too early to dress for the party, so Alice took Andrew for a walk on Nikki's three-acre property, listening to crickets chirp and frogs croak. The property had a lot of fruit trees and she stood under a mango tree and held his hand. "I want to ask you a question and I need a straight answer."

One corner of his mouth pulled into a slight smile. "I only give straight answers."

"Did you have anything to do with my getting the job at Franks? And before you answer, remember I had no marketing or advertising experience."

He chuckled, reached up and held onto a tree branch. "Yes. When Ben sent me your resume, I immediately told him to hire you."

"And he just went along with your decision?"

"I told him you were a quick study and I'd train you myself. I have absolutely no regrets."

She took a cleansing breath. "Thank you for taking a chance on me."

"Are you kidding? I didn't take a chance." He let go of the branch and faced her. "You go at everything with such gusto, no one loses with you. Do you know that because of you, the company got three more accounts? Ben wasn't joking when he said we'd be working on two new accounts when we get back."

At his words, a warm glow flowed through her. She leaned in and placed her head on his chest. She could take all the gossip at the office because she knew when they all realized what she'd done for the company they'd come to appreciate her, or not. She didn't care one way or the other. "Thank you."

"No, Alice. Thank you."

Basking in his embrace, she didn't move as the island breeze rustled the trees. Dark clouds moved from the full moon, lighting their way back to the house.

Andrew went inside to be with the children and Nikki walked out to the verandah, where Alice sat on a lounge chair.

"You work hard and play hard," Alice said.

"I work hard. Play hard, not so much. I'm so glad you came. I have to say, I give my stamp of approval. Andrew is really a nice person. You could crush him and he wouldn't whine."

Alice laughed. "I'd never hurt him. You know, I wish this feeling of peace and tranquility that I'm feeling right now would never go away."

"Trust?"

"For once in my life, yes. I trust him."

Nicholas, Nikki's long time boyfriend joined them on the verandah and Alice laughed and rose to greet him. "Oh my God. Look at you. You look more handsome than ever."

Nicholas fit the tall, dark, and very handsome profile to a T.

He laughed, hugged her, and lifted her off her feet. "And you're just as beautiful as the first day we met. You don't age." He placed her back on her feet.

"You're too kind, my friend."

He stood looking at her. "How can you come home for just a weekend? This is Jamaica. No one comes home for just three days. There's too much to do."

"I know, but we'll be back in a few months and Christmas."

He kissed her cheek. "You're forgiven."

Andrew came out. "Andrew, this is Nicholas. Nikki's... I should be saying husband. They've known each other long enough."

Nicholas laughed. "It's not from lack of trying. She just won't set a date."

"So there's talk of a wedding?" Alice asked looking at Nikki, who rolled her eyes.

"You would be the first one to know," she said.

"We met in the living room," Andrew said, coming to stand beside her.

It was time to get dressed for the party.

Getting dressed for the party, the children walked into Alice's room. "Are you guys going out?" Phillip asked.

"Yes, we are going to a party." She sat on the bed and lifted them both to sit beside her. "I have something to tell you both and I want you to think before you answer, okay."

They both nodded.

She held out her hand for them to look at the ring on her finger. "Uncle Andrew has asked me to marry him," she hurried to say. "It won't be for now, but I want to know if you guys are okay with him being your stepfather." She looked from one to the other, mainly at Phillip. He screwed his mouth and wrinkled his brow, then looked at his sister.

"You guys like him, don't you?"

They nodded.

She waited and wondered if they knew how important their answer was to her.

"Daddy will still be our daddy, and we'll still spend time with him?" Phillip asked.

"Of course. Andrew doesn't want to replace your father. He just wants to be in your lives. You will still spend as much time with your father as you wish. You can call him as often as you wish."

They both nodded. "You can marry him," Phillip said.

"Yes," Alia said.

Alice smiled at her children and hugged them to her. "Thank you both. It means a lot that you like him and want him in your lives." She kissed their cheeks multiple times, then stood and ran her hand down her red strapless silk dress. "I love you both very much." Her happiness spiraled upward. *What more could I ask for?* She had a fantastic job, two wonderful children, and a man who seemingly loved the very earth she walked on. Hand in hand, all three walked out to where Nikki, Andrew, and Nicholas waited for her in the living room.

Andrew got up when he saw her. His smile was wide as he took her hand with quiet assurance. "Every time I see you, you look more beautiful."

She smiled up at him. "It's because you love me so much."

"Now you get it." He was now sure of his rightful place with her.

They both kissed the children goodnight and told them not to stay up too late.

Nikki was dressed in a navy blue gown with spaghetti straps and a string of delicate pearls around her slender neck. A wisp of dark hair framed her small face. She took the hand offered by Nicholas and walked toward his car.

"By the way," Alice said to Andrew as they settled in Nicholas's Porsche. "You look very dashing."

"It's your love radiating through me."

She laughed.

It took them all of ten minutes to get to the party in Beverly Hills. Inside the mansion of one of Nikki's colleagues, Alice and Andrew were introduced to as many people as were there. Champagne was pushed into their hands while they chatted with doctors, lawyers, and businessmen. Eventually, their new acquaintances drifted in different directions and Andrew led Alice onto the dance floor.

The music took her back to another time and place when the Drifters sang and Percy Sledge warmed and melted hearts with romantic ballads. Otis Redding took them to the dock of the bay holding hands, hugging, laughing, kissing, and melting into each others arms.

She remembered when she had her first and only beer; when she had her first kiss making her knees weak in a twisted sense of time.

Time stood still, then raced—racing too fast. Stop! Stop! Her mind shouted. She didn't want to go back. She didn't want to think about *him*, not tonight. Not ever in that way again.

Tonight was special, maybe more special than days gone by. She leaned her head against Andrew's chest and encircled his neck with her arms as they waltzed.

He tightened his hold on her waist and gently kissed her cheek. "You'll be all right. I'm not going anywhere," he whispered as if reading her thoughts.

She nodded as the kiss from his warm mouth lingered on her cheek. "This is the kind of music I grew up with."

"Me too," he replied, leading her off the dance floor. They sat in the garden on a marbled bench under the stars. "It brings back memories?"

She sighed and nodded. "Unwanted ones of better times, I suppose. But I'm making some wonderful ones with you." She smiled and gazed into his twinkling green eyes. She wasn't afraid. He had a big hand in her getting her self- confidence back.

Suddenly she realized that all the years that Harvey had told her that she never finished anything, that she couldn't make it without him, had melted away. He'd told her that even though they were divorced, she'd come running back to him when she couldn't find anyone else. She gazed lovingly at Andrew, who reciprocated with soft eyes. "We have the children's blessing," she said, drawing a slow steady smile of happiness.

He got up and pulled her to him. He'd peeled back her layers of fear of him, exposing everything she was—her strength, her conviction. He watched and listened to her laughter and knew that he had her heart and soul. "My life is complete," he said, kissing her under the full moon in a garden filled with the scent of roses. "I love you with all my heart."

"And I you. I'm so glad we came here."

He lifted her off the ground and spun her around. And she laughed like he'd never heard before, light and true. He placed her back on her feet and covered her mouth with his, tasting a fountain that he'd spend the rest of his life drinking from.